MW00479833

Bryan M. Powell

Undetected

Bryan M. Powell

Undetected

to Brongker
+ Jenie
God bless

by Bryan M. Powell

Fiction, Christian - Fiction, Mystery Adult – Fiction,
– Fiction
Cover design by Bryan M. Powell
Photography by Photography by McCarthy

Manufactured in the United States of America
ISBN: 9781704345420

Cast of Characters

Trace O'Reilly – After being hit and nearly killed by a drone missile, Trace is left to face new challenges and old habits.

Lily O'Reilly – Her life changed drastically for the worse, but her faith in God never wavered.

Will O'Reilly – It didn't take long for Will to realize his life had taken a dramatic turn. It was time to take responsibility for his actions.

Troy Ashcroft – Caught in the vortex of disaster.

Olivia Emerson – As the head of the newly formed NRA, National Resistance Army, Olivia must return to the life she'd rejected and trust the people she once hated.

Secretary of State Norman Bleakly – As the newly sworn in President, Bleakly is swift to wrest power from the states and form a new government; one in which he holds all the power.

Amanda Borden – A mysterious woman with many secrets. As President Bleakly's chief councilor, co-conspirer, and lover it was her job to keep an eye on her half-brother.

Millie Kendall – Sitting outside the Oval Office, she was in the ideal position to learn the President's closest secrets ... secrets the underground desperately needed to know.

Chapter One

"In secrecy, error undetected will flourish and subvert."
J. Robert Oppenheimer

S treaks of red and orange light stabbed Trace's eyes as consciousness seeped back into his brain.

With his ears ringing and the knot on the back of his head throbbing every time he moved, he knew one thing ... he was alive. That was a small consolation, however. Peering through pinched eyes, he realized his desperate situation. His arm was in a cast. The other arm was handcuffed to the bars of a hospital bed.

As the cobwebs cleared he remembered lying on the smoldering concrete. He remembered the heat-seeking missile blast, searching for Cami, and the emptiness of not finding her.

Then the lights went out.

He struggled against the restraint, but it held fast. Someone stepped close and adjusted the dosage of pain medication and he felt himself drifting.

Unaware of the passage of time, he awoke as an orderly detached him from the bed and placed him in a wheelchair. "Okay, Mr. O'Reilly, you're getting out of here."

"Where am I? Where are you taking me?" he muttered, his mind still not functioning at full capacity.

"Rehab."

"Re what?"

"Rehab. You're going to the orientation facility to be reeducated at government expense. I know, I know, you're going to thank me, but save it until afterward. Consider yourself one lucky man."

Trace tried to look at the orderly, but his neck was stiff from lying in bed for weeks. "Lucky? How so?"

"You're lucky they didn't try you for subversion and shoot you. So, like I said, you're one lucky guy. Now take my advice. Let them reeducate you, do your job and live out your days in peace."

There was no use questioning the orderly any further. His life had just taken a major shift and he was no longer free to make his own decisions.

After being assisted to a wheelchair, he was wheeled to the loading dock of the hospital where several armored cars sat. Their doors yawned open inviting his and a group of other detainees to get in. Once they were secured with chains to the vehicle's floor, the guards took their positions and waited for the convoy to depart.

"Where are they taking us?" Trace asked the guy next to him.

"To the inner city, that's where the reeducation facility is located. They want us to change the way we think." His African-American voice was laced with bitterness.

"And how should we think?" Trace asked.

The whites of the black man's eyes glowed with anger. "They want us to swear allegiance to the new republic," he said sarcastically. "I'll die before I swear to that. I didn't survive two tours in Afghanistan defending the stars and bars just to be told it didn't matter."

The guard, who'd been standing outside the door leaned in. "That kind of talk will get you shot. Now shut up!" He slammed the door with finality.

***

The armored caravan pulled away from the hospital and wove its way through the littered streets of a city.

From his view, that area of town wasn't anywhere Trace recognized. They hit a pothole and the hard bench chewed into his tender hinder parts. Finally, when they'd reached their destination, the vehicles ground to a stop. The driver swung the door open and climbed out.

Since Trace was first in, he had to wait until last to be unchained. As the guard did so, he sneered at Trace and said, "Get out."

Surrounding the vehicle stood a cadre of armed soldiers wearing International Guard uniforms. It was clear to all they had no intention of letting anyone escape.

Trace bit back a snarky remark knowing it would only result in a kick in the gut or a fist in the face. The moment he stepped from the vehicle, his legs buckled making him wonder how long he'd been in the hospital.

Breathing in the polluted air, he took in his surroundings. The crumbling building in front of him had at one time been a high school, but that was long ago. In the years following its abandonment, it had fallen into disarray. Its decrepit walls were sprayed with antigovernment slogans, gang symbols and an assortment of vulgar slogans.

"Line up, feet together, hands by your sides. Anyone stupid enough to speak without permission will be shot." The commander of the unit left no doubt he meant business.

Trace joined the line of men and was shoved up the steps into the building. No sooner had he entered than the stench of mold and urine assaulted his nostrils. Clutching his stomach he felt like vomiting but fought it back down. It was obvious the plumbing wasn't working and he wondered what else the new government couldn't keep up with. At least the electricity was working, albeit, poorly, as evidenced by the dimly lit halls. It reminded him of the prison he'd escaped from.

A uniformed soldier with an M-16 shoved the man in front of him and the line began to trudge down the corridor. Ahead, a guard held a door open.

"In here," he ordered.

The men followed his instructions and took their seats in what used to be an auditorium. Stepping behind a podium with a single microphone, the guard began, "Listen up. What you are about to experience will open your eyes to the evils of your democratically elected government. They have deceived you into believing they had all the answers; that your vote counted, that you could obtain the American dream. All it got us is war, poverty and a global epidemic. Yes, you heard me. I said a global epidemic. All those bodies out there." He jerked his thumb in the direction of heaps of burning corpses. "That was your government at work. They created this mess. They wanted it, and that is what's left. So sit back, let this and other videos help you understand, we are here to save the planet and make things right."

For the next two hours, Trace and the others listened to a parade of environmental extremists and anti-capitalists rant against the evils of capitalism, the free market system, national borders, and a myriad of other social ills. When they'd finished, they sent the men to a converted classroom with wooden bunks and ordered them to bed down. The following day began where the previous day left off with more reeducation classes.

What began as maniacal rhetoric soon turned into ridiculous drivel. After a week Trace had heard it so much that he could quote the mantra by heart.

However, he knew the truth. It all started with Scott Wan. He had the evidence, or at least had it until a missile struck just ahead of his car. As he listened, one big question pressed into his mind. Why had God spared Cami's life only to have it ripped from her, from him?

The longer he lay on his bunk, the angrier he got. He was mad at whoever fired that missile, at God for letting it hit them, and at himself for being stupid enough to think he could rescue Olivia and her maid. What was he thinking? He had walked into a trap and it cost Cami's life and his freedom.

To top it all off, Scott Wan worked for the government. For all he knew, the government he'd sworn to protect had turned on him. His anger turned sour. Doubts turned to bitterness and bitterness to cynicism.

By the end of the two month reeducation period, he was ready to chuck it all; his patriotism, his faith, and his sobriety.

Chapter Two

Two months earlier …

The atmosphere inside the Situation Room scintillated with energy as President Richardson and his closest advisers considered their options.

News reports of the bird attacks sweeping the nation were coming in at such a rapid pace that it was impossible to keep up with the situation.

"Mr. President, we have reports of flocks of wild birds attacking other birds. Whatever is driving them mad is also causing them to spread their disease to other birds."

President Richardson looked at his adviser with grim determination. "Have you been able to speak with the Vice President?"

The color from his adviser's face paled. "No, sir. He was on the golf course when the attacks began. None of his protective detail survived and I fear the worst."

"And the Speaker of the House?"

"They were both playing in an invitational fund raiser … sir."

Rear-Admiral Brooks, commander of the Pacific fleet stepped up. "Sir, we have reports that the disease is spreading faster than—"

Mayor Watson, the chief executive of the District of Colombia interrupted the conference. "Sir, did you implement the Grid Protocols?"

President Richardson wheeled around to face the woman. Her fiery eyes bore holes in him. He had already discussed the matter with the Secretary of State and tabled it.

She continued, "Because, I've got International Guard troops roaming *my* streets in armored vehicles pointing 50 mm machine guns at *my* citizens ordering them to get off *my* streets."

Hands held up in his defense, President Richardson took a step back. "Mayor Watson, I assure you this was not—"

All at once, the President's head of security stepped inside the Situation Room.

He touched the President's elbow, turning him around. "Sir, I need you to follow me."

How had it come to this? How had he let things get to this point? In an instant, he saw his country slip into anarchy and it was under his watch. He had sworn an oath to protect the constitution and the citizens of this nation from all enemies both foreign and domestic. But who would have thought that the attack would come in the form of birds?

Needing no explanation, POTUS prepared to leave, then paused. "Ladies and gentlemen, please stay calm, and follow this gentleman. Your families are being taken to secure locations as we speak, but we need to follow protocol."

The Presidential detail formed a wedge and began to lead the President and his advisers down the wide corridor. They had gone only a few paces when they were met by a dozen men wearing military uniforms and sporting M-16's.

"Stand aside," the head of security demanded.

The commander of the armed men squared himself in front of the Presidential detail. "Not so fast. We are under orders to take President Richardson and his cabinet into custody." His tone left no doubt he meant business.

"Under whose authority?" POTUS shouted over the sound of raised voices.

"By order of Secretary of State Bleakly. He has exercised the Twenty-fifth Amendment of the Constitution and has removed you from office."

"On what charges?" the head of security bellowed.

"You'll have to take that up with him. Now stand down."

Rather than follow his orders, he and the rest of the protective detail pulled their weapons and pointed them at opposing men. Someone tossed a stun grenade into their midst followed by blinding teargas. In an instant, the air became unbreathable. Shots fired and within the span of sixty seconds several of the President's advisors and all of his protective detail lay dead.

Choking from the cordite and teargas, the President was unable to fight off those who came to arrest him. He and the few cabinet members who'd survived were forced into two vans and taken to an undisclosed location.

***

With the government in complete shambles, the Vice President and Speaker of the House dead, the Secretary of State was the next in the line of succession, and he was more than ready to accept the mantle of leadership.

As word of President Richardson's arrest reached SOS Norman Bleakly's ears, he gave a nod to chief Justice Myers. The black robed man handed Bleakly a tattered Bible and said, "Repeat after me."

Bleakly followed his instructions and recited the 23 words which changed a man's destiny from a common citizen to the most powerful man on the planet.

President Norman Bleakly smiled following the swearing in ceremony. The helicopter, in which he flew, had a new designation. It was now Marine One and it came with four F-22 Raptor Fighter jets to escort it to Washington, D.C.

Everything was right on track. It was time to implement phase two of the Grid Protocols for his country ... his nation ... his people.

And there was no one left to stop him.

Chapter Three

"A criminal can lead a Dr. Jekyll-Mr. Hyde life, undetected by neighbors, co-workers, even family."

As the helicopter carrying Norman Bleakly dipped over the horizon, Olivia turned to her new associate.

"We need to put some distance between us and this lab. I'm sure by now Bleakly has ordered this place to be obliterated."

Fortunately, Conner had skills not listed on a résumé. He reached under the dashboard of Lily's car and pulled out a fist-full of harness connectors. Using his pocket knife, he sliced the ignition wire and the battery wires and touched them together. Sparks jumped and the engine turned over.

A satisfied smile stretched across his face. "Just like riding a bicycle. Now get in."

Incredulous, Olivia took her seat and slammed the passenger door. "Drive!"

Conner popped a wheelie and sped off. An instant later, two missiles struck the CDC anti-bio lab. The blast shook the car sending it careening sideways. It was all Conner could do to keep it on the road. Fishtailing, he raced ahead of the fireball and flying debris. After a few miles, they began to breathe easier.

Suddenly, a flash appeared in the sky followed by another missile. It struck thirty feet in front of them blasting a twenty foot hole in the asphalt. Conner swerved around as rocks and pieces of concrete ripped through the super-heated air.

"What was that?" Olivia screamed.

Once Conner regained control of the vehicle, he glanced into the rear-view mirror. "That was your government's dollars at work if I'm not mistaken. But not to worry, it was the last of the missiles that drone had."

"What if there was another drone?"

"Good point, Olivia. Just to be sure, I'm not taking any chances." As they approached an intersection, Conner yanked the wheel hard to the left and fishtailed through a stand of Joshua trees. The narrow road led deeper into a mountainous region surrounded by high cliffs and perilous drop offs. A few miles later, the road widened and they found themselves staring at the mouth of a collapsed mine.

Dust swirled as the car came to an abrupt stop. "Is this what I think it is?" Olivia coughed.

Conner extricated himself from the car and eyed the demolished mine entrance. "Yep. That it is."

"A lot of good it's going to do us. The Chinese are all dead, their money is scattered to the four winds, and this deed ..." She pulled it from her pocket and let the sheets of paper flutter away. "These are just as worthless as that mine."

Stepping closer to the pile of rocks, Conner offered her a wry grin. "Not so fast, my lady. I happen to know this mine holds the key to our future, if you're willing to dig for it."

Olivia let out an exaggerated huff. "I'm not so desperate as to start digging through rubble with my bare hands."

"You would if you knew there was a couple million dollars not fifteen feet from where you stand." As he spoke, he hoisted a football sized rock over his head and tossed it to the side.

"And how would you know?" she said, following his example.

"Because, I put it there. Before the virus struck, my crew and I recovered the bodies of a couple of unfortunate guys who fell victim to the Bird Flu virus. They were the two guards who drove a Garda truck full of money. Now are you interested?"

Olivia grabbed a rock and tossed it aside. "Very!"

***

Thinking he was hallucinating, Will tried to focus on the sounds outside the truck.

He'd been in total darkness for hours and had lost all sense of time. In the stifling heat and close quarters, he'd resigned himself to the fact that he was going to die. Hearing voices, he listened harder. It wasn't his imagination. There really were people out there, and they were digging.

The thought suddenly occurred to him. What if they were the same people who tried to kill him and Lily?

What if they had already done so? The idea of his sister lying dead in that awful facility made his blood run cold.

As he considered his options, a shaft of light sliced through the darkness. Whoever was outside had reached the truck and was working to free the door. He thought about the gun left by the man in the front of the cab. But even if he could break the glass window and get it, was he willing to kill another human being? No, he'd just have to wait and see. If they were Lily's killers, he was ready.

He took a seat on a stack of money bags and waited. His wait was interrupted when the rear door squeaked open and a flashlight blinded him.

"Who are you?" a male voice demanded.

Holding his hands between himself and the beam of light, Will stumbled forward over the bags of money. "I'm Gill ... I mean, William O'Reilly." He tried to sound brave, confident. But in reality, he was scared spitless.

"I remember you. You're the guy who beat me up outside the AC unit a few hours ago."

It was Conner.

The tables had turned and Will feared the worst.

"How did you end up in the back of this truck?" Conner asked, his voice carrying a sense of wonder, of admiration.

Will climbed out on stiff legs and stretched. "Lily and I returned to get our friend, Troy Ashcroft—"

"I know the guy. What's that got to do with—."

"Shut it Conner," Olivia snapped. "I want to know how he got here."

Will let out a weak chuckle. "Like I was saying, Lily and I came back to the lab and rammed the front of the building. We jumped out leaving the keys in the ignition and began to search for Troy. When we found him, he was in bad shape. I returned to the truck to get a bottle of water and climbed in the rear compartment," he tipped his head in the direction of the truck. "In the meantime, Mr. Wan jumped in the cab and backed out. When he did, I hit my head on something. The next thing I know, I'm stuck in there with a dead man." Will's knees buckled and he slumped to the ground.

Olivia grabbed his arm and guided him to a sitting position. "You're one lucky guy. That's all I've got to say."

Eyeing Conner, Will's fists formed into two iron sledgehammers. "What was that you were saying about a missile? Were you talking about my dad?"

Hands raised, Conner said. "Hey, now wait a minute. It wasn't my fault. It was Troy's fault. He jumped me from behind. We fought. What was I to do?" His hands moved animatedly. "He pinned me to the counter, his hand slipped and hit the trigger to the missile. I don't know if it hit your dad or not. I think it missed, but even if it landed close, I … don't … know … how—" his voice trailed off.

"You killed them!" Will jumped to his feet and lunged at Conner.

Olivia drew her weapon and brought it down on Will's skull. Flashes of red and orange streaks blurred his vision and he felt himself land hard on the ground.

Chapter Four

Will awoke to the sound of a guttural growl.

His eyes popped open and he found himself staring into Wag's bared teeth as he strained at his leash. Wag's raspy breath enveloped him. Reeling back, he found his arm handcuffed to the bumper of the truck. Wag lunged at him barking and tearing at him with his paws.

"Wag, Wag, it's me, Will," he said trying to calm the animal down.

Wag's wild eyes showed recognition. Relaxing his stance, he licked the slobber from his jaw, and sat on his haunches. He let out a soft yip, then lowered his head.

Cautiously, Will extended the back of his hand and rubbed the fur behind Wag's ear.

"Ada-boy," he whispered, "What's gotten into you?" Wag stood and nudged him with his nose. "Where did you come from anyway?

Olivia stood and stepped closer, her shadow blocking the sun. "He just appeared out of nowhere. While I was hiding in the lab, I saw him tear a piece out of Bleakly's arm. After that, he ran back inside the building with three men close on his tail." She let out a wicked chuckle. "Smart dog. He led those guys right into a trap. Those DNA pod creatures were all over them before they knew it. They didn't have a chance. Then he made a beeline back outside and tried to follow the helicopters. That was the last I'd seen of him until he showed up here. Conner chained him up before he attacked us. Is he yours?"

Will shook his head and moaned. Rubbing the knot on the back of his head. "My sister sorta adopted Him. He actually belongs to Cami Stetson."

His hand slid down to Wag's leg where the DNA pod jabbed its probe. It was irritated and festered. "I wonder if that DNA thing infected Wag with some sort of virus. Look at this." He separated the fur.

Olivia leaned in to get a closer look. A sharp object protruded from the wound.

With care, Will pulled it out and inspected it. The probe reminded him of a scorpion barb. "Cami will sure be upset if she knew what had happened to you, old buddy."

As if thanking him, Wag licked his hand.

"Looks like you've got a friend for life," Conner observed as he unlocked the handcuffs.

Will rubbed his wrists and let out a weak chuckle. "Yeah, I wonder what Lily would think about that." Standing, he asked, "Do you know what happened to her and Troy?"

Conner slouched against the truck and offered him a warm bottle of water. "For what it's worth, I'm sorry about your dad. As far as Lily is concerned, she wasn't as lucky as you. Bleakly arrested both of them. He said something about taking them to Grid Twenty-Six, wherever that is."

Will ran his hand across his face and started to leave. "I've got to find her."

Olivia grabbed his arm halting him mid stride. "Wait, you can't go out there. It's not safe. Those people who've taken over our country will arrest you just like they did your sister."

"That's if they don't shoot you first," Conner added as he dusted the dirt from his pants.

Olivia ignored him. "I've been monitoring the news. The bird epidemic swept the country. They've arrested President Richardson claiming he was somehow responsible. To make matters worse, Bleakly just finished a news conference. Apparently the Vice President and Speaker of the House had fallen victim to the bird attacks and he was sworn in as the President. His first act was to implement a program called the Grid Protocols."

Will's eyes switched between Olivia and Conner. "I can't believe what's happening."

"Believe it," Conner stated flatly. "Bleakly has been planning this for years. I should know. Scott Wan and I were in on the initial planning." He let an oath escape his lips. "We never thought it would go this far. I figured Scott would sell out his boss and the whole thing would backfire."

"It backfired all right," Olivia cut in. "Backfired on our country. We've got to stick together, form a plan, join forces with other survivors and take our country back."

Will let out a sideways smirk, strode to the back of the truck and hauled out a bag of money. "And how do you propose we do that? With this?" he asked, shaking the canvas bag.

Olivia snatched it from his hand. "Yes. This money will buy a lot of friends. Aren't you forgetting I'm a

Beretta? My father built one of the largest crime syndicates in the southwest. I could make a dozen phone calls and raise an army a thousand strong. Within a few weeks, we could mobilize and be ready to act as soon as the time is right."

Will knew something of the Beretta family. Even though he'd never met Olivia, it didn't take a rocket-scientist to see the resemblance. If anyone could pull together the old waring rivals, it was Olivia Beretta Emerson. And he was ready to join her ranks. "I agree. We need to build a coalition, find paramilitary groups and form a network," Will said, with renewed confidence. "But a frontal assault won't work. We've got to infiltrate their command and control units. Find their weaknesses; look for ways to take over from within."

Olivia smiled. "I like this guy," she cooed. "Let's get to work."

Patting Will on the back, Conner and Olivia began digging the rest of the rubble away from the truck. It was going to be a long day.

Chapter Five

"I imagined that I could turn the earth undetected."

Patti Smith

As the helicopter rose and the CDC facility receded from view, Lily felt the urge to jump.

She'd seen armed men pounce on Troy with extreme prejudice, while others chased Wag back into the CDC building. Her brother was nowhere to be found and she felt a gnawing suspicion that something bad had happened to her dad and Cami. In a matter of minutes she'd lost her brother, her father, and her home. Her stomach churned like a cement mixer. Fighting the urge to retch, she forced down the acid in her throat and swiped her tears aside. She refused to show these people weakness. She had to be strong, she had to resist, but her heart felt like it had been ripped from her chest.

The helicopter's bare-boned frame pitched and rolled tossing her around like a rag-doll. When it landed, Lily jumped out and immediately emptied what little she had in her stomach on the tarmac. After a moment, she regained her senses. A man grabbed her arm and yanked her to her feet. With a shove, he forced her to get in line with a number of other prisoners.

"Move out," he ordered.

She and the others shuffled forward until they reached the steps of a sand-bagged facility. It was surrounded by a concrete wall and topped with automated machine-gun placements located every twenty-five yards. This was no small operation, she mused.

Voices rose and she turned to see Troy being dragged from the other helicopter.

"Get your hands off—"

His protests were smothered by the laughter and curses of the men who held him. He struggled to his feet, lowered his shoulder and lunged at the guards. Lily gasped as the men struck him with the butts of the weapons.

"Take him to the pit," the unit commander ordered.

The pressure behind her eyes broke as tears flooded her eyes. Her vision blurred as Troy was dragged unconscious into another building. She felt her chest constrict.

"Inside," a guard ordered, ripping her attention from Troy.

Barely able to see through her tears, she stumbled up the steps. A female guard shoved her into a room.

"Take a seat," she barked.

Lily lowered herself onto a rickety aluminum chair. It was still warm from the last prisoner. Before she could relax, a guard hollered, "Next!"

It was her turn. She stood on rubbery legs and entered a curtained area where she was given a tattoo on her forearm, an orange uniform and a pair of rubber sandals. Once she was processed, she was ushered to a duce and a half military truck with a canvas top.

"Get in." The female guard's voice seemed cold, uncaring.

Fearing she'd be beaten, she and a group of other women climbed inside. They too sported a number tattoo. It was clear, they were going nowhere without this new government knowing it.

"Listen up," a female guard's commanding voice silenced the whimpering. Heads turned. Her icy glare left no doubt in Lily's mind who was in charge. "After your trial, you will be taken to our orientation facility. Once you have served your sentence, you will be assigned a job and sent to one of our work sites within the twenty-six grids. Any questions?"

There were none.

Chapter Six

The moment Troy opened his eyes he knew he was in trouble.

As the fog in his mind cleared, he remembered being forced into a helicopter over Lily's protests. He vaguely remembered the helicopter taking off. The stone-hard faces of the men sitting around him stared down as the ground receded. Even the medics who treated his wounds seemed uncaring.

The knot on the back of his head reminded him he'd not given up without a fight. As the terrain changed, something told him he was being taken … to Corcoran, California's most notorious prison.

He'd sent many men there, now it was his turn. Without the benefit of a trial, he was assigned a cell and a number. His only crime was that of being in the wrong place at the wrong time. Sitting among a mixed group of detainees, Troy found himself confronted with a toxic mixture of socialism and radical environmentalist doctrine.

A shaved-headed millennial stood before the group in camouflage cargo pants and a tan tee-shirt with sweat stains. Her tattoos and piercings were intended to make a statement; this is my body I'll do with it as I please.

"Citizens of Mother-Earth, greetings and welcome to your new home." The stud, which pierced her tongue, made it difficult for Troy to understand every word, but he got the overall gist. This person had drained the Kool-Aid pitcher.

"You will no longer address each other as him or her, sir or ma'am. You are prohibited to call yourself a man or woman, a male or female. You are a person. If you insist on identifying yourself as a male or female, you will be subjected to an intense reeducation course. Also, because humankind has destroyed Mother-Earth with their fossil fuels, their nuclear waste and carbon footprint, we, members of Earth First will help show you the error of your ways."

The speaker droned on about how it was man's fault for all the ills of the world. She was partly right, Troy thought. Adam and Eve violated God's only command. They brought sin and death into this world and with it, all the ills, the pain, the bloodshed. He could easily trace a crimson line of destruction all the way back to the Garden of Eden. Were it not for that one disobedient act, we would not be in the mess we're in today, Troy thought. But to blame it all on modern technology was pure madness. After an hour of hearing her drivel, Troy lifted his hand.

"Ma'am," he said to the gasps of those around him. "I think you have a few valid points, but I have just one question."

The young millennial glared at him. "What is it?" clearly not used to being questioned.

"If, as you say, evolution is true, and if, as you say, it is the survival of the fittest who get to rule the world, then isn't it logical to say, that we, the human race are the fittest, the most evolved species on this planet and as such, the masters and rulers of this earth? And if so, can't we choose how we use the resource of this earth?"

"Mister, you're out of line." The young woman's face turned the color of chalk as she realized she used a male nomenclature. She tried to correct herself, but Troy was not finished.

"On the other hand," he continued, "in the beginning, God created man and woman. They were named Adam and Eve. And God gave them dominion over all the earth. He told them to multiply and subdue the earth. This planet is our God-given home. And yes, there are those sloppy industrialists who have polluted it, and have stripped its trees, its soil, its minerals. But I also submit for your consideration all the good men and women have done in the name of science, medicine, technology. We have reduced poverty, fed millions, extended life expectancies, stopped rogue nations from attacking their neighbors—"

"And imposed their capitalistic, racist, homophobic, anti-socialistic rhetoric on the global community," the young millennial retorted.

As four guards grabbed Troy and dragged him away, his last cries were, "We came to liberate, not dominate."

The room fell silent as the doors closed. Finally, a chant began and grew in intensity. It was Troy's last word which resonated throughout the meeting room.

"We liberate, not dominate."

The shaken millennial lifted her hands to silence the crowd, but was drowned out as the voices of the people grew louder. Frustrated, she stepped off the podium and spoke to the commander of the International Guards who stood next to her. Her words could not be heard, but her intent was clear.

With a nod, the guards pointed their weapons and opened fire. Amidst screams and cries was heard, "We liberate, not dominate."

Then silence.

Chapter Seven

"It is impossible for true beauty to go on undetected."

The Author

The paramedics, assigned to Cami by the Secretary of State, fought valiantly to save her life.

When the ambulance from Sacramento arrived she was stable but needed immediate surgery. She was taken to Mercy General Hospital where, only months earlier, Trace had been. Now it was her turn. After several hours of surgery she awoke in the recovery room confused and alone.

"Where am I?" Her muffled question was answered by a strange woman.

She stepped into Cami's line of sight and placed her hand on Cami's forearm. "You're one lucky woman. When they brought you in, you were barely alive."

Cami tried to piece together the recent events, but they fluttered around in her head like scraps of paper in a wind tunnel.

"Whoa … what happened?"

The woman patted her arm gently. "All in good time, Cami. All in good time. Right now, you need to concentrate on getting better."

"Who are you and how do you know my name?"

"My name is Amanda Borden. I'll be your personal trainer and assistant."

"But, but—"

Peering down benevolently, Amanda said, "Miss Stetson, you are the nation's brightest star and I am here to help you shine."

Cami's heart-rate hiked causing the heart monitor to sound an alarm. A moment later, a nurse entered the room. Amanda stepped aside to let the nurse do her job.

"I thought she was having a—" the nurse's concerns were broomed aside.

"No need to worry. I was just telling Miss Stetson the good news."

The nurse smirked. "The good news is, you're alive. That's more than you can say about a lot of people."

"Get out!" Amanda's voice turned icy.

In an instant, the nurse's face turned ashen and she scurried from the room.

Amanda huffed as the door closed. Turning on the charm, she said, "These people," she shook her head. "They have no class. Now, you just relax, get some rest. We have much to do in the coming weeks and you'll need your strength."

Another condescending pat and Amanda swept from the room, leaving Cami with more questions than answers.

Chapter Eight

When the newly sworn in President arrived back in Washington D.C. he was pleased to learn most of the states were functioning well under martial law.

In a few days, the Grid Protocols would be approved by the surviving members of congress. It was a new day in the life of the nation.

As POTUS stepped off Air Force One, he was greeted with cheers and the usual bevy of questions from the fawning press.

He strode to a podium fostering a bank of microphones. Immediately, a number of top military brass and a few members of congress assembled behind him. With his sister, Amanda Borden, at his side he began. "Ladies and gentlemen of the press and my fellow citizens. Our country has just suffered the worst disaster since September eleventh." He let the weight of those first words settle across the air. "But we are a strong nation. We have sustained the deadliest attack Mother Nature could throw at us and we have prevailed."

Another pause.

"Today, I stand before you as living proof that mankind is the master of its own destiny. Instead of cowering in fear, we have conquered it. Instead of letting circumstances control us, we have wrest control of these spiraling circumstances and snatched defeat from the jaws of defeat."

Amanda cleared her throat and Bleakly glared at her. He stepped back and whispered, "What'd I say?"

"Read your notes. Don't go off script," she admonished under her breath.

He returned his gaze to the teleprompter. "As I was saying, we have snatched victory from the jaws of defeat. Together, we will build a better future, a better tomorrow, a better nation. To quote a President of the past, 'We will make this country great again."

A crowd of supporters with signs bearing the slogan, Better Future, Better Country, Better Tomorrow, began marching across the tarmac. As expected, the national media quickly focused on the message.

President Bleakly gave them a two thumbs up and slid into the Presidential limousine. As the vehicles headed to the White House, Amanda, sitting next to her brother, glared at him.

"What was that all about?" she demanded.

Bleakly turned, his eyes slightly unfocused. "What was what about?"

Amanda breathed a curse. "That little slip of the tongue. If it wasn't for me leaking your notes to the press your administration would be dead on arrival."

POTUS shrugged off her comments. "I've got it under control."

Amanda lifted his arm and pulled his sleeve back revealing the raw flesh left from Wag's teeth. "Just like you've got this under control?"

He yanked his arm from her grip. "It's nothing."

"Yeah, nothing that a few Rabies shots won't cure."

"It's not that bat, I mean bad," he corrected himself.

"That woman," Amanda said, still holding her brother's gaze.

"What woman?"

"The one you found along the highway. She's the one who donated her blood ... the one with the immunity to the virus. Isn't she?"

Bleakly nodded. "What about her?"

"You need to get a transfusion of her blood. Better yet, you should marry her."

Bleakly's jaw fell open. "Marry her!? I don't even know her."

"Doesn't matter. If we are to succeed in this ... we need to solidify your position. Now I want you to do exactly what I say and leave the rest to me and Mother Nature."

"I've seen what you and Mother Nature can do. And frankly, it frightens me."

Amanda let out a wicked, full throated laugh. "Yes, me and Mother Nature. What a dynamic duo."

Chapter Nine

"Look and you will find it – what is unsought will go undetected." **Sophocles**

It had been weeks since Lily and the other female detainees had been delivered to a local jail.

Her trial date was still a month away and she knew what was coming. Sitting in her overcrowded cell, Lily assessed her situation.

It was bleak.

She'd lost contact with her family, she'd been arrested for trespassing, and her lawyer was a total jerk. It was obvious, he cared nothing for her or the other women he represented. He was either driven by fear of being arrested or motivated by greed. One thing was clear; he was not going to win her freedom.

Finally, when her day came, her lawyer accompanied her to the courtroom. When her name was called, her attorney nervously took his place next to her. His plaid sports coat was a bit too short for his arms and didn't button around the middle. The bow tie he'd chosen was poorly knotted and failed to match any of the colors in the ensemble.

"Your client has been charged with criminal trespass, destroying government property and lying to a Grid Authority official. How does she plead?" the judge asked.

"Guilty," her attorney said, having not consulted her.

Lily's mouth gaped, "But, but—"

"Shush," the lawyer whispered. "If you claim innocence, it will go much harder. Just keep your mouth shut and let me do the talking."

With her eyes stinging, Lily sucked in a quaky breath.

"I might add, your honor, this is Miss O'Reilly's first offense and under the circumstances I recommend leniency."

The judge muttered something indistinguishable and leered at Lily. "I commend you to Corcoran State Penitentiary for a period not to exceed one year." His gavel came down with a bone-chilling crack.

Lily tried to grasp what had just happened, but all she could hear was her own sobs and the resounding crack of the gavel. The floor tilted and she felt herself falling. Were it not for a female guard who grabbed her by the arm she would have smacked her head on the hardwood floor.

"Come with me," she said and yanked her through a door.

Over her shoulder, she could see her incompetent lawyer. His shoulders scrunched up apologetically. "I'm sorry," he mouthed.

Lily was so shocked; she couldn't form a cogent thought, let alone an appropriate insult to hurl at the man. With a yank, the guard tugged her through a doorway and down a long corridor.

The rest of her day was a blur. After waiting in a cold, windowless holding cell for the other detainees to learn their fate, she and the others were loaded on an aging school bus. Once they were settled, six armed guards took their places in front, in the middle and in the rear of the bus. The driver depressed a button and the door closed. He pulled away from the curb and joined the traffic going west.

Lily wanted to ask her seatmate a dozen questions but the guards made it clear, no talking, no singing, no sudden moves. As the bus hummed along the highway, Lily tried to remember the last verse of scripture she'd committed to memory. It was sketchy. Memorizing the Bible was more difficult than memorizing facts and figures. Lord, help me! I really need you, she prayed.

As she waited, the verses in Isaiah 43:2 came to mind. *When thou passest through the waters, I will be with thee; and through the rivers, they shall not overflow thee: when thou walkest through the fire, thou shalt not be burned; neither shall the flame kindle upon thee.*

Lily let the words resonate in her mind. Pinching her soaked eyes tight, she tried to focus on that one thought … God is mindful of me. A sweet peace enveloped her and she drifted off to sleep.

Chapter Ten

After weeks of drifting in and out of consciousness, Cami's mind finally cleared. Her condition improved enough for her to eat solid foods and begin a regiment of physical therapy. But her memory was a different thing. She had no recollection of the events prior to her waking up. All she knew was that she'd been in a traumatic accident.

It was Amanda who help filled in the blanks. Miss Borden was a middle-aged woman with the energy of a millennial. From the moment Cami regained consciousness, she was there. It was her tough-love and unyielding drive that pushed Cami through physical therapy and the long days of rehabilitation.

When she was not in therapy, Amanda spent hours answering Cami's questions. Questions such as; 'How did the accident happen? Was anyone else involved in the accident? What was my life like before the accident?''

Amanda demonstrated the patience of Job as she filled in the details of Cami's life. 'You were trying to escape the Bird Flu virus when you were struck by another motorist. Unfortunately, the other motorist was killed. As to your other life, the one which ended tragically when the virus struck, you worked for a media firm as their spokesperson.'

No mention of Trace O'Reilly, no mention of Lily or Will, no mention of Sacramento.

Her narrative went on for weeks. It wasn't long before Cami began to believe it. It made sense. All around her was evidence of the truth of her statements. Millions of people had died as a result of the virus. There was one thing, however, she did remember. She had volunteered her blood to be used to create an antidote to counteract the virus. That act alone had catapulted her to stardom.

***

As her physical condition improved, she exchanged her hospital gowns for evening gowns.

The long days of indoctrination, of watching the news and reading about city-wide riots had changed her. In the six months since she was brought to the hospital, a lot had changed. Once the riots subsided and a state of normalcy returned, the nation woke up under a new regime … The National Grid Authority.

As Press Secretary and the face of the nation, Cami found herself being wined and dined by government and media personalities. Living in Grid One, formerly known as Washington, D.C., afforded her access to the power-brokers and decision-makers governing the new republic … The Republic of North America.

***

"Hold still," the hairdresser gently admonished.

Cami squirmed to see herself in the mirror. She liked the new look. Shorter is better, she thought. *It makes me look five years younger.*

Amanda breezed into the salon. "Oh, look at you!" she squealed. "If Norman doesn't notice you, I'm going to personally fit him with bi-focals."

Cami felt heat creep up her neck. "I should be the last person on his mind. That man has his hands so full. I can't believe he hasn't had a nervous breakdown."

"His hands are not so full that they can't grab ahold of—"

"Now, now, Amanda, let's keep it clean. I don't want to be a distraction. He's got plenty of other things to think about besides me. Anyway, I'm his press secretary. How would it look for the President of the United States having a liaison with one of his staff? It is out of the question."

"Not in this present day and age, my dear," Amanda cooed. "We're living in the twenty-first century, girl. Get with it."

Cami eyed her coolly. "It's not going to happen. Anyway, he's not my type."

Amanda guffawed. "Not your type, hmm? Like that dumb detective—" she clamped her hand over her mouth like she was seasick. "I mean—" The phone rang saving her from doing any more damage.

She snatched it from its cradle. "Uh-huh, I understand ... yes. But ... I was—"

The phone click off so loudly that even Cami heard it. "I take it someone is—"

"Hush," Amanda cautioned. Pulling a note pad close, she wrote, "We are being watched ... and listened to."

Cami felt the blood drain from her face. She snatched the pen and pad from Amanda's fingers. "Why? Who?" she wrote.

Amanda countered with a coy smile. "Not to worry. It's just big brother ... *my big brother.*"

Suddenly, it wasn't fun anymore. Cami grabbed Amanda by the arm and led her to the bathroom. After turning on the spigot, she said, "Are you and the President somehow related?"

A wicked smile curled Amanda's lips. She turned off the water and fisted her hip. "No need for secrecy. Yes, he's my brother. What of it?"

Cami crossed her arms over her chest. "You could have told me. Why the cloak and dagger? And why are you so gung ho about hooking me up with POTUS?"

The air between them scintillated with raw energy. "Look, Cami. All this," she extended her arm indicating the apartment, her clothes, her jewelry, the security detail et al, "is on loan. Just keep doing what you're doing."

Then she flung the bathroom door open and marched stiff legged from the apartment.

Once the air cleared, Cami plopped down on the lid of the commode, her mind reeling.

Chapter Eleven

"If left undetected, sin, like a cancer, can eat you alive."

The Author

W hen Trace first heard he was assigned to hard labor, he thought he might be smashing rocks with a sledge hammer.

Nothing could have been further from the truth. In the last six weeks since his reeducation ended, he'd been sent to a worn down factory in the middle of Detroit. His job, though not technically challenging, was physically demanding. The twelve-hour shifts and a foreman breathing down his neck to work faster drove him to the breaking point.

When the whistle blew signaling the end of the shift, he was more than ready to leave. He collected his lunchbox and jacket and joined the other men as they trudged to their barracks. As he rounded the last corner, a sign above the local bar caught his attention.

Free Beer, the blinking neon light flashed.

All at once, the old demon of alcohol wrapped its icy fingers around his mind and squeezed. Forgetting it was booze that had destroyed his relationship with Cami twenty-five years ago, and wrecked his marriage; he followed the other men into the bar.

Peering through the blue haze, he spotted the bar, behind it stood a buxom barmaid. She was a strawberry-blond with fiery red lips and dark eyes. She smiled at the last customer then stepped over to where Trace stood.

"What'll it be, honey?" her sultry voice sang over the laughter and honky-tonk music.

Trace inhaled, forgetting how toxic the air in a bar could be. It left him coughing his lungs out. Wiping his eyes, he tried to speak, but his vocal chords refused to cooperate.

"I got you covered, sweetie." She lifted a heavy glass mug, tipped it to the side as she filled it with a rich, golden liquid. After slicing off the foam with a ladle, she placed in on a napkin and slid it in my direction.

"Drink up. You look like you could use it."

His mouth salivated so much he could hardly swallow. With effort, he forced his shaking fingers around the handle and lifted it to his lips. It was the first beer he'd had in many years. The alcohol hit him like a mule kick.

He was hooked.

All the lessons, the promises to the AA group, to Cami … to God, were swept away by the time he'd reached of bottom of the glass.

Three mugs later he'd lost all restraint. He only hoped he'd be sober enough to show up for work the next day. If he failed to report to roll-call, he'd be sent to prison or worse … shot.

Life was cheap in Grid Twenty-Four.

***

The following day, Trace awoke to the shouts of angry men.

They were calling for everyone in his barracks to assemble and he was late. His mouth felt like he'd swallowed a pillow filled with angry bees. Sitting up, he tried to clear the cobwebs. The room tilted and he heaved. After emptying the remaining contents of his stomach on the wooden floor, he wiped the slobber from his lips with the sleeve of his shirt.

Fighting back another wave of nausea and the constant pounding in his head, he quickly dressed, pulled on his boots and stepped outside. In an instant, the bright daylight pierced his eyes, and his knees buckled as the weight of the sunrays pressed down upon him. He cursed the day, then regretted it.

Trying not to draw attention to himself any more than he already had, he tugged his grungy hardhat lower to block out the light and got in line.

While the unit commander read off the day's assignments, he tried to focus. "How'd I get home?" he muttered.

The man next to him shrugged. "That guy in row four, third one back. He dragged you to your bunk."

Trace tried to catch a glimpse of his benefactor, but it hurt to move his eyes. Twisting his neck was out of the question. "I'll have to buy him a beer after work," he whispered back.

The man smirked. "Beer's free, remember?"

Trace nodded, then pinched his eyes closed with a groan.

Later that day, after their shift ended, Trace found the guy who helped him get to his bunk.

"Hey Sammy," he hollered.

The man glanced up but kept walking. "You talking to me?" he eyed Trace with suspicion.

"Yeah, you're the guy who got me out of the bar last night, right?"

He nodded slowly, "Uh-huh, what of it?"

Trace stepped closer. "I just wanted to say thanks for looking after me. Why'd ya do it?"

Sammy shook his head. "You're Trace O'Reilly. I remember you from your detective days. A buddy of mine named Jimmy used to talk about you all the time."

"Jimmy? Are you talking about Jimmy Barlow?"

"The one and the same. Said you two were partners."

"Yeah, partners in the sense of detective partners. Not—" he let his sentence end without further explanation.

"Do you remember pulling a woman and kid from a burning car?"

Trace rubbed the stubble on his chin, trying to remember. "It was a long time ago."

"Yeah, about thirty-one years. I was the kid you guys saved. So I guess I owed you one. The way I figured it, that was my way of saying thanks."

Trace nodded at his logic. "Okay, so we're even."

"Yeah, s'pose so."

After an uncomfortable pause, they parted in different directions. Sammy to his squalid barracks, Trace to the bar.

***

Trace had just taken a seat and ordered a cold beer, when the football game, which had been playing on the big screen TV, was interrupted by a Grid Authority Public Service Announcement.

The room erupted in curses.

Glancing up, Trace's heart froze.

Cami's face filled the screen.

He thought he'd lost her, that she was dead. This was the first time Trace had seen her since the missile attack. Now he was faced with a new reality. Cami was not only alive, but she was the government's spokeswoman.

As she began to address the nation, the curses and cat-calls quickly turned to whistles. "Hey, honey. You can come home with me anytime," one man shouted.

Others laughed and taunted the television.

Unable to hear, Trace leaned over the bar and yelled, "Turn it up. I want to hear what she has to say."

The barmaid frowned, grabbed the remote and increased the volume. Even still, it was hard to hear every word over the room noise.

"My fellow countrymen, on behalf of the President, and his administration, we would like to extend our deepest sympathy to those who lost loved ones following the recent outbreak of the Bird Flu Virus. We are a nation in mourning. As such, we need time to heal, to refocus, to catch our breath. The events following those dark days have swept across this nation at such a rapid pace that even we are just now coming to realize how deep the conspiracy to overthrow our government went. The fact is, our elected officials lied to us. They led us to believe we were safe from biological and chemical attack. We were not. They wanted us to trust them for our safety, for our security, for our future. They were wrong. Fortunately, President Bleakly has acted swiftly in quelling the virus. As you know, I, myself, have poured out my life's blood to serve as an example of patriotism. I am asking you, my fellow countrymen to accept the new protocols and the ID chip being implemented on a national level. Do not resist! It is for your good and the good of the nation."

While Cami continued the propaganda, the men in the bar grew restless. The barmaid flicked the television off. "I'm not saying it's good and I'm not saying it's bad, but these PSA's are hurting my business," she offered Trace an inviting smile.

He took another sip and set the mug down. "How long have these PSA's been going on?"

She looked at him like he'd come from Mars. "Where've you been all this time? *Miss Stetson* has been parading her tush all across this country trying to drum up support for the new *el Presidente*."

Staring at the blank screen, Trace tried to remember the last few months. It was all a blur. "When I got out of the hospital, they sent me to reeducation class. After that, I've been working day and night."

The barmaid nodded. "Yeah, that pretty much sums up life in the grids anymore. We work, we sleep or get drunk, whichever comes first, and we get up and do it again."

The beer no longer interested him. He stood, grabbed his coat and lunchbox and headed for the door. Once outside, he took in a cleansing breath. As his mind cleared, he realized how tired he was, and how dumb he was. Shoulders slumping, he trudged back to his barracks, and flopped on his bunk. His last conscious thought was Cami's face.

Chapter Twelve

The noise inside Corcoran State Penitentiary never stopped.

Lily placed her hands over her ears to block out the vulgar shouts and incessant curses, but it didn't help. California's state-of-the-art prison was the noisiest place on earth, she thought. Only a week had passed, and yet it felt like nine months. To pass the time, she began marking the wall with small scratches; one mark for every day.

Meal time was the worst. Those senior inmates intimidated the younger ones, stealing their food and making their lives a living Hell. Lily tried to shut it out, but the abuse continued.

After taking a seat, she tried to offer a prayer of thanksgiving, but the words just wouldn't come. So she just bowed her head.

"Hey, we got us a prayer here," a raspy, smoker's voice called out over the cacophony of laughter and curses.

Lily's eyes popped open. The people sitting across from her gaped at her like she'd committed murder.

The voice belonged to Sister Soldier, a big boned woman with tattoos covering most of her body. She loomed over Lily with menacing eyes. "You got a prayer for me?" Her cackle brought smirks from the others. "Here, let me give you something to pray about."

In a flash, the woman scooped up a handful of baked beans from Lily's tray and slathered them across Lily's chest and face. Lily sprang to her feet, gasping. Fingers trembling, she pulled her blouse away from her skin as the steaming hot mess scalded her. Fighting back tears, she snatched up a napkin and wiped her face, but the woman would have none of it.

She grabbed Lily's plate and slung it at her. But Lily saw it coming and ducked out of the way. The plate struck the woman next to her. A moment later, the cafeteria erupted in a brawl.

Whistles blew and an alarm sounded. Guards of both genders rushed in to quell the violence. Before Lily knew it, she and Sister Soldier were being dragged from the dining hall.

Lily was shoved into a holding cell and told to sit down and keep her mouth shut. She slumped against the wall and slid down, her heart still pounding. An hour later the warden entered the cell and glared at her. "Miss O'Reilly, what are we going to do with you? You pick a fight with the meanest woman in the facility and expect to be treated like royalty?" It was not a question.

Lily tried to speak, but the warden waved her off. "I'm sending you to the pit. Maybe you will learn a little respect around here." As he spoke, a guard they called Fat Louie, and another guard entered. They reminded Lily of Mutt and Jeff; two mismatched tin horns created by cartoonist Bud Fisher. Only there was nothing comical about these two men.

"No, no!" Lily tried to push them away, but their hands clamped around her arms like vise-grips.

They jerked her to her feet. "Come with me," Fat Louie said.

It suddenly occurred to her, that he said, "me," not, "us." Dread enveloped her as the fat man dragged her down a long, dark corridor. His unrelenting leer sent chills over her. When they reached a section of the prison which reminded her of the Bastille, the guard swiped a pass-key though a slot and swung the door open.

"Get in," he ordered.

Before she could take a step, he shoved her forward. Rather than slamming the door behind her, he stepped in behind her. "Lesson one, don't resist. Lesson two, don't say a word."

Lily braced herself as the man reached for her blouse. Sucking in a sharp breath she imagined herself in another place ... a place far away where evil doesn't exist, where justice prevails.

***

Lily woke with a jerk.

Something furry brushed against her legs and she curled up and into a tight ball. Whatever it was, scampered across the floor. It sounded like it was trying to climb the wall, but in the darkness she couldn't tell which wall. She pushed herself into the corner, keeping her hands and feet tucked under her. She wanted to scream, but knew it wouldn't do any good.

Pinching her eyes closed, she prayed until she drifted off to sleep.

Hours later, she awakened feeling dirty both inside and outside. She stood on cramped legs. In the corner of her cell was a filthy sink and a roll of paper towels. It wasn't much but it was better than nothing. Using the tiny bar of soap, she did her best to bathe. The paper towels disintegrated as she dried off. With each sheet she pulled up, another one popped up. By the time she'd finished, she'd used up the entire roll. She knew she would need them in the days ahead. Since the cell lacked any other hygiene products, she spread them out to let them dry.

When she'd finished, her bath, the cell looked like a Chinese paper factory rather than a prison.

As the days dragged on, memories of that night haunted her. Visions of Fat Louie's wicked face hovering over her came into view. She felt nauseous and dreaded the worst. What was she to tell Troy? How could she admit what had happened to her? Guilt gnawed at her like a dog with a bone. Could she have fought him off? Should she have tried? She made up her mind, if Fat Louie came at her again, she'd either kill him or he'd kill her, but she'd not go down without a fight.

A week after being in the pit, a female guard unlocked Lily's cell and swung the door open. "Stand!"

Lily knew to obey without question.

"Turn around and extend your hands."

Lily obeyed.

The guard clicked a set of steel bracelets around her wrists and spun her around.

"Step forward."

Lily complied. Wherever she was taking her, she hoped it was far from Fat Louie's reach. But that was not to be.

***

As the female guard led her from the pit, Lily caught a glimpse of Fat Louie.

He glared at her lustfully. Determined not to let him intimidate her, she returned his cold stare. All she had were the handcuffs. If it came down to it, she'd use them to choke the man to death.

Fortunately, it didn't come to that. She was led down a brightly lit corridor with polished floors and a number of locked doors. She could hear the groans and mutterings of those behind the doors and wondered who they were and what they'd done to deserve such harsh treatment. When they reached her cell, a female guard stopped and swung the door open.

"Get in, wait until the door is closed, then back toward me."

Lily followed her orders. The guard released the cuffs, freeing her hands and then closed the outer door. She turned and peered through the small reinforced window. She had to admit, things were looking up. Her cell was clean, as were the sheets and toilet. It was relatively quiet, at least at that time of the day. Then it dawned on her; this was the inmates' break time. Standing on her tiptoes, Lily peered through the slats in the outer window.

Great, a room with a view, she thought.

From her vantage point in cell R-123, she could see a sliver of sky and a slice of real estate called the 'Yard.'

The fifty by fifty foot pen was encircled by a chain linked fence topped with razor wire and guarded by heavily armed men. It was here they let a limited number of inmates stretch their legs and get some much needed fresh air each day.

Lily soon realized the two hour stint was a privilege that could be revoked with the slightest infraction. Her slot was right after dinner; a time when she felt the evening sun, the winter winds and the loneliest.

Her nine by six foot cell came equipped with none of the comforts of her posh condo. The hundreds of thousands of dollars she'd spent to renovate it and furnish the loft space were long gone as well as her million dollar nest egg. Using the side of her sandal to make a mark on the wall, she counted down the days. She only had 355 more days to go if her calculations were correct.

Sitting in her cell, Lily imagined what it must have been like for her dad when he was incarcerated. Both were falsely accused, both were mistreated. Although his outcome turned out quite differently, they both found themselves running for their lives through the sewers of the prison. She hoped her release would happen before it came to that.

***

Lily's days quickly fell into a predictable routine.

After breakfast, she and the other detainees were taken to reeducation class where everything she believed was challenged; her understanding of history, her country, even her faith. It was all she could do to keep from screaming out the truth, but she knew the moment she did that, her days would be numbered.

When class was finished, Lily was returned to her cell and given, "vitamins." The result was sleep, not better health. She'd tried not taking them, but found the guards forced them upon her if she resisted. When she awoke, she discovered places on her arm where someone had injected her with a needle. She soon lost her appetite and what food she did eat, she couldn't keep down. She became listless, irritable, even paranoid.

The pattern continued for weeks, then ended without explanation. Whatever they were doing to her had either been a success or failure. She didn't care as long as she could think clearly.

The only source of stimuli Lily had was looking through the small reinforced window into the wide corridor. Occasionally, she'd catch a glimpse of Fat Louie. When she did, she'd reel back to the furthest wall.

Her breathing shallowed and her palms slicked. Still suffering from guilt, she'd spend the night sobbing her eyes out. Her only solace was the few scriptures she'd memorized. One particular verse kept coming to mind. It was Jeremiah 29:11. *"For I know the thoughts I think toward you, saith the Lord, thoughts of peace, and not evil, to give you an expected end."*

She didn't know what that verse meant, but she clung to it like it was her only lifeline.

Chapter Thirteen

"Fears are undetected robbers, robbing us of our future and are mostly rooted in our past." **Evinda Lepins**

The loud speaker crackled to life.

"Inmates in Cell Block 9B, stand in front of your doors and prepare for dinner."

The announcement sent a cold chill cascading over Lily. As she waited her turn to be released, she sent up a short prayer. "Lord, protect me."

The cell door clicked open and she and the others formed a line and began walking. She entered the cafeteria with mixed emotions.

Although she craved the interaction with the other detainees, she feared another encounter with Sister Soldier would be deadly. She'd seen what the woman could do with her bare hands. Other inmates could testify to the woman's brutality as well. Sister Soldier made it clear, it was she who ruled the dining hall. Anyone foolish enough to break her rules found themselves at her mercy.

Today was no different.

It was rumored that she and Fat Louie were working together. Whenever a pretty young female inmate stepped out of line, she fell prey to her and her evil partner.

Sister Soldier stood with her arms crossed glowering at the slow moving serving line. A young newbie, unfamiliar to the rules, failed to give her server proper respect. Before she had time to set her tray down, Sister Soldier had her by the throat. Lily watched as the guards, like sharks smelling blood, began to circle.

"You didn't say thank you to your server," Sister Soldier's voice sliced through the cacophony, silencing the room.

Lily glanced around. She could see the fear in the young girls' eyes. The calloused inmates went about their meal with passive indifference. But Lily knew if she didn't intervene, the girl would suffer at the hands of Fat Louie. She'd be taken to the pit, beaten, violated, and left in darkness for days.

Before anyone could stop her, Lily stood and began to sing the thank you song. It was part of their dinner routine, the only difference was, it was before, not after dinner. Soon, the entire dining hall joined the chorus.

The look on Sister Soldier's face was rewarding, but it only lasted as long as they were singing. When the chorus ended, she made a bee-line for Lily. Lily's blood curdled as the big woman plowed through the room like a human wrecking ball.

Just before she reached Lily's table someone stuck their foot out. Sister Soldier tripped and fell taking tables and chairs with her. She fumbled to her feet, slipped and fell again. Laughter began to percolate across the room. With effort, she hoisted her girth up and stood, glowering. By now, her crisp orange uniform was covered with the contents of the trays. Her hair dripped with a greasy substance.

Fat Louie colored the air sailor blue. He shoved the laughing inmates aside and came to her rescue. As he neared, someone else extended their foot sending him tumbling. The two caught each other and before anyone could stop them, they slipped and fell like two lovers on an icy lake.

In a heartbeat, the women surrounding them pounced like a pack of wolves. Using whatever they could find; plastic forks, trays, fingernails, the inmates poured their contempt on the two.

Like a raging bull, Sister Soldier stood and bellowed, "Silence."

The room fell silent except for a few snickers.

With effort, Fat Louie pushed himself to his feet. It was obvious he had suffered the worse at the inmate's hands. "All outdoor privileges are revoked," he bellowed.

Lily joined the crowd as a chorus of, "To the pit," grew in intensity.

Soon the dining hall vibrated with the mantra drowning out Sister Soldier's demands for silence. It was clear she had lost control.

"Guards," Fat Louie called.

Immediately, the place swarmed with angry guards. The chant morphed into, "Lock her up, lock her up."

With the situation in a near riot, Fat Louie was forced to follow protocol. He pulled out a pair of hand cuffs and slapped them around Sister Soldier's wrists.

Fearing he'd be tripped again, he ordered the guards to form a circle. Like a football team going for the goal line, they dashed toward the door.

The moment the door closed, the room erupted into cheers. When the celebration subsided, the young girl squeezed in next to Lily. She'd gotten a fresh serving of food and claimed Lily as her only friend.

"Thank you for what you did." The girl's eyes danced with admiration.

Lily retook her seat. "I only did what was right."

"Yes, but it was you who stood up to that woman, not anyone else."

"True, but I'm sure I'll suffer the consequences for my action in the days to come."

The girl glanced around at the sea of faces. They were smiling, laughing, talking animatedly. "I don't think so. You've got a room full of supporters. If they try that again, we'll all stand up for you. By the way, my name is Nadia."

Lily washed the last of her meal down with a swig of orange juice. "Nice to meet you, Nadia. I'm Lily."

The two exchanged hugs. "I hope you're right."

Lily returned to her cell knowing she had a friend, but she also knew the authorities had someone they could use as leverage against her.

***

The following day, her routine took a drastic change. Before breakfast, two guards arrived at her cell, cuffed her and took her to the Debriefing Room where she was shackled to a table. For the next three hours she was subjected to bright lights, loud music and continuous demands for information. Information she couldn't give. Her interrogators were intent on finding out all she knew about Olivia Beretta Emerson.

Lily's knowledge of the woman was limited to only a few brief minutes, yet they demanded she tell them over and over about those minutes in the CDC lab.

After the interrogation, she was returned to her cell. She had missed lunch and supper.

The following morning, the routine began where it left off.

More demands.

More shouting.

More loud music.

At one time, she overheard the guards arguing. One of them let it slip that Mrs. Emerson was wanted for conspiracy to overthrow the government. That information alone made it worth resisting.

Finally, after weeks of being interrogated, the interviews ceased leaving Lily to wonder if someone else had given the authorities the information they sought.

The one thing she wished more than anything was to learn the whereabouts of Will or Troy. But as hard as she tried, she could find out nothing. It seemed they had simply disappeared.

Hope faded and she lost the will to live. Her appetite waned. Her prison issued orange uniform sagged on her like an over-sized raincoat and she began to lose muscle mass.

Chapter Fourteen

Hearing voices in the hall, Lily stood and peered through the small window in her door.

She caught a glimpse of a man being dragged from his cell. Her heart ached for him even though she didn't know him. His prison clothes hung on him like a gunnysack, and his arms were bruised and lacerated from a steady diet of beatings. She pinched her eyes closed and whispered a prayer. "Lord, please show this man your mercy. He has suffered so much. Give him grace to endure whatever happens to him." When she looked again, the guards and the man were gone. Slumping down, she pulled her knees to her chest and wept softly.

Several hours later, she uncurled herself and stood. The guards were returning with the man they'd taken earlier. Cupping her hands on the glass, she watched them place the unconscious man on his bunk.

Moments before the door slammed shut she caught a glimpse of him. It was no surprise what she saw. His bearded face was a mesh of lacerations. Angry purple and blue bruises swelled his eyes closed.

***

The following day, the guards returned.

A cold knot formed in her stomach and she wondered if they'd come for her or the man across the hall.

When they opened the cell across from hers, she breathed a long sigh of relief, then she chided herself. She had no right to feel relief at someone else's suffering. The thought of that poor man enduring another round of beatings made her blood run cold.

As they swung the door open, she got a better look at the prisoner. The swelling around his eyes had gone down enough for her to see that they were blue. His body, though bruised, showed he was at one time in good physical condition and there was a familiar scar above his right eye.

All at once, the man looked directly at her.

It was Troy.

He had survived the long nightmarish ordeal.

Using her hands to get his attention, she flashed the sign, 'I Love You.' In like manner, he flashed it back before the guards led him away.

In the weeks to follow, they developed their own form of sign language. Left fist, right finger meant 'A'. Left hand one finger, right hand one finger meant 'F' and so forth until they spelled the whole alphabet. 'Z' of course created a number of challenges, so they settled on two fists. Seldom, however, did they ever need a 'Z' in their communication as most of the time their messages were rudimentary.

"R U OK?" he asked.

"I am. How R U doing?"

"I'll survive," he spelled "I heard we were taken over."

Lily waited for a guard to pass before answering. When her chance came, she said. "From within. The new gov controls everything; water, el., commerce, even the highways." She'd learned this by listening to the other detainees talk. It took time for her to spell each word as the guards kept a constant rhythm between the far ends of the corridor.

"Who's running the country?" Troy asked.

"Bleakly. He's the President."

"What happened to the President? The Constitution? The government?"

Lily hated being the bearer of bad news, but that's all she had.

"Gone?"

"Why were they beating you?" she asked.

"I refused to submit. And I fought them when they tried to inject me with that tracking device."

Lily's lower lip trembled at the thought of him being tortured and beaten.

"How long will you be here?" he asked.

She fingered spelled ninety-one days if my calculations are right. "After that, I'm not sure." She wanted to tell Troy about being assaulted, but the memory was too painful, too raw to put into words.

After a long pause, Troy responded with three simple words. "Keep the faith."

That was all Lily had to cling to … her faith.

Chapter Fifteen

"The stealth bomber is supposed to be a big deal. It flies in undetected, bombs, then flies away. I've been doing that all my life."   **Bob Hope**

The phone outside the Oval Office rang several times before Millie picked it up.

Millie lifted the phone from its cradle. "Office of the President, Millie Kendall speaking."

It was Amanda Borden, the President's half-sister and chief adviser. "I need to speak to Norman … immediately." Amanda demanded.

She was the only person who called the president by his first name. It was clear she thought she was the power behind the man.

This will be interesting, Millie thought.

"He is meeting with—"

"I don't care who he's with. I need to speak to him now!"

Millie felt heat creep up her neck. "I'll let him know you're on your way.

She pressed the button on the phone and POTUS picked up. "Sir, Miss Borden wants to see you."

The President let out a curse. "Uh, thank you."

A moment later, three wealthy supporters shuffled from the Oval Office. Before the door closed, Amanda marched in and shut the door without giving Millie a second look. The two men and one woman exchanged glances.

Millie stood and ushered them down the hall. "My apology, obviously Miss Borden has an urgent matter which couldn't wait."

The three supporters accepted the quickly woven excuse and exited.

As they left, Millie pressed a hidden button which activated a listening device. It recorded every word POTUS said. In her position as the President's personal secretary and gate keeper to the President's schedule, she'd been quietly monitoring his activities since the takeover. Her clearance level afforded her access to top secret information. Information she passed along to her friends in the underground.

"What should we do with the former President and his remaining cabinet?" Amanda asked.

The shuffle of papers filled the silence. "I don't know. What do you suggest?"

Not missing a beat, Amanda continued, "I personally think a public execution would be in order. The public already blames him and his administration for the bird flu debacle. Why not give them what they want … an eye for an eye, a tooth for tooth and blood for blood."

"I'm not sure that's such a good idea. This isn't France and it wasn't the French Revolution. My coming to power was within the bounds of the constitution."

"True, but if the public ever discovers the truth, we'll have Hell to pay. Getting rid of your competition only makes sense." Amanda cooed.

Bryan M. Powell

What was it about Amanda that had such sway over the President's mind? What spell had she spun? Millie wondered. One thing she knew, she had to act fast if she was going to save former President Richardson's life.

She immediately drafted an inner White House memo recommending the former President be moved to Corcoran State Penitentiary and placed on suicide watch. She signed the President's name and sent it to the respective parties. With any luck, the transfer would go without a hitch.

Just before she returned to her work, she noticed a request for a Good-Will prisoner exchange. The request came from two squabbling western grids. Numbers Twenty-Four and Twenty-Six wanted to swap a dozen technical and medical personnel for twelve computer analysts. Their names were listed on the memo and a separate document was attached requiring the President's signature. She added the named Trace O'Reilly to the shortest list and signed Bleakly's signature. She shoved them inside an envelope marked, "Official Requisition", and placed it in the out box. Returning her attention to the conversation, she continued to listen.

"One other thing," Amanda continued.

"What is it?" POTUS sounded irritated.

"I still think you should propose to Miss Stetson."

Millie nearly fell out of her chair.

It sounded like the President did too.

"Amanda! We've been over this a dozen times. We're not compatible." He sounded defeated. Like a man resigned to bachelorhood.

"No, you're not." Amanda said. Her voice sounded as smooth as a baby's bottom. "But we both know your numbers are tanking. Plus, it would do you good. You're too up-tight. You've been working so hard recently. You're due for a heart-attack or a nervous breakdown. Marrying Miss Stetson would provide the nation a good excuse to support you and give you some spring in your step. And there's that other matter; the one involving your posterity. You want to have a child with this woman, one that will be immune from all such diseases. It will be your legacy."

Silence filled the space while Norman considered her suggestion. "Tell you what, I'll ask her, but I doubt she'll agree."

"Oh, she'll agree. I'll see to it."

The phone rang and Millie removed her listening device from her ear and answered the phone.

As she fielded two more phone calls, Amanda stepped from the Oval Office. She indicated she wanted to say something, so Millie put the call on hold.

"Yes?"

"The President isn't feeling well. He is not to be disturbed under any circumstances. If you need anything, *anything*, call me first." Her tone sounded huskier than normal.

Millie knew not to ask any questions and responded with a simple, "Yes, ma'am."

The elevator doors opened just as Amanda approached. It reminded Millie of a scene from the movie, *Get Smart*. Amanda stepped inside and then turned. A moment later, the doors slid shut and Millie breathed a sigh of relief. She needed to get the information to her contact outside the White House and she needed to meet with Cami before Amanda got to her. With the clock ticking, she private messaged Cami hoping it would not be picked up by those who monitored Cami's Facebook, email and Twitter accounts.

Chapter Sixteen

It wasn't unusual for Cami to get emails from her fans, but a private message from Millie caused her breath to catch.

As the administration's spokesperson, Cami's strictly screened email box overflowed with requests for interviews, one-on-ones and special favors. She was expected, even encouraged, to respond to as many as possible. She usually graciously refused most requests.

Having daily contact with her made Cami wonder why Millie didn't just speak with her the next time they met. Sensing urgency, she eased her office door closed and clicked on Millie's name.

The message read, 'Hey, let's do lunch.'

Cami smiled at the request. She typed, "Any time." And hit send.

To her surprise she got an immediate response.

'Today at noon. Meet me at the Le Bon Cafe'.'

Pleased with the chance to get away from Amanda's stifling presence, she made a mental note not to mention her lunch arrangements to anyone.

Turning her attention to the latest press release, slated for the next news cycle, she lined out a few words and scribbled her own in the margin which represented administration in a better light. Then she forwarded it the news outlets. Between phone calls asking for an interview with POTUS and special interest groups demanding to see her boss, her morning whizzed by.

By noon, her stomach growled, reminding her of her lunch appointment. She'd seen Amanda several times throughout the morning and knew she was in no mood for another confrontation. Rather than get involved in a long explanation, she grabbed her purse and sweater and left through the back entrance.

Taking the sidewalk, she quickened her pace. It felt good to be outside, to stretch her legs, not to mention her lungs. Unlike other days, the autumn air was brisk, the leaves showed signs of wear and tear. She loved this time of year with its festivities and its parties. It wouldn't be long before they would be celebrating both Christmas and New Years; one without the fear of birds.

She wove through the pedestrians, businessmen in tailored suits, professional women in form-fitting skirts and blouses, and occasional gathering of tourists until she reached her destination. Slightly out of breath, she stepped into the cafe'. The air conditioning fought to keep the place cool despite the crowd of diners. Across the room sat Millie, a petite, athletic type, studying the menu.

She stood as Cami approached and greeted her with a bright smile and quick hug. "So glad you could make it on such short notice. Any problems getting away?"

Cami took a seat and she shook her head. "No, I just didn't tell anyone, especially Amanda. The woman is like a shadow."

Nodding, Millie smiled, not commenting. After placing their orders, Millie glanced around, leaned in closer, and said in a conspiratorial tone, "Cami, I have something to discuss with you of a very sensitive nature."

Cami played with her water glass for a minute. "I knew you wanted something. What, you want me to put in a good word—"

Millie brushed aside the comment. "It's nothing like that, Cami." Glancing around, she tried again. "I'm going to tell you something in the strictest of confidence. Can you keep a secret?"

After a beat, Cami relaxed her grip on the water glass. "Yes, I suppose. As long as it's not some crazy plot to overthrow the government," she said, toying with her napkin. She noticed Millie didn't smile.

"I'll take that as a yes. Truth is, I do have connections to some powerful people who are very concerned with the direction of the country."

She had Cami's full attention. "Oh?"

Millie pressed ahead. "Actually, I am with the CIA, or what is left of it. I was assigned to follow the activities of the secretary of state before the bird disaster."

Suddenly, Cami's throat felt like sandpaper. She took a sip of water. "Go on," she encouraged her.

"You've got to promise you won't breathe a word of this to anyone. Can I have it?"

After a beat, Cami nodded. "Yes, I promise. Why? What's this all about?"

Their meal arrived, but Millie didn't eat. She continued without giving her soup and sandwich a second look. "My contacts need access to the grid codes."

Cami took in a sharp intake. "The grid codes? That's treasonous."

Hands held up to calm Cami before she caused a scene, Millie continued. "I have information that your fiancé is alive."

Palm to her mouth, Cami couldn't hide her surprise. "Trace is alive!?"

"Yes, but he is under constant surveillance. Any attempt to contact him would result in his and your death. Now do I have your attention?"

Nodding, Cami leaned closer. "Can you get a message to him?"

Millie shook her head. "No, but I monitor all chatter concerning him and some very important political prisoners. Now I need your help. I need you to get inside the Oval Office and get the codes."

"I can't do that. No one is allowed in his office without him being there. That is with the exception of Amanda. It seems she has his complete attention."

Finally, after her soup had gotten cold, Millie lifted her spoon and took a sip. While the two women ate, Millie continued to lay out her plan.

"She doesn't have the President's full attention ... you do, Cami. You see, Amanda has talked POTUS into asking you to marry him."

Cami choked and grabbed her glass of water. She gulped a few swigs to clear her throat. "She what?" Cami said in a controlled scream. "How would you know that?"

A few heads turned.

"Keep your voice down. Someone might hear you."

Cami closed her eyes and shook her head. "I can't believe this."

"Believe it. POTUS's office is bugged." She smirked. "Actually, every square foot of the White House is bugged. I overheard him and Amanda discussing it. You see, he needs to change his persona. His poll numbers are in the teens and he wants to change that."

Cami's hand grabbed Millie's and squeezed. "His poll numbers are not in the teens. I read the daily reports. They are somewhere between—"

Millie's eyes bore into with fresh intensity. "They are being manipulated, just like everything else. It's all lies. Believe me. He knows he is sitting on a powder-keg. If he doesn't unify the nation, he is facing a revolt."

"So why would marrying me change that?" Cami couldn't believe she was having this discussion.

"Because … you are the darling of the nation. Everyone loves you. Marrying you will give him credibility, not to mention a child."

"I could never marry him. Not knowing Trace is somewhere, locked away in a prison."

"You won't have to marry him. Just get close enough to him to steal the codes." As she spoke, she slid a burner phone across the table and stood. "Who knows, maybe you have been brought into the kingdom for such a time as this."

The image of Esther standing in Ahasuerus' courtyard praying for courage to enter without the king's permission scrolled across her mind like a movie.

"Think about it. When you're ready, use this phone and say the words 'Till death do we part.'"

Cami glanced down at the phone and mulled over the words. When she looked up, Millie was gone.

Chapter Seventeen

"For the wrongdoer to be undetected is difficult; and for him to have confidence that his concealment will continue is impossible." **Epicurus**

When Millie returned from lunch, she found a brown paper sack sitting in the middle of her desk.

Curious to know its contents, she inspected it for a note. There was none. "I wonder what this is and who sent it," she muttered.

Curious, she unfolded the top and peered inside. It was a bottle of pills, the kind you would expect from a typical pharmacy. Her heart rate spiked as she withdrew the bottle. It contained a month's supply of pills. The label on the outside indicated the pills were for Amanda.

The elevator dinged and Millie dropped the bottle back inside the bag, but not before snapping a mental picture of the label. Zyprexa. *Hmm, I'll have to look that up.*

A moment later, Amanda stepped from the elevator. Her eyes fell on the bag in Millie's hand. She snatched it up. "Don't you dare breathe a word about this," she seethed. Then she disappeared inside the Oval Office.

The listening device cracked slightly and she heard Amanda's silky voice. "Norman, I've got something for your headaches." A bag rattled and Millie figured it must be the one from the pharmacy. While the conversation between the President and Amanda continued, Millie booted up her computer and typed in Zyprexa. Immediately, the screen registered several sites for the drug. It wasn't for headaches. It was a powerful drug designed to control schizophrenia, manic depression and bipolar disorder.

"So that is why POTUS has been acting so strangely." She noticed the subtle change of personality over the course of several months. She chalked it up to the pressures of the job. Some men thrived on such demands. Others sought relief from booze or worse … women.

Millie made a mental note of it, erased her search history and pulled up a file containing the President's schedule. While she skimmed through the following day's activities, Amanda strode from the Oval Office.

"He's not to be disturbed."

I think he already is. Millie hoped her mind wasn't bugged.

Chapter Eighteen

I t had taken Olivia longer than she'd expected to contact her father's old friends and rivals.

Having to deal with the curfew, roadblocks and a general government takeover, she found it difficult to move within the shadows and outside the law. First, she had to build trust between her father's former syndicate associates. That took money ... lots of it.

Fortunately, she had a truck load of it, literally.

Then she had to establish a network of communication between all the parties involved. That was where Conner shined. His old contacts inside the White House security detail proved invaluable. Using a number of old satellites which the military discarded, yet remained in orbit, he was able to circumvent the grid and move money and information without detection.

Using Conner's connections with the military establishment, he acquired surplus solar panels, miles of cable, computers. With it, he built a power system. The next problem was water. Again, his connections and Olivia's money provided the answer. He purchased drilling equipment and pipes on the black market and hired roughnecks to run the rigs. Santa Vern was not only rich in uranium, but it had a vast supply of natural gas which they parlayed into a major money source.

Within nine months, they'd transformed Santa Vern into a thriving community, off the grid of course. The former nuclear dump site had grown from a dusty ghost town to the new Las Vegas. It boasted twenty casinos and scores of hotels, restaurants and bars. Surrounding the town was a twelve-foot copper fence, patrolled by armed guards. In the center of it all was a tower one-hundred foot tall which sent out an electronic pulse, thus making the town a dead-zone.

That was just the beginning of Olivia and Conner's plan. They'd made contact with people inside the Bleakly administration who were willing to form a shadow government. Using the information they provided, Olivia began to discover all was not well within the administration. There were rivalries, deprivations, even infighting; all of which she used to her advantage.

Using the Santa Vern Saloon as a front, she'd built a network of informants who kept her in constant contact with the outside world. Located in a backroom behind two steel-reinforced doors, Olivia governed her clandestine underground in the spirit of Luciano Beretta. Her goal was simple; the overthrow of the government and to take back her country.

***

In the months after the implementation of the Grid Protocols, nearly every citizen had been forced to receive an ID chip which contained both the virus and its antidote.

Anyone attempting to cross from one grid to another without permission died from the infection. Fortunately, Olivia, Conner and Will had escaped before the International Guard caught them.

While she and her team were busy building their National Resistance Army, or NRA, the country was undergoing its own change. The United States of America had been renamed The Republic of North America. It had been divided into twenty-six separate grids; each vying for power and position.

Individual grid authorities often joined forces with neighboring grids to starve out the smaller ones. Already, Grids Twenty-Two and Twenty-Five, which consisted of the mid-west, had combined to force Grid Twenty-Four, the states of Minnesota, Wisconsin and Michigan, to capitulate their vast water supply in exchange for wheat and crude oil. Now they had their sights set on Grid Twenty-Six . . . California and Washington.

This Olivia knew, and now it was time to act.

***

It was time for Olivia to use her power and change the playing field.

She stepped from her office and strode down the hall to a conference room where a large group of men gathered to drink, smoke and curse the administration. It was one of the few places where the freedom of expression still existed.

"Gentlemen," Olivia's commanding tone brought the smoke-filled room to silence. "As you know, we are facing a formidable challenge. Grids Twenty-Two and Twenty-Five have decided they want access to our ports and we are in their cross-hairs."

"Why don't we just let them have it?" The question came from Clemente Rodriquez, a longtime rival of the Beretta Crime Syndicate.

"Because Clemente, we would only be helping the grid authorities gain a stronger foothold on our country."

"And what's so bad about that? We can still do business just like always. Drugs, Protection, Extortion, Influence, it's all the same. It's just coming from the grid authority rather than the feds."

In a heartbeat, the room broke into shouts and arguments. Some men agreed with Rodriquez. Others argued against him.

Bang!

A shot rang out settling the crowd and pulling everyone's attention back to Olivia. She jammed her Colt 45 back in its shoulder holster. Hands on her narrow hips, she glared at the men sitting before her. "Aren't you forgetting what those men did to you, to your country, to your families? And I don't mean your crime families. I mean your wives, your children, your grandchildren. They have taken over and relocated them to major population centers to fill the jobs left behind after the Bird Flu disaster. And they are forcing them to work for nearly nothing. Doing what? Developing more ID chips and building weapons they can use against us."

A stir rippled throughout the room. She was right and they knew it. She had seen the underbelly of the Grid Administration; she knew what they were capable of doing. The secret to saving her country was to find a way to cross the borders, link up with other underground freedom fighters, and attack their command and control centers and take their country back.

They would deal with drug and crime issues later.

"Gentlemen, I didn't call you here to fight over who controls the cocaine trade. I called you here because we have a common enemy." Heads bobbed and a low ripple of agreement spread throughout the meeting room. Even Clemente had to agree with that. It was true; the enemy of my enemy is my friend.

"I have information that there are several people within the Bleakly administration who agree with us and who have not received the nanochip. They can cross the grid borders without being detected or infected."

Enthusiastic murmurs rose at the riveting news.

"Why are we just now hearing about this?" An angry man shouted … his face red from too much alcohol.

Hands raised to quiet the growing impatience, Olivia looked to Conner. He stood and hiked up his holster laden belt. His show of prominence was not missed by those closest to him.

"Because, it took months for us to develop our sources inside the twenty-six grids. I also have it on good authority that government has developed a serum, an antidote to combat the virus which they are withholding from the public. They have been field testing it on the political dissidents in the prison in Corcoran State Penitentiary," Conner's words silencing the crowd.

Not one to mince words, John Conner eyed the crime-kingpins and syndicate leaders with a steely gaze.

The next question came from a man in the back of the room. "So who are these human guinea pigs and how does that help us?"

Shifting to address the man, Conner continued. "We know of at least two people. Their names are Lily Peterson O'Reilly and a former detective named Troy Ashcroft, but there may be more."

"What about President Richardson? Has anyone heard from him?" Another drug lord asked.

He eyed Olivia who shook her head.

"Our contact within the administration tells me that Bleakly was planning a public execution. The latest news I have is that President Richardson and a few of his cabinet members were shipped out west. I don't know the exact location but I'd really like to learn where."

"Where are you getting your information?" Clemente demanded.

The men grew restless. They wanted answers and they wanted them now. Olivia was not ready to give it to them. Squaring herself, she said. "I have a source high up within the government. That's all I'm going to say, but trust me, this person is in a position of great influence."

"We can't just sit here and let the grids have our country. When are we going to do something?" Clemente pushed back.

"I am not at liberty to disclose much, but I will tell you this. I have approved a mission which is being carried out as we speak. It will test our ability to penetrate the enemy's reaction time and possibly set some important people free."

Chapter Nineteen

"In today's regulatory environment, it's virtually impossible to violate rules ... but it's impossible for a violation to go undetected." **Bernard Madoff**

A rusty haze hung over the Detroit District blocking out the sun, giving its inhabitants a sense of continuous gloom.

The former vibrant city, at the center of Grid Twenty-Four, had been reduced to a grungy industrial wasteland. Long lines of tattered workmen left their tenement houses each morning to begin another twelve hour shift. They assembled into blocks of fifty, five rows of ten men, surrounded by International Guard soldiers.

Since water was their main commodity, their job was to build the parts for water treatment plants springing up along the Great Lakes. Selling water in exchange for wheat and crude oil became an obsession with the Grid Authority. Nothing else mattered, not even the survivors of the Bird Flu virus.

Trace tossed his empty bottle of Jack Daniels into the ditch as he staggered along the dusty road. For the last nine months, he'd questioned everything he'd believed; his faith, his God, his love for Cami. All had been ripped away in one ground-shaking blast.

Yes, he'd survived.

He'd survived the virus.

He'd survived the missile attack.

He'd survived the last nine months.

But that was little comfort. He was an empty shell going through the routine of living, of surviving.

He stopped to lace up the ill-fitting government-issued boots. Lifting his head, he squinted at the lines of other emaciated men headed to the factory. It was going to be a killer of a day, he muttered.

A guard nudged him in the ribs with the butt of his weapon. He glanced into the man's eyes. There was something unearthly in his expressionless face.

"I'm going," he said, staggering into position.

Ahead, lay rows of former automobile assembly plants. Their tall chimneys belched out sulfurous smoke making the atmosphere surrounding the city even more unbreathable. Whatever rhetoric the environment wackos espoused in the early days was quickly abandoned as the demand for fresh water grew.

When Trace and the others finally reached the assembly line, he slouched into his seat and waited for it to start. A low rumble shook the floor as the conveyor belt began to move.

An hour later, one of his coworkers reached too far and his hand got caught in the gears. He screamed and tossed his wrench into the flywheel, stopping the conveyer belt. His sudden action brought a swift reprisal, as a number of guards swarmed him. Using a taser gun, they tried to shock him into submission, but he continued to fight back. All at once, a shot rang out and the man slumped to the concrete floor.

"Okay, there's nothing to see here," the squad leader barked as a crew of men gathered up the bloody corpse and tossed it into a wheelbarrow. "Get back to work."

The conveyor belt jolted to life and Trace resumed his task. With practiced skill, he placed the green and red diodes into place, zapped them with his soldering gun and pulled his hands back. It was a mundane job, but at least it was out of the elements and his pay-grade allowed him some freedom of movement.

Following a thirty minute lunch break, Trace retook his seat and waited for the line to resume when he heard, "Hey O'Reilly?"

It was his supervisor, a short, stocky man with a shorter temper. He enjoyed taunting Trace about his 'religion' as he called it.

"Heard from God lately?" A sneer tugged at the corners of his unshaven jaw. Two fierce eyes peered from under a set of bushy eyebrows begging Trace to lash back.

Trace straightened as onlookers awaited the inevitable confrontation. "Yes sir, Mr. Foreman." Everyone addressed him as such. Clearly the man enjoyed the sway he held over his beleaguered work crew.

"Oh? And what did *He* say?"

Not missing a beat, Trace smiled. "He says you're going to—" a fist interrupted what he was going to say.

Lights flashed as Trace's head jerked back. Landing face first on the oily concrete, he felt his world tilt. He forced his arms under him and pushed himself up to a sitting position. Leaning against an iron pipe, his mind staggered back to the time he'd stepped into the prison cafeteria to face Rocky. If only he'd been left to die there, he wouldn't have met Cami or Lily or Will.

But he had.

And now they were gone.

In their place he'd found his way back to the bottle. It seemed to be the only sedative that worked to mask the pain of loss and loneliness. He pushed himself to his feet and faced the foreman. "Take your best shot," he said, defiantly.

The foreman pulled his fist back and swung a pile driver. Just before his fist connected, Trace stepped aside. The fist struck the pipe he'd leaned against. The man screamed in agony, gripping his broken hand. With one powerful uppercut, Trace decked him. His neck snapped back and his head slapped the concrete. A pool of blood began to ooze from the wound and Trace reached down to check the man's pulse. It was weak, but at least the man was alive.

"O'Reilly," the unit commander hollered. "Get your lousy tail upstairs. The boss wants to see you."

With a shove from his nightstick, Trace stumbled forward and headed to the administrative office. Each step darkened his heart. *God, why did you allow Cami and I to get struck with that missile? Why didn't you intervene? It doesn't make any sense. And what's become of Lily and Will?* All he had left was bitter memories.

Stepping into the administrative office brought back memories of the days as a detective. Men and women sat in tight cubicles huddled over telephones.

Trace gave the boss's door three sharp raps.

"Enter," came an angry retort.

Trace took a steadying breath and stepped inside. "Sir, did you call for me?" It was a dumb question, but in his condition, that was the best he could come up with.

The superintendent, a tall, bare-boned man with piercing blue eyes, reminded him of a gestapo commander. The man pushed back from his desk and glowered at him.

"Yes, O'Reilly. I wanted you to get this first hand rather than you hearing it through the grapevine."

Trace braced himself for the verbal punch in the gut. He was probably chosen to go on work detail up in the Upper Peninsula . . . a region where men went to work and never returned. Or possibly he was being singled out to go to the battle front where he would be expected to defend his grid to the death. As far as he was concerned, death would be a welcomed relief compared to the hellish conditions he was forced to endure. He braced himself for the dreaded news.

"O'Reilly you and a few other detainees have been singled out to participate in what the grids are calling a Good-Will Citizen Exchange Program. What that means is, you're being sent to Grid Twenty-Six. You will go directly to the transportation depot and leave within the hour." His boss finished by signing the bottom of a sheet of paper and shoved it across his desk. "This is your new assignment."

Trace leaned forward and took the sheet. "What will I do in Grid Twenty-Six?"

"I have no idea, nor do I care. I just know I have one less drunk to deal with. Now get outta here."

A cold knot formed in Trace's stomach. He folded the sheet of paper, stuffed it into his pocket, and asked, "Sir, where is Grid Twenty-Six?"

His boss let out an exasperated huff. "You should know. It's California and Washington State. Isn't that your old stomping ground?"

Trace nodded absently.

"You should thank your lucky stars. Someone upstream is looking out for you. Now get out of here."

Chapter Twenty

It was an unusually warm day and Lily stood basking in the sunlight.

The guards controlling Cell Block 9B allowed the inmates to stay outside in the 'Yard' a little longer than normal. That change caused an overlap in the schedule.

Hearing sharp commands, Lily turned to see a line of men being ushered into the 'Yard.' One of them was Troy.

As soon as he and the others were allowed to move about freely, she made a beeline for him.

"Troy," Lily buried her face in his rickety chest. Tears streamed down her cheeks as she held him. His bony chest heaved. "Troy, what have they done to you?" she stepped back to get a better look at him.

His Adam's apple bobbed as he took a hard swallow. "Oh, it's nothing, Lily. I've had a touch of dysentery," his voice shaky, his skin yellow. Instinctively he placed his hands on his stomach.

"Troy, you've got to get some medicine or you'll die."

Nodding, he continued. "They promised they'd give me all the meds I need, but—" His sunken eyes strafed the area.

"But what? What are you not telling me?"

Troy's lower lip trembled. "I haven't told you this because…"

"Because what?"

He took a shaky sob, and forced out the words he dreaded saying. "I think I'm responsible for killing your dad and Miss Cami."

His words sent a shock wave through Lily's system. Her eyes rounding, she covered her mouth and tried to keep from screaming.

"You did what? How? Why?"

Troy gave her a weak smile. He'd lived with the guilt following his dad's death for so long that when he saw John Conner, he snapped. He'd chosen vengeance over his love for Lily. Now he had to bear the consequences of that action. "I caught Conner following Trace and Cami with a drone. I didn't realize it was armed with a missile. We fought. Something happened. I guess I hit the triggering mechanism. The next thing I know, I'm watching the missile with your dad's car in its cross-hairs. I think they took a direct hit." His throat constricted and collapsed into a heap of quivering flesh.

For a moment, all Lily could do was gape at him. How could she love the man who'd killed her father? Her thoughts swirled like insects around a streetlight. Finally, she laid her hand on his heaving shoulders. "Troy, look at me."

He took a halting breath and looked up. "Troy, something's happened to me. A few days after I was taken here, I was sent to the pit."

Troy held her gaze.

Lily's lower lip trembled as she told him how Sister Soldier and Fat Louie had worked together to get her sent to the pit where he raped and beat her.

"Sometimes things happen, things out of our control. Sometimes bad things happen to good people. You were doing what you thought was right and I can't fault you for that. But I didn't fight him. I should have—"

"I'm going to kill him—"

Finger to his lips, she silenced him. "No, not another word. I forgive you. Can you forgive me?"

Pushing himself up, Troy enfolded her in a warm embrace. "I love you, Lily. None of this was your fault."

"I love you too."

Glancing from side to side, he lowered his voice to just above a whisper. He pointed to a small scar on his forearm. It matched the one on Lily's.

"Do you remember the day this all started? The day you and Will came back for me?"

Lily nodded slowly. "Yes, why?"

"Do you remember getting pecked by one of those birds?"

She squeezed her eyes shut, trying to recall that day. It was all a blur. "No."

"Well I do. You were helping me out of the building when two smaller birds, I don't think they were blackbirds, but still, they had those red eyes." Holding his one hand up and making an open fist. "I felt a small prick and looked down. He got me on the arm." He held his arm so she could get a better look at the pock mark.

Lily held his gaze and then inspected her arm. "You know, now that I think of it, I do remember something stinging me. I thought it was a piece of glass. It must have been a bird too. But what does that have to do with them not giving you the medication you need?" Her voice rose, heads turned. She realized she'd drawn the attention of more than a few inmates.

Taking her by the arm, Troy led her to an empty space near the back of the 'Yard' where few gathered.

"Because, I think the doctors have been running tests on us. I think they have been using us as guinea pigs to develop an antidote for the Bird Flu virus. That may be why we haven't been given the nanochip."

Pulling him close, Lily's breath shallowed. "Is that why you've been so sick?" Remembering her own bout with dysentery.

"Yes, and…"

"And what? Troy, you've got to tell me. What's going on?"

Troy's eyes shifted from side to side. A guard was coming. Time had run out. "This morning, someone put a note in my mashed potatoes which said, 'Help is coming.' I don't know what that means, but you've got to hang in there."

The whistle interrupted them.

"Ladies, line up," a female guard called. Within thirty seconds all twenty inmates had formed into two columns.

"Attention."

They snapped to a crisp stance.

"Move out," the lean Block commander barked and the column marched back into the cool shade of Cell Block 9B.

Chapter Twenty-One

"I crossed my fingers, hoping my mocking his speech would remain undetected." **A. Nonymous**

Being shackled to the floor of a military vehicle with nine other men wasn't Trace's idea of traveling first class.

The sun beat relentlessly on the canvas tarp covering the rear quarter of the truck like an angry eye. Inside, the air reeked with human sweat and urine making Trace's stomach churn.

In the months since his reeducation and assignment to Grid Twenty-Four, Trace had no way to shave or cut his hair. He barely recognized himself let alone any of the other men riding with him. Why was he chosen for this Good-Will swap? He had no special skills like that of the other men. Whose idea was it to take him from his cushy life as an underpaid, overworked factory worker to some skilled labor job? He had to wonder if there really was a God who still cared for him. He'd given that idea up a long time ago.

He shook his head and smirked, causing the man next to him to stare at him.

"What are you looking at?" Trace demanded.

The man shrugged. "Oh nothing. Just another drunk."

The comment struck him like a sledgehammer. It was true. Like a hog returning to his mire, he'd slid headlong into his old ways. Guilt stabbed his calloused heart and he began to weep.

The men around him guffawed, but he didn't care. He felt dirty. He was dirty. He'd broken every promise he'd ever made. Pinching his eyes tight, he began to pray, *Lord, I am such a wretch. I have sullied your name and defiled your temple. I am no longer worthy to be called your child. Make me one of your servants.*

All at once, he felt the loving arms of his Savior reach out and embrace him. He could almost hear the Father say, *"Bring forth the best robe that I may put it upon my son; and put a ring on his finger and shoes on his feet: and let us kill the fatted calf and be merry: for this my son who was dead, is alive; he was lost, and is found."*

Taking a cleansing breath, Trace felt as if he'd been washed. Although his outward circumstances hadn't changed, he'd been changed. God had breathed a fresh breath across the strings of his soul; stirring them back to life and his heart began to sing.

***

After hours of bouncing along the highway, the convoy slowed and joined a long line of vehicles waiting to cross the border.

As they neared the check-point, it came to an abrupt stop. The temperature inside the rear of the truck rose, making the air unbreathable. Through the slats in the canvas, Trace could see rows of guard shacks where border patrol officers with German shepherd dogs moved between the vehicles. On either side of the lanes were concrete barriers angled so as to make each vehicle swerve to the left and then to the right. Ahead were machine gun emplacements surrounded by mounds of sandbags. Sitting behind them were scores of International Guard soldiers wearing dark sunglasses and protective armor.

On the far side of the border a dozen people stood waiting. They appeared to be professionals; doctors, engineers and educators.

Unable to wipe the sweat from his eyes, Trace and the others waited for their transfer papers to be completed. Once the Customs and Border Security Commander was satisfied all was in order, he gave the order to deactivate the nanochip in each person's arm so they could cross the border safely.

A flurry of activity caught Trace's attention. Pitched voices outside the truck rose as men argued over the details of the exchange. Without warning, the canvas tarp flew back. Bright sunlight spilled in temporarily blinding Trace and the others. Shielding his eyes from the stabbing rays, he bit back a curse.

The silhouette of a large man pushed his way into the interior and began unlocking the detainee's chains.

"Everyone, outside! Line up. No talking," he ordered.

Having been the first to load in, Trace was the last to exit the vehicle. When he finally stepped down, he filled his lungs with fresh air and looked around.

After doing a quick count, he realized why the delay. Grid Twenty-Four had sent a dozen men while his group sent only ten. *Funny thing,* Trace considered. *Those men certainly look better fed than the motley crew I'm in.*

A technician moved with practiced skill from man to man checking their ID chip until he reached Trace. Movement caught the man's attention. He turned as the twelve men on the opposite side pulled automatic weapons from under their shirts. They opened fire spraying lead at the guards manning the 50 caliber machine guns. Others tossed hand grenades and smoke bombs before taking out the nearest guards.

In less than sixty seconds the partisans had killed all the border guards. The irony stench of blood and cordite filled the air stinging Trace's nostrils, causing him to double over. He slumped to his knees and heaved what little he had in his stomach. Expecting a bullet to end his life, he kept his head down and waited for the end to come.

It didn't.

A shadowed figure stood over him momentarily blocking out the sun. Trace glanced at the man, then had to cover his eyes as grey smoke wafted across the battle scene.

"Are you Trace O'Reilly?" he asked, his tone flat, unemotional.

Pushing himself up on weak legs, Trace leveled his gaze. The man clearly felt no concern for the loss of life. His steely gray eyes reminded him of a killer shark. The scar across his jaw bespoke of many a fierce battle.

"Yes, I'm Trace O'Reilly."

The leader softened his stance. "I'm Joe Franklin, the leader of this motley crew." He waved his hand in a grand display.

Trace remembered him from his days on the police force. Joe had been an active city councilman in Sacramento during the prosperous days of Governor Sanchez. Since then, he'd made a name for himself as an urban developer. His money and influence put him on the fast-track for mayor had it not been for the Birds. Now he used his connections in another way. He joined the ranks of the resistance.

Olivia quickly saw Joe's potential and tasked him with intercepting the Good-Will prisoner swap.

Trace extended his hand. "I remember you. Thanks for stepping in. I wasn't too happy about being sent to grid Twenty-Six."

Joe cut him off with a wave. "Just doing my part. I kinda like making trouble for the grids." He chuckled. "Okay men, load up."

As they led Trace to one of the APC's, he said, "Wait, my nanochip, It hasn't been deactivated."

Turning, Joe said, "Nigel, take the scanner and deactivate this man's chip."

A young man dressed like a mujahedeen fighter, found the scanner in the hand of the dead technician. He picked it up and stepped closer to Trace.

"Hold out your arm."

Trace complied. With a quick swipe and a soft beep, the chip was rendered inoperative.

"Okay, it's done. We'd better get a move on," the younger man said.

"Where are we going?"

Not answering, Nigel turned and began to help the other detainees into the back of an APC. Once they were settled, six men with guns climbed in and pulled the iron door shut.

Nigel squared himself and addressed everyone. "You people are now enemies of the state. We are about to take you into the dead zone called Santa Vern. Anyone unwilling to join the resistance may stay behind."

"Do we have a choice?" Trace asked.

Giving him a crooked smile, Nigel patted him on the shoulder. "No, but if you stay here, they'll probably shoot you."

Trace tried to swallow, but his mouth felt like cotton. "I think I'll go with you guys."

"I thought you'd see it our way."

Chapter Twenty-Two

The meeting between Olivia and the leaders of the underground droned on into the evening.

As several plans were offered and rejected, patience grew thin and tempers flared.

"Gentlemen, we don't have the resources to launch a full-scale attack on all twenty-six grid headquarters."

A hand rose in the back of the crowd and a newcomer spoke. "What about the raid on the border?"

Olivia scanned the crowd looking for the man who'd asked the question. "What makes you think there is one? If there was such a mission it would be on a need to know basis and you're not—"

Boom!

The room shook from several flash-bang grenades. The lights blinked out. Machine gun fire crisscrossed the room as scores of International Guard soldiers, DEA and Homeland Security agents swarmed in. Streaks of orange and red tracers interrupted the spray of bullets. Women shrieked, men moaned and bodies fell slicking the floor with blood. A large explosion outside the saloon rocked the building sending heavy smoke and debris into the air like a giant furnace. Tanks and heavy artillery opened fire killing and maiming anyone unlucky enough to be caught in the crossfire. Within minutes of the assault, the streets were littered with bodies.

The few survivors were herded to the entrance of the Santa Vern Saloon and summarily shot.

"What about these two?" One of the members of the assault team asked his commander.

Olivia and Conner stood, their hands laced behind their backs, their mouths duct taped.

Giving the two a disgusted look, he said, "Take them into custody. Let's let the interrogators have a crack at them. We need to know who else is a part of this conspiracy."

The man saluted his commander. Looking at Olivia and Conner, he said, "Looks like it's your lucky day. You get to spend the rest of your miserable lives as guests in Corcoran State Prison." His mirthless laugh faded quickly.

Giving Conner a sharp jab in the ribs with the butt of his weapon, he shoved him and Olivia into an armored vehicle and slammed the door.

***

The afternoon sun glared down on the kennel outside the uranium mine where Wag lay chained to a post in the ground.

The wound he'd received from the DNA creature festered, sending sharp spikes of pain up his leg. The taste of Secretary of State Bleakly's blood still lingered in his mouth from where he'd bitten him. Memories of being kicked still haunted him. Until the day of the bird attack, his life had been relatively normal. Now all he wanted to do was to attack anyone who threatened him.

Even the occasional Good Samaritan, who would toss him a scrap of food, got a deep, chesty growl.

It was as if he was being punished. The longer he existed at the end of a chain, the more his domesticated side yielded to the wilder, untamed side. Hunger and deprivation took over leaving him a snarling beast.

As a soldier walked by his kennel, he tripped, dropping his dinner plate and spilling beans and cornbread on the ground. The food landed just out of Wag's reach. Smelling the meal, he lunged, snapping his chain. Within a few seconds, he'd lapped up the food and went searching for more.

Following his nose, he headed to the back of the mess tent, where the cooks had just finished cleaning up. He gorged himself on leftovers. Forgetting he was unchained, he wandered over to the shade and curled up for a long afternoon nap.

Hours later, he awoke to the aroma of fresh–cooked stew. He stood and edged closer to the cook tent.

"Get out of here you stinkin' dog." The man's angry words caused Wag to snap and snarl.

The cook picked up a steaming pot of beans and tossed them at him. It missed and landed on the ground. In an instant, Wag pounced on it.

The sudden urge to see Cami or Lily permeated his thoughts. Sniffing the dusty air, he caught a whiff of a familiar scent. He bounded up the ridge and turned south passing two APCs as they reentered the canyon.

***

"Halt!" Joe ordered.

Trace and the others got out of their APCs and viewed the carnage left behind by the International Guard soldiers. There was little left of Santa Vern. A dark cloud of smoke gathered above the buildings. Burning vehicles and twisted broken bodies lay in heaps where they were thrown.

"What happened?" he asked, not believing his eyes.

Joe released a string of expletives. "I have no idea. Apparently someone tipped off the grid authorities."

Nigel stepped up. "Your orders, sir?"

He shifted to face the younger man. "No need to go any further. Let's get out of here."

"Where to commander?" He asked.

Getting back in the armored personnel carrier, Joe said, "To the uranium mine ASAP. We'll hide there until I get word about what happened. For now, we need to get these vehicles out of sight."

"The uranium mine?" Trace asked.

"Yeah, while you were enjoying yourself in Detroit, we were working our tails off transforming the mine into the underground's headquarters. We've stockpiled tons of munitions and supplies."

Trace smiled, "I always thought that place was good for something," and climbed into the APC.

Forty-five minutes later, the heavily armed vehicles rumbled through the gate and didn't stop until they'd reached the heart of the mine. A couple men pulled a canvas tarp over the entrance and soon the desert winds blew away all evidence of their arrival.

Chapter Twenty-Three

"As far as we know, our computer has never had an undetected error."   **Conrad Weisert**

Millie couldn't believe what she was seeing.

The satellite imagery was grainy but clearly recognizable as the nation's most wanted men gathered on a hill overlooking Santa Vern. If the Grid Authority got the location of those men, it would be only a matter of time before another attack order was issued.

Within a matter of minutes, the rest of her friends in the underground would be dead. She already felt terrible for not knowing the attack order had been issued on Santa Vern. She knew one was eminent, but she somehow missed the exact time. That cost the underground many lives.

She had to act fast.

The phone rang jolting her from her thoughts. "Office of the President," Millie stated in a professional tone.

"This is watch commander Westbrook. I just sent the POTUS a video. Did he receive it?"

He hadn't. Millie had intercepted it. It was that video she was reviewing when the call came in. Because lying was a part of her job, she felt no computation to answer in the negative.

"Watch Commander Westbrook, has this video been scanned for viruses?"

"Uh, uh, I don't know, ma'am. I'm just relaying information given to me by the Global Satellite Observation Unit."

"Okay, then. Before you send the President some corrupted file, I suggest you send the original data to me and let me check it for any malware and encrypt it."

"Ma'am, that file I sent you is the original."

"Commander Westbrook, are you telling me you tried to pass off some piece of junk without first checking to see if it possibly had a Trojan Horse hidden in it?" She enjoyed dressing down the underlings working the security protocols. Most of them were as green as a spring leaf and as dumb as a stump.

"Yes, ma'am. I mean, no, ma'am," his voice faltered.

"All right then. I'll cover your stupidity this time, but don't you ever call here again without doing your job or I'll have your head. Do I make myself clear?"

The shaken watch commander stuttered a weak, "Yes, ma'am." She ended the call and peered at the file.

Satisfied she had the only evidence of the escapee's whereabouts; she quickly deleted the file and replaced it with old footage. After saving the altered file, she parked it in an obscure data base and returned to eavesdropping.

POTUS was in deep consultation with Amanda … again.

***

Crack!

Millie jumped as Bleakly's hand struck the desk.

"How in Sam-Hill did they escape?" He demanded. His pitched voice reverberated through the closed door.

Amanda tried to calm the commander in chief down, but it only made matters worse.

"I, I don't know how it happened. Someone must have tipped off the authorities. They didn't know what hit them." Amanda was clearly shaken.

"That's not acceptable," the President raged.

Bleakly's temper tantrums were legendary within his inner circle. His appetite for power was insatiable.

In an attempt to pacify Norman's outburst, Amanda said, "On a brighter note, we were able to round up a number of underground leaders meeting at Santa Vern. We are holding them, awaiting your orders."

POTUS's tone softened. "Good, I will personally oversee their interrogation. When I get through with them, they will wish they were dead. Maybe we can find out who masterminded the attack on our borders."

"All right, I will make that my first priority following Cami's town hall meeting. She is scheduled to be on national television within the hour. I'm so excited. We've been working on it for weeks. Are you going to watch?"

Bleakly gave an impatient huff. "Yes."

"By the way, when are you going to ask her to marry you? The clock is ticking, you know."

Another huff.

"After the interview." He sounded nervous.

Millie could just about hear Amanda shaking her head in a womanly way. "Men, you're all bluster when it comes to blowing things up, but when it comes to matrimonial warfare, you have no guts."

POTUS changed the subject. "And where is former President Richardson? I called the prison in New York and was told he'd been transferred. I didn't order a transfer … did I?"

The rattle of paper caused Millie's heart to palpitate. Had they learned she'd forged his signature? She casually lifted her purse from the floor and fished out her lipstick. If she felt threatened, she would apply red lipstick to her lips. That would signal to her counterpart in the adjoining room to detonate a series of IED's.

Her hand paused in midair.

Millie could see her counterpart reach for his special cell phone.

All he needed to do was press the call button and the IEDs hidden throughout the city would ignite. In the pandemonium Millie would have time to escape. With a little luck and some help from operatives strategically placed at the exits, she would be able to disappear.

Another beat ticked and Millie heard Amanda's whiny voice.

"Norman, you signed his and his cabinet member's transfer papers a week ago."

"I did nothing of the sort," his sharp reply, peppered with vulgarity, caused Millie's skin to crawl.

"Yes, Norman, here are the papers. That's your signature. No one can write as poorly as you. So it has to be yours."

Bleakly growled.

Millie lowered the lipstick and began to breathe again.

"That doesn't make sense. Why would I do such a thing?"

"I don't know, Norman. Sometimes I wonder about you. It's a good thing you have me watching out for you."

Millie could almost see the two lovers standing arm in arm. Despite their sibling relationship, she always knew there was more to it than just familial love.

"As to the prisoner exchange debacle, I want every last guard involved hanged."

"That won't be necessary." Amanda countered.

"And why's that?"

"Because Norman, they're all dead ... ambushed. The underground knew the exact time and location of the transfer. The moment the border guards deactivated the force field, they made their move."

Bleakly fouled the air with expletives. "How did that top-secret information get leaked? I gave the commander an explicit order to lock those men down until the transfer was completed." he raged.

"I don't know Norman. I'm just telling you what your gutless underlings refused to tell you."

The President continued to fume while Amanda tried to appease him. "Look, getting back to Miss Stetson. Why don't I set you two up for a quiet evening together? Let her see your good side. Show her you're not such bad a guy."

Millie wished she could see through walls as Amanda purred her way closer into Bleakly's personal space.

"After all, you're charming, good looking, rich and powerful," her voice took on a soft, sultry tone.

It was an odd thing to listen to the President and his sister carry on a conversation. It was also curious that Millie had never seen the two of them together outside the White House. There was a rule whenever the President was alone in the Oval Office with Amanda. No one was to interrupt them.

Suddenly, the door flew open and Amanda marched out. "He is in no mood to be disturbed," she hissed and stomped to the elevator.

Chapter Twenty-Four

A sharp rap on the Green Room door quickened Cami's pulse.

"Come in," she said, trying to calm her nerves. After her lunch with Millie a day earlier, she'd grown to hate her job; the interviews, the lies, the fear of being caught. She feared if she didn't escape soon, she'd be discovered and executed.

Millie's words rang in her ears.

A familiar face poked around the partially open door. "Miss Stetson?"

It was Amanda.

"Miss Stetson, they are ready for you."

Cami smiled. They'd been working on this live town hall interview for months. It was the first of a string of town hall meetings scheduled to be held throughout the mid-west. Although she knew the questions had been closely screened and she'd been coached by a professional, she was still nervous. The words, 'be calm, act natural,' rang in her ears. However, just below the surface, her mind boiled a cauldron of mixed feelings. The thought of doing a dozen of these events made Cami's stomach flip.

She inhaled and let it out slowly. "I can do this," she told herself.

She stepped into the hall where nearly one-hundred hand selected citizens sat in a semi-circle. Cameras panned the area giving viewers at home a front row seat.

Once everyone was in place, the cameraman held up three fingers and counted backward.

"Three, two ..." Cami couldn't here one, but knew from experience the cameras were rolling. Every word would be sliced, diced and analyzed by those who opposed the Bleakly Administration. Her influence, as the face of the administration, added credibility, warmth, personality. When she spoke, people listened and ratings skyrocketed.

The sign flashed, 'Applause.' A chorus of cheers from the audience rose as they greeted her warmly.

The moderator cleared his throat, quelling the audience. After making a few opening remarks, in which he set the ground rules, he turned to Cami.

"Miss Stetson, thank you for making all this possible. We common folk appreciate having a government which is open and accessible. You being here speaks highly of our leadership."

Cami smiled and thanked him.

Another round of applause.

Standing, she began a practiced stroll around the stage taking in the scene, smiling into the camera. She had the nation in the palm of her hand.

Returning her gaze to the audience seated around her, she began, "My fellow citizens and viewers at home, we welcome you to this, the first of many town hall meetings. We hope our little chats together will show you that you have nothing to fear from your government. It is our honor to hold your sacred trust. As the Japanese declared in their constitution in 1946, 'Government is a sacred trust of the people.'"

Again, the 'Applause,' sign flashed and the audience dutifully responded.

Cami lifted her hand and pointed to a woman dressed in a cotton blouse. "So Miss Stetson, what is the state of our nation?"

She'd been asked that question or one like it so many times she could answer it by rote.

In a clear, confident voice, she said to the caller, "The state of our country is strong. Under President Bleakly's leadership, it is in good hands. Yes, we've gone through some rough times, and yes, we've all lost people who are dear to us, but we have walked through the fire, swam through the flood, climbed the highest mountain, and have come through stronger than ever. What didn't break us, molded us, reshaped us … sharpened us. And we are ready to face the next challenge."

She paused to take a sip of water from a plastic bottle.

On cue, a man in overalls asked, "And what is the next challenge?"

Facing the camera, Cami looked into the soul of the nation. "The next challenge is unification. We have grid leaders at each other's throats. We have dissidents spreading lies, undermining the very foundation this nation was built upon; life, liberty and the pursuit of happiness. We need to set aside our petty differences and come together under one flag, the flag of the Republic of North America. After all isn't that what our founding fathers fought and died for?"

It wasn't a question which needed an answer.

A special phone line had been installed to allow citizens from across the country to call in their questions. Of course, the callers had been screened, their questions edited and fed to Cami before the show began.

As the interview wrapped up, the station manager inserted one last question ... one that was missed by the program's censors.

"Miss Stetson, I love what you've done with your hair," the caller said.

Not expecting the compliment, Cami instinctively touched the silky lock which flowed over her shoulders. "Why thank you," she said, a slight query in her tone. Dropping her defense, she asked, "And your question?" expecting the usual seminar question.

"My question is, why is President Bleakly arresting and imprisoning anyone who disagrees with his administration? Didn't you say—" The line went dead before the caller could double down.

"I'm sorry, but I think our caller's phone didn't have a good connection. I think what our caller was asking goes to the very heart of the issue of unity." Softening her tone, she looked directly into the camera. "My friends, our nation has been through a terrible ordeal. Many of us have lost family and loved ones. Today, we stand at the brink of a bright new future; one without the morays of disunity and division. It is through the vision and strong leadership of President Bleakly that we find our nation stronger, more unified than ever. Isn't that what we all want; one nation, indivisible, with freedom and justice for all?"

"And cut," a technician announced.

Cami stood, yanked the microphone from her blouse and threw it on the sound stage. "Who the heck let that caller get through?" she spat.

The red faced moderator scurried to the Green Room. It was clear, someone had dropped the ball.

Finally, after an uncomfortable silence, Cami huffed and marched stiff legged off the stage with Amanda close on her heels.

"Cami, Cami," she called.

Cami turned, fire burning in her eyes. "What!?"

"You did great—"

"I don't want to hear it. That caller nearly undid everything I accomplished with that question."

Amanda caught up to her, still gulping air. "But you handled it like a pro." Lowering her voice, she added. Norman wants a word with you. So take a breath, get your emotions under control and let him take the lead."

"This better be good," she huffed and continued to the dressing room.

Chapter Twenty-Five

"So, if you feel a smile begin, don't leave it undetected,
let's start an epidemic quick, and get the world infected."
Russell Conwell

Driven by instinct, Wag headed across the mountain range in search of Sacramento.

By the time he'd reached the foothills, night had overtaken him. Using his nose, he only had the easterly breeze as a point of reference to guide him across the prairie. As he neared a range of mountains, a howl broke the silence. It was a pack of wolves.

And they were hungry.

Sensing imminent danger, Wag took off in an open run. But after weeks of deprivation, his energy soon flagged. With the wolf pack rapidly closing the distance, his chances of survival were quickly ebbing.

All at once, a dark figure appeared on the top of a boulder. It was the alfa male. He snarled viciously and leapt directly in front of Wag. A moment later, the pack had him encircled.

They immediately began testing his strength. First the youngest male approached in an effort to prove himself. Wag lunged at him, his teeth bared. The younger wolf backed away. The next in line stepped up to prove his prowess. Wag lunged, this time the more mature wolf stood his ground. The circle began to shrink as the wolves moved in for the kill. One wolf snapped at Wag's heels. He wheeled around and caught the eager attacker off guard.

Then it was the Alfa male's turn. He broke through the tight circle and crouched low, ready to spring. His jaw snapped wildly and his eyes bore a deadly glare. Wag tried to defend himself, but the powerful male was no match for him.

As the two animals locked onto each other, a shot rang out, sending the wolf pack scurrying. The Alfa male, sensing the presence of a human being, turned, poised to attack the lone intruder.

A shadow moved revealing a man with a rifle. Undeterred, the leader of the pack lowered himself and pounced. Another shot split the night air and the wolf yipped. He was wounded, but not mortally. Still baring his teeth, he struggled to his feet and lunged again.

Another shot.

This time it struck the beast directly in the throat. Blood spurted as the wounded animal thrashed around in the bushes. Soon the quivering ceased and the night reclaimed its stillness.

Wag lay panting in the dirt. He'd been torn, but not seriously.

Kneeling, the bearded mountain man scooped Wag up as if he were a puppy. "C'mon boy, let's get you looked at." With ease, he carried him back to his campsite

The oil lantern illuminating his tent cast an ominous glow and created an inky stench, but Wag was in no condition to care. He held still while the man inspected his wounds. As he poured some ointment and salve on the torn flesh, he sang a calming tune. When he'd finished, he smiled at his work. "I think you'll live ol' buddy."

A five foot rusty chain, which they used to attach him to the post, still hung from his collar. Wag waited patiently until the man clipped it off.

"There, you should travel a lot lighter without that thing dragging you down. You'd have probably outrun that whole pack if it weren't for that darned thing."

As the man droned on, Wag curled up in a corner and drifted off to sleep. When he awoke, the fire had died out and the man was nowhere to be seen. The few scraps of food the man left from his breakfast lay a short distance away. Wag scarfed them down and sniffed the air. A storm was brewing from the east. Needing no encouragement, he resumed his journey.

By mid-day, he'd reached the outskirts of Sacramento. The further he traveled, the more familiar the buildings and streets became. All at once, he recognized his surroundings. Expecting to find Cami or Lily waiting for him, he bounded up the steps and pounced on the front door. It was locked and he let out a sharp yip.

Nothing.

His continued barking only brought an angry "Shut up!" from the neighbor.

As the evening shadows lengthened, a car pulled up and a woman got out. Fearing the stranger, he backed into the shrubs and waited. The moment she opened the door, he plowed inside.

Chapter Twenty-Six

"You did a great job, Miss Stetson."

Hand to her chest, Cami spun around.

President Bleakly stood in the doorway where Amanda had been only a few minutes ago. Her heart did a backward somersault. She took a calming breath and tried to relax. She had a role to play. Despite his foibles, his warm brown eyes and tender smile caught her by surprise. In a way, he had replaced Senator Sanchez as her mentor and surrogate father; the father she'd never known. It was that missing figure in her life which made her so vulnerable to strong men.

Trace being the one exception.

Gulping air, she said, "I, I didn't know you were watching. That last caller nearly blew it," feeling hives creep up her neck.

He waved the comment aside. "You handled it like a pro."

Where have I heard that? She wondered.

"Did you know, from the time you took the assignment to be my spokeswoman, my poll numbers have been steadily climbing?"

She knew it was a lie, but chose not to upset the tomato cart. She held his gaze a tad longer than she expected to before saying, "Thank you," her dry throat barely allowing the words to form. "But I didn't really take the job. It was sort of thrust upon me, if you'll remember."

Finger raised, he continued to hold her attention. "True, but you *did* volunteer your blood to science. Without it, we might never have beaten back the epidemic."

Cami's shoulders rose and fell. "I suppose you're right. At the time, I had no idea how my world would change after the accident."

Squaring himself in front of her, he tilted her head back and peered into her eyes. "You are a brave woman. That's one of the things that got my attention. I wish all of my staff were as courageous as you. Just think of the good we could do for mankind"

Cami tried to smile, but her lips refused to cooperate.

Taking her by the elbow, he guided her from the dressing room, down the hall and into a waiting limousine. "Mind riding with me back to the White House?"

How could she refuse?

As they exited the building, a cadre of uniformed men snapped to attention and gave a sharp salute. He returned it sloppily and held the car door for her. She slid in and tried to calm her nerves. Taking a seat next to her, he continued, "Now that we have assured the people we mean them no harm, it is time we move to the next level."

The driver swung the passenger door closed with a soft thud sealing the limo like a coffin. Cami pushed further in until she bumped the other side. The cool touch of leather sent a chill up her arms and she tried to brush them away. Knowing what was coming intensified her anxiety.

POTUS reached across the space between them and took her hand. He softened his tone as he turned toward her. Cami found herself sinking deeper into his warm brown eyes. "Miss Stetson … Cami, it pains me to inform you that we have found the body of Mr. O'Reilly."

Another lie. Or was it? Had they just executed him? Was he lying in a shallow grave somewhere? Tears glistened and ran down her cheeks.

Cami heard the words … knew they couldn't be true, but still they struck her with the force of a mule-kick. "I, I don't understand," she sputtered.

"Yes, well, there is a lot we don't understand about the last nine months. The Bird Flu epidemic, as you know cost this country dearly. I, myself, have suffered much." Tears welled in his eyes. His lower lip quivered slightly. "My wife, my daughter—" he sucked in a deep breath in a failed attempt to regain his emotions.

The absurdity of the moment could not have been missed. She knew he was lying; about Trace, about his family, about his poll numbers. How long had they been lying to her? She had to keep up the ruse. She had to get her hands on the grid codes. That was now clearer than ever.

Finally, the President spoke; his words pressed through his constricted throat. "I know this might not seem like the best time, but I feel the urgency of the hour. The world is changing. Events around us are forcing us to make decisions based upon what we know, not on what we want. If we are going to weather this storm, we need to present a unified front." By now his voice had cleared. His eyes regained their clarity, their vision, their innate determination.

Cami listened, expecting what she knew to be his grand proposal. "Cami, did you hear me? I want you to be my wife. Will you marry me?"

Feigning shock, she fought to keep a straight face. "I, I don't know what to say." Her words came out, dry, raspy.

"Then just say, 'yes.' I'll make all the arrangements. We will have the grandest wedding. It will rival those of Queen Victoria and Lady Diana. And we will live out our days in luxury." A deep laugh percolated from within his chest, primitive, guttural, ancient.

Chapter Twenty-Seven

"Doctors can make mistakes and diseases can remain undetected."   **A. Nonymous**

After being dropped off at her condo in D.C., Cami took a long bath and tried to get her emotions under control.

Thirty minutes later, she emerged from the spacious bathroom wrapped in a thick terrycloth bathrobe, her hair still damp. She curled up on the couch and stared aimlessly into space. It was useless to watch the state controlled television. She tried to read, but her mind kept returning to Bleakly's proposal. Could she go through with it? Could she really marry him? Could she actually steal the codes?

A rash of emotions swirled in her head as she contemplated her situation. The condo, the car, even her bank account were just a few of the many perks provided by the Grid Administration. But they came at a price. As long as she toed the party line and kept up all pretenses, she remained the darling of the administration. She'd seen what happened to those who questioned Bleakly's authority.

They disappeared.

The question the last caller asked probably got her a lifetime membership in prison or worse ... a bullet in the back of the head. Despite her attempt to deflect the question, it had its intended effect. In the silence of her apartment, she began to ask herself, what am I missing?

Why did the Bleakly administration react so violently to criticism? Why did they resist any descent? And why did he lie about Trace? If indeed, he was lying. Surely she could check out his story. Was that why he was so insistent on their marriage?

The notion of marrying anyone other than Trace had never occurred to her. She'd dreamed of the day when she would give her heart and body to him; when she would say the words, 'I vow to love you, Trace O'Reilly, in sickness and in health, for richer, for poorer, for better, for worse.' And hear him repeat those words and seal them with a passionate kiss. But that day would probably never come.

Not now.

Not ever.

On one hand, she knew she could never love Norman Bleakly. On the other hand, her country needed her. It was her blood which saved the nation, her blood which ran through the veins of each and every citizen.

As she toured the country she was exposed to prosperity and poverty, great progress and severe loss. Her heart ached for the people … her people. Her once great nation had been reduced to twenty-six squabbling grids. Would playing her role give her access to the Oval Office? A plan began to emerge. It was possible, but she had to try.

***

"Amanda, what do you think?" Cami asked, the moment her personal assistant entered the condo.

She'd just returned from the White House and was fixing herself a drink from the bar located at the far end of the living room.

After a beat, she turned and offered Cami an innocent expression. "About what?"

Cami knew Amanda was behind the whole thing. She also knew her condo was bugged.

"About marrying POTUS?"

Finger to her chin, Amanda considered the question. "I think you should."

"Aren't you the slightest bit jealous? You spend practically every waking minute with the man. Maybe you should marry him."

Amanda finished off her Gin and tonic and opened the refrigerator. She stood, considering Cami's statement. Then she retrieved a bottle of wine and poured two glasses. Handing one to Cami, she said, "Don't be ridiculous."

Cami set the glass aside and watched her for any sign of betrayal. "Well, why not? You have as much claim on him as me?"

Amanda leveled her gaze. "You mean you don't know?" her tone turning incredulous. "Norman and I are brother and sister. Actually, he's my half-brother, to be exact; same mother, different fathers." Amanda emptied her glass and refilled it. "Cami, can I be perfectly honest with you?"

Seeing Amanda's face darken, Cami knew it was serious. "Yes, I suppose."

Amanda glanced around as if someone was watching. She lowered her voice and began. "Norman is not well. Actually, he's dying. If he doesn't get a liver transplant, he will die."

Unable to hide her surprise, Cami's mouth fell open. "No, I had no idea. How long have you known?"

"It all started shortly after he was bitten by a dog. Can you believe it?"

Without divulging too much, she continued. "He was leaving the CDC Bio facility in Santa Vern when some mangy dog attacked him. At first we thought the dog had rabies, but the doctors ruled it out. After a bunch of tests, we discovered the dog must have been infected by methyl mercury, a compound found in fish." Amanda paused and wiped her eyes.

Cami's interest piqued at the mention of Santa Vern, but she kept a straight face. "Go on," she encouraged.

"With all that was happening during those early days, the doctors didn't catch it until the damage was done. He has hepatitis B."

"Meaning?"

"Meaning it's gone to his head, literally. If he gets a new liver the doctors are hoping they can reverse his psychological condition. As it stands, he is showing early signs of schizophrenia."

It took several minutes for Cami to absorb this. She was either a very good liar or they were desperate. "And so you want me to marry Norman because—"

"Because I can't. I mean, I can't give him one of my livers. We are not compatible."

"And I am?"

"What a twit," she mocked. "Of course you are. As the President, Norman couldn't accept a liver from just anyone. You, on the other hand, as his wife could. So you see, you have to marry him."

Cami forced the tears back. No wonder she spent so much time with Norman. She'd been covering for his shortcomings. They must have been planning this not long after the takeover.

Standing, she walked to the double-glass doors leading to the balcony. "I need some air," she said, attempting to change the subject.

Once outside, she inhaled deeply. The fresh autumn air cleared her mind. "I vaguely remember having an apartment in Sacramento, and a dog. What was his name?" she paused in thought. "Oh yes, Wag, that's it. Wag the Dog. You know, as in the movie?"

Amanda shook her head. "I hate dogs. So does Norman." Apparently she hadn't seen the movie.

"It seems so long ago now." Cami continued her nervous chatter. "Surely there are a few people still living in my community who knew me back then. And since I haven't completed the unification tour, you could include it on our itinerary. Right?"

The corners of Amanda's lips turned down.

Sacramento had never been a destination point. Never been included on the list of cities, making Cami wonder why.

She caught a flash of something in Amanda's brown eyes. Was it anger? Frustration? She couldn't tell. But she knew the wheels were turning in Amanda's head.

The brisk air between them scintillated with nervous energy. Finally, Amanda spoke. Her saccharin sweet tone didn't go unnoticed by Cami. "Tell you what, why don't I run it past Norman. If he signs off on it, you and I will take off in one of his jets. We can skip around your little provisional town, have a cup of coffee at a quaint shop, see if your apartment has been ransacked. Then we'll fly back. Why not? It'll be fun." As she breezed from her condo Cami couldn't help the feeling that she'd been played. Not just a few minutes ago, but for the last nine months.

Curious to find out what really happened since the accident and subsequent memory loss, Cami reentered the living room and booted up her laptop. As soon as she was on line, she began to search the internet for answers.

Chapter Twenty-Eight

Pulsating music drowned out Conner's screams, but it didn't matter.

No one knew he was there and even if they did, they could neither stop the torture nor help him escape. He would die in that place and he knew it. He also knew he would not give them what they wanted.

"Hit him again," the President said.

The chief interrogator gave him a cruel grin and swung his fist at full force; striking Conner in the midsection.

Blood spurted from his mouth and ran down his chin, staining his shirt. He had already soiled his pants, but he was in no condition to care. With his hands tied to a rope suspended from the ceiling, he hung inches from the concrete surface. The full weight of his body bore down on his wrists. Bolts of pain shot up his arms.

After days of beatings, Conner had given them nothing; no names, no locations, no plans. He had trained for such treatment, but his will to resist was weakening.

Bleakly stepped closer, he grabbed Conner's hair and yanked his head back. Conner's swollen eyes parted a sliver. "John, I am a reasonable man. You could have saved yourself all this trouble. Just tell us what we want to know and all this will stop."

Conner spit a wad of bloody saliva. It splattered squarely on the President's face.

Calmly, Bleakly pulled a handkerchief from his pocket and wiped it off. With a sigh, he said, "I'll take that as a no. You leave me little choice but to put you out of your misery."

Pulling a 9mm Ruger from the holster which hung on the interrogator's hip, he charged the weapon and pointed it at Conner's temple. "Now, if we have no other business here, I bid you farewell."

"I have—" Conner tried to speak, but his parched throat prevented him from saying much. He forced a swallow and tried again. "I . . . have . . . information," he choked out.

Bleakly eased the weapon back an inch. "Get him some water."

The interrogator found a half empty bottle of water and handed it to his commander and chief. Dangling it in front of Conner's eyes, he taunted him. "Give me some actionable information and I'll spare your life."

Conner cracked an eye again, and tried to lick his lips, but his tongue stuck to the roof of his mouth. Forcing himself to focus, he squeezed out the words, "Scott Wan."

The general tipped the bottle over Conner's face, allowing the crystal fluid to seep into the creases of his mouth. Conner sputtered, and opened his mouth like a young bird begging for more.

Then he pulled the bottle back. "Want more?"

"Uh, huh."

"Then tell me more."

Conner pinched his eyes tighter. If he gave them what they wanted, they would probably shoot him anyway. But he wasn't ready to die; not for a failed cause, and the NRA was a failed cause. "Scott Wan is dead."

Exasperated, Bleakly threw the water bottle across the room. It bounced and tumbled into a corner. "Is that the best you could do? He got what was coming to him. Serves him right for going behind my back and making a deal with the chinks. What I want to know is, was Dr. Jovanovich experimenting on dogs?"

Conner lifted his head. "How should I know? You and Scott were funding that operation. You of all people should know."

"I didn't know everything," he said, slightly distracted.

Looking at his interrogator, POTUS said, "Cut him down. I'll deal with him later."

With a nod, the man whipped out a knife and sliced the ropes holding Conner up. He fell to the concrete floor like a sack of potatoes.

"Take him to Cell Block 9B."

"But sir, all the cells are full."

Not missing a beat, the President said, "Throw him in with another detainee. They won't mind the company."

"What about the woman?"

Bleakly paused, lost in thought. "Uh, what woman?"

"You know, Olivia Emerson, the leader of the underground."

Hand to his forehead, the President seemed to waver. Then he shot him an impatient glance. "Oh yes, her. Have you interrogated her?"

He nodded.

"Has she given you any actionable information?"

"Nada."

Bleakly huffed. "Put her in Cell Block 9B, too. I'll decide later if I want to make an example of her or send her to one of our factories. Heaven knows we could use everyone we can get."

***

While Lily deciphered Troy's last message, her attention was arrested by the shuffle of feet and the crisp snap of an electronic lock.

It had been a while since any new prisoners had been brought to her cell block, and she was not expecting any visitors. She hoped it was not the guards coming to interrogate her. The thought of Fat Louie attacking her again chilled her to the bone. Having spent weeks subjected to bright lights and pounding music Lily dreaded a repeat performance.

Out of curiosity, she stood and peered through the mesh window in the door. To her surprise, the guards were dragging two people, a man and a woman down the hall. It was obvious the man had suffered the worst of it. His face was unrecognizable, and his head was a mass of bloody matted hair. Lily wondered if it would have been better to have died rather than endure such punishment.

The other person, a woman in her mid-thirties, appeared to be badly shaken. She too had suffered at the hands of a professional sadist. At least her face wasn't marred. An icy chill ran down her back.

"Stand back," the guard ordered, his hand resting on his holster.

Lily took four steps back and bumped into the wall. It was as far as she could go. The guard swung the door open and motioned her to take a seat on her bunk. Lily complied, though her mind screamed, "I'm still standing.'

"Not one word or you'll lose your outdoor privileges," the guard warned.

The threat of losing their two hour stint outside would turn most detainees into jellyfish. Lily took a seat on the corner of her bed. Her ragged fingernails snagged the rough horse-hair blanket and dug in.

As one guard eyed her lustfully, two other guards dragged the woman in and tossed her limp body on the bunk next to hers. "You two get along now and don't get into any cat fights. You know where that will land you," the guard said.

Lily nodded. She knew what the guards did to those women who became uncooperative. You fight them you end up in a dark hole. No sun, no fresh air and little water. She willed herself to smile and sat back until the guards left and all was quiet.

The bunk across from hers was built on hinges. When it was down, it made her already confined space even smaller. It didn't take Lily two seconds for her to recognize her cellmate. Sharing space with another detainee was one thing. Sharing it with Olivia Beretta Emerson was quite another.

Chapter Twenty-Nine

"Only hidden and undetected oratory is really insidious."
Mortimer J. Adler

The news about POTUS haunted Cami.

She had to learn more, but with internet strictly controlled, she wasn't sure if she could glean any more than what Amanda told her. She started with mercury poisoning, then moved to hepatitis B and what it did to the liver. Finally, after navigating through the internet looking for anything about Santa Vern or the CDC Bio laboratory, and finding nothing, she tapped on a few newspaper articles dating back to the day of the bird attack. It was clear from what she read that the bird attack did not emanate from the President or his administration.

Before the investigative reporter, who had been following the story disappeared, he had gotten his hands on the memo Dr. Jovanovich accidentally sent to Mia Wan. It and other damning information convinced her that the current administration was built on lies and deceit. As she scrolled through the memo, her screen went blank.

Frustrated, she banged on the keys trying to retrieve the article. "That does it," she muttered. With a quick glance over her shoulder, Cami picked up the burner cell phone Millie had given her. She hit redial and the call went through. Someone picked up, but didn't speak.

"Till death do we part," she said, and ended the call hoping her cryptic message went unnoticed by those monitoring her activities. Then she took the phone apart and flushed each piece down the toilet.

***

Minutes earlier, in a concrete room with no windows, a team of computer analysts and surveillance operatives wearing headsets stared at a bank of computer screens.

A light flashed on one of the screens and an analyst tapped it. After a moment, he lifted the phone which had a direct line to the President, and, as instructed, spoke in a controlled tone. "Sir, we have someone trying to log on to an internet connection through a private server. Should I shut them down?"

POTUS had just returned to the Oval Office from the west coast where he had been personally overseeing the interrogation of Conner and Olivia. He inhaled and let it out slowly. "What are they searching for? Can you find out?"

Scrolling through the metadata, the analysts sought a pattern. "Yes, they are searching for old newspaper articles, Fox news transcripts, national talk show host's newsletters, that sort of thing."

POTUS stopped and took another breath.

"Got a name?"

"Yes, sir. It is Miss Stetson. She's at it again," he said nervously.

The last time that happened, they used shock treatments to knock her memory out. This time, they'd have to try a new approach.

"Do you have the Revised History File ready to upload?" The RHF was the regime's newest propaganda program designed to reinvent history, especially the history of the last few years. With it, they'd painted an entirely different picture of the country. The trick now was to convince Cami of its veracity.

"Yes, sir." It sounded like POTUS was on the move again.

"Good, do it now. I don't want her to have access to real time information."

"Yes, sir." His fingers flew over the keys programming the information they wanted Cami to read.

Just before the President ended the called, he added, "Keep me informed as to Miss Stetson's activities. If anything changes, you know where to find me.

The line went dead.

Chapter Thirty

A cold knot formed in the pit of Troy's stomach. He'd been finger spelling a message to Lily across the hall when he heard one of the guards speaking.

"Okay, Conner, this is your lucky day. You get to live." He laughed at his stupid joke. The other guard smirked. Apparently their sense of humor had descended to the lowest level.

Conner groaned as the guards dropped him on the extra bunk.

"You two get along or you'll end up in the pit," he warned.

Troy didn't care. He'd gladly spend the rest of his life in the hole if it meant getting even with Conner for what he did to his dad. Grinding his teeth, Troy drew himself up in a tight ball and waited.

For what, he wasn't sure.

By lights out, neither Troy nor Conner had moved. His temper had cooled to a slow burn, but the desire to deal a fatal blow to Conner still lingered. Occasionally, Conner would mutter incoherently. His bruised and bloody face made speaking nearly impossible.

It wasn't that long ago that he looked the same way . . . just a piece of quivering human flesh barely hanging on to a shred of life, Troy thought. Hadn't this man suffered enough? Maybe the same memories which haunt me haunt Conner. Maybe it was one of those situations where bad things happen to good people. His father's last words were, "You must forgive him. He's only a boy."

Those words still rang in his ears. The only difference was, Conner wasn't a boy, not any more. Had he not been tracking Trace with a drone armed with a missile, they might not have fought. He might not have accidentally hit the firing mechanism. And Trace might still be alive. The parallel couldn't be missed.

How could I forgive him after all these years?

Troy's heart slammed against his chest. He knew what he had to do, yet every fiber of his body resisted the Spirit's promptings.

He'll kill you as soon as he recovers, his mind screamed. *The moment he wakes up, he'll be on you like a tick on a dog.*

"Water." Conner's lips barely moved.

Conner's swollen eyes remained unfocused. Troy was grateful for that.

"Water," he repeated.

Troy's heart shattered.

Taking a small paper cup, Troy filled it with lukewarm water from the tap. He lifted it to Conner's lips. At first, he winced and pulled back. Troy knew what it was like to try to drink when every joint in your body screamed in pain.

He tried again. This time Conner lifted his hands to clasp the cup. It was then, Troy saw his fingers. Every fingernail had been pulled out. Tears gathered in Troy's eyes and ran down his cheeks. *This man has suffered far more than me.*

But not more than Me, the Lord prompted, *and yet I forgave you.*

Troy's pulse quickened. "Yes, Lord."

Conner's eyes widened. "Thanks," he muttered.

"Don't mention it."

As he crumpled the paper cup in a ball and tossed it into the trash can, he made a decision. *This man has to live. He has got to survive and tell his story. Together, we will defeat the animals that did this to him, to us, to our country.*

***

Thud!

Troy's eyes popped open.

Conner had fallen out of his bunk. His labored breathing continued and Troy held his position ready to lash out if the man tried anything. A few beats passed and Conner hadn't moved. Troy peeked over the edge of his bunk. Conner lay in a fetal position where he'd fallen and shivered uncontrollably. Careful not to step on him, Troy leaned down and tugged his blanket over Conner's shoulders.

Suddenly, a hand reached out and latched on to Troy's wrist. Conner's swollen eyes cracked open revealing a pair of burning embers.

Troy's breath caught. "You fell out of bed, man. I was just covering you up."

Conner rolled over and pushed himself to a sitting position. Resting his arms on his knees, he let his head flop against his bunk.

Troy was pretty sure his cellmate hadn't recognized him. It would only be a matter of time before he did, however. When that happened, things could get dicey. If he was going to show Conner any kindness, it would have to be now, before the old animosity reared its ugly head.

In the silence, Troy thought he heard him crying.

"Hey buddy, it's not so bad once you get used to it in here." Troy tried to put a good face on a bad situation. The truth was, this was a bad place.

"Why didn't you kill me?" Conner asked between sniffles.

The question stunned Troy. *Had he known all along? Did he know now?*

"What are you talking about, buddy?"

Conner pushed himself up and eased his weight on his bunk. "You're not fooling anyone, especially not me, Troy. The whole reason I'm here in the first place is because of you." His voice had cleared.

Troy couldn't believe what he was hearing. "Are you here to kill me?"

Conner shook his head, dully.

"I'm in no condition to kill anybody, especially you."

"I don't get it. If you're not here to kill me, why are you here? Besides the usual reasons." Troy asked.

The corner of Conner's swollen lip hiked up and he let out a hoarse chuckle. "You just don't get it, do ya? You and your girlfriend have been used as guinea pigs.

You two are the only people who can cross the grid borders without being detected. Before they captured me the underground was planning your escape."

"The underground? You mean to say there is hope for our country?"

Conner slumped back. "Not now. Our movement called the NRA, the National Resistance Army was attacked by the International Guard. They wiped out nearly all of us," he coughed out another chuckle. "We've been trying to locate you two but had no idea where you were until we got an encrypted message from an imbedded operative." He took a labored breath.

Troy softened his expression. "So you're not here to kill me?"

Shaking his head, he continued. "No, you should be the one doing the killing. I killed your father and for that, I am deeply sorry. The memory of that terrible day still haunts me."

Conner became quiet.

Troy knew he was hurting. So was he. He knew the anguish it caused to kill someone.

All at once, the bitterness and hatred seeped from Troy's heart leaving it feeling empty. He took a heavy sigh and looked up.

Finally, Conner roused. "Could you find it in your heart to forgive me? It would mean a lot to me before I die." He coughed and wiped his mouth. A bloody smear stained his shirtsleeve.

Troy almost could see his Savior's eyes peering down at him from the cross, almost hear Him saying, *'Father, forgive him, for he didn't know what he was doing.'*

Troy's eyes glazed. He took a shaky breath and stood. Extending his hand, he took Conner's and gave it a manly squeeze. "Conner, because I have been forgiven much, in the name of Jesus, I forgive you." His throat clamped shut.

"Thank you. Now I don't have much time left." A coughing spell interrupted him and Troy handed him another cup of water. "Thanks. Your girlfriend, Lily, that's her name, right?"

Troy nodded.

A smile lifted the corner of his lip. "Nice name. Anyway, Olivia is in her cell telling her what I'm about to tell you."

"I'm listening," caution colored his voice.

"Okay, here's the deal. There is a number of high priority detainees located in this prison. There has been a plan put into action to help them escape. In the next few days our guys will replace the prison guards. I can't tell you how they'll acquire the uniforms, but suffice it to say, the guys who will be guarding us will soon be the good guys. Do what they say. It's the only way we're going to get out of here. You got that?"

"But why us?"

"Like I said, you two are the only two people who can cross the grid borders without detection. Years ago, the North American Electrical Reliability Corporation (NAERC), was located in Atlanta, Georgia, but more recently its mainframe has been relocated just outside of St. Louis, Missouri. Under Bleakly's Grid Authority, the former electrical power corporation wields its influence over all aspects of American life; from power production, to distribution, and cyber information gathering. It's interconnected, integrated systems control the twenty-six Power Grid Stations through a satellite uplink.

The plan was to get you out of here, give you a crash course in espionage and insert you inside Hub Central where you would hack into their computer system and shut it down."

Hands held in surrender, Troy stopped him. "Wait, wait. I know nothing about grids or computer technology."

Conner swiped his protestation aside with a hand. "Not to worry, we will train you. Once we get our hands on the grid codes, you can shut it down. When that happens, the partisans will mount an all-out, coordinated attack against the International Guard."

"You mean we'll be fighting our own countrymen?"

Conner shook his head. "No, the International Guard has been infiltrated with middle-east insurgents. It's all a moot point anyway since the underground has been wiped out."

The explanation made sense.

Troy had noticed the difference long ago.

Conner's breathing shallowed, his faced paled.

"Oh no you don't. I'm not letting you die that easily, Conner. Here take this," handing him a cup of water.

Conner sipped, then coughed.

"Just let me lie still for a while. Maybe get some food in my stomach." He slid back down and laid his head on the pillow. Troy tucked the blanket around his shivering body. "Man, you're burning up. I've got to get you to the infirmary."

"No, I'm too busted up. Anyway, they don't care about me."

Sitting back, Troy watched Conner drift off to sleep. Breakfast came and went and Conner hadn't moved. By lunch time Troy was getting worried. Finally, Conner stirred. "You know any Bible verses?"

The question took Troy by surprise. "Yeah, a few … why?"

He shifted to see Troy, he continued, "I think I'd like to know more about being forgiven."

Troy slid off his bunk and took a seat next to Conner and began.

Chapter Thirty-One

"Stress can often times go undetected in those who feel they have a good control over life."   **A. Nonymous**

A s the hours passed, Lily watched Olivia drift in and out of consciousness.

She hoped and prayed she didn't die. She wanted to know what happened after she was taken away from the bio lab. Maybe she had news of her father, or Will.

A tap on Lily's door brought her upright. "Wake up, it's breakfast time," someone yelled.

Since the dining room brawl, they were confined to their cells and served meals through the bars. Today was no different. Two trays were slid through a narrow slot. Lily took them and placed them on the small table affixed to the wall, then thanked God for the food.

Olivia roused as the aroma of coffee, scrambled eggs and bacon filled the small cell. Rolling over, she sat up and rubbed the kink in her neck.

"You're ... you're that girl." Her bleary eyes narrowed.

Lily felt heat creep up her neck. "What girl?"

Still suffering the effects of electric shock treatments and water boarding, Olivia shifted, placed her elbows on her knees and cradled her head in her palms. "You're the one I was talking about before—" her eyes welled. Hand to her mouth, she began to weep. "All those people, all our planning," she sputtered between halting breaths.

"What people? What plans?" asked Lily, confusion racking her brain.

After several minutes, Olivia regained her composure, and cleared her throat. "Young lady, I don't know if you remember me or not. We met at the CDC lab, my name is—"

"I remember you. You're Olivia Beretta Emerson." Lily interrupted. Her tone was cautious.

"Yes, I regret to say I am. You may take some comfort in knowing the man who tried to get me to sign over the deed to Santa Vern, the one who caused you and your family a great deal of pain, is dead; been that way for some time."

Lily handed her a plate and slouched next to her.

Olivia continued, "I was hiding in that facility and watched Bleakly and his goons arrest you and your friend." She shook her head and let out a hoarse chuckle. "Your dog, what's his name?"

"Wag."

"Yes, Wag. He got a good piece of Bleakly's flesh. I just hope he was carrying that virus and infected him."

"Wag did that?"

"Yep."

"I had no idea. I was wondering what became of him, and Will."

Olivia lifted a piece of flimsy bacon and bit off an end. "I can't speak for Wag, but I do know what happened to your brother."

Lily sat up straighter. "You do?"

She nodded. "Yeah, he had the happy luck of being locked in the back of that Garda truck. Conner and I had to dig him out."

"You mean you and Conner were working together?"

"We weren't back then. But we are or at least, were. That was until Bleakly and his ilk attacked us."

Lily ignored her last statement and asked, "What about Will? Is he okay?"

Olivia took a sip of lukewarm coffee and wrinkled her nose. "Needs more sugar. Yes, he is doing just fine."

"And Wag, what became of him?"

A shadow crossed Olivia's face. "Your dog got real mean and we had to chain him up."

Tears swelled in Lily's eyes. "But you said he bit the President."

She smiled wickedly. "Yeah, he got him real good. I'm real sorry they captured you and Troy." Olivia took another bite and forced it down.

"What about my dad? Do you know anything about him?" Lily's throat clogged with emotion.

Olivia shook her head. "I don't know. But I do know that Miss Stetson survived the missile attack, so it's possible."

Lily lifted her tray and scraped the remaining scrambled eggs together and scooped them into her mouth. Chewing thoughtfully, she said. "How do you know Cami is alive?"

Olivia gave her a wink. "She's the President's spokeswoman. She's on national television nearly every day. I must say, they are feeding her a heck of a lot better than they are us."

Lily let out a weak chuckle. "You got that right."

"You know, John and I had been trying to get a message to you, but we had no way of getting it to you."

Her eyes rounded.

"The authorities have been experimenting on you. If my guess is right you and Troy are immune from the virus. We were planning your escape when we were attacked. Most of the underground leaders were killed."

Lily felt the blood drain from her face. "Why us?"

"Because, you two can cross the borders undetected. We were going to use you two to disable the Central Hub Station, but I guess all that went up in smoke when they captured us."

Lily sank back on her bunk. "How were you going to get your hands on the grid codes?"

Olivia finished her meal and set the tray aside. "That, my girl, is a secret. But trust me, if they haven't been captured, we have people in very sensitive positions who can do just that. Now help me lay down. I'm ready for a nap."

A claxon sounded calling Lily's cell-block to exercise time. Lily extended her hand and helped Olivia to her feet. "Recess. Enjoy it while it lasts."

***

Hearing footsteps outside their cell, Olivia's eyes popped open.

She had drifted off to sleep after their return from the 'Yard,' and hadn't moved. Sitting up, she glanced around. Confusion marked her face.

"How long have I been out?"

Lily dragged her eyes from the notepad she'd been doodling on. "Let's just say, you missed swim time, and story time. Has anyone ever mentioned you snore like a bear?"

Olivia threw the covers off and lowered her feet to the floor. Standing, she held the edge of the bunk frame until the blood reached her head. "I'm rather muddleheaded, but I feel much better now."

"Good, I was getting worried." Handing her a tray of leftovers, Lily plopped down next to her. "I do have one question. If you know so much about what's going on out there. Why haven't you told me where Will is? Is he in prison, too?"

Olivia held Lily's questioning gaze. After a beat, she released a slow breath. "I'm afraid on that point I will have to decline. His role is too sensitive for you to know."

Lily's eyes misted. "I miss him so much. I don't know what I'd do without him."

"Honey, you can't think about that now. We need to stay focused and wait. It won't be long."

Taking a halting breath, Lily rubbed her hands down the front of her prison uniform pants. "Okay, but you've got to promise me one thing."

Olivia lifted her chin. The lines in her face deep with concern. "What is that?"

"Promise me when this is all over you'll help me find my brother. You've got to promise me."

The corners of Olivia's lips tilted upward. "Okay, Lily. I promise."

Lily wiped the tears from her eyes and asked. "Are those guards out there our guys?"

As she spoke, two guards strode passed their cell talking quietly.

Olivia stood on her tiptoes and peered at the men who'd just walked by. Frowning, she shook her head. Not yet, but soon."

Lily nodded and took a seat on the bunk.

Chapter Thirty-Two

"Saddle up boys," Joe Franklin ordered.

In the weeks since Olivia and Conner's capture, Joe had demonstrated strong leadership skills. He had organized the remaining fighters into units and had personally trained them in hand-to-hand combat along with battle-front techniques and handling high explosives. As new recruits arrived, he assigned his best men to repeat the process. Soon, the NRA functioned as a well-trained army.

His next goal was to test the grid borders for weaknesses. When he found one, he sent a squad to exploit it. The problem was finding reinforcements to replace the fallen who were killed and wounded in these skirmishes. Experienced fighting men were at a premium. So when a retired military service man or woman showed up at camp, they were immediately assigned leadership roles and sent out on a mission.

The volunteers who had chips had to undergo painful and dangerous surgery to keep the chip from activating. If they were not removed properly they would ignite, killing the host and giving off a signal which would alert the authorities. Having a shortage of qualified surgeons limited Joe and his team.

If they were to be successful in taking their country back they needed someone inside the main grid hub who could move around without being detected. To his knowledge, there were only two people who fit that description. He had to get them out of prison.

"Where to commander?" Trace asked,

In the weeks since his rescue, Trace had regained his strength and had proven to be an important member of the partisan unit. He chuckled at the name they'd chosen for his unit. *The Brewers*, after the Brewer Blackbirds which were responsible for much of the death and destruction which spread across America.

Franklin ignored the question. He'd find out soon enough. Thirty minutes later, Joe and a team of eight fighters rumbled across the desert. Sitting in the front seat, Joe turned to his men. "I've got credible intel that a convoy of new uniforms is headed to Corcoran State Prison. I plan to relieve them of their burden."

"And how do you plan to get them?" One of the men asked as they checked their weapons.

Franklin's stubbly chin jutted out. "That depends upon how cooperative the guards are. Either way," he continued in a gravelly voice, "we kill them." His matter of fact tone let everyone know the seriousness of the situation. It was a 'take no prisoners' mission.

Joe and Trace had bonded early as each had experienced loss. Trace lost Cami to a drone attack, Joe lost his wife and children to a gang of thugs as they left church. They threatened to arrest him if he didn't surrender his car. When he refused, they shot him. Fortunately, the bullet missed any vital organs. His wife and kids were not so lucky.

Were it not for the kindness of a passing stranger, he too would have bled out. After weeks of recovery, he was finally able to leave his friends and hide out in the foothills. He vowed to avenge his family and he was doing it with systematic ferocity.

"The caravan carrying the new uniforms is expected to make a pit stop along old US 65 between Wheatfield and Sheridan. That's where we'll take them. We have the advantage of driving a grid APC so that should draw them in close. But once they see we are partisans they will probably try to radio it in. Nigel will use his skill to jam their radio. The rest is up to us. We take the uniforms and get the heck out of there."

Nigel, a strapping young man, whose strong jaw was covered with a heavy beard, leaned forward. His piercing blue eyes bespoke of maturity beyond his years.

"I double checked the jamming device, sir. It works like a new pair of crutches." Nigel's smile warmed Trace's heart, but left him wondering if he really knew about jamming devices. Facing Trace, he extended his hand. "I don't think I've introduced myself. The boss has me out on patrol most of the time. You're, Trace O'Reilly, correct?" His iron grip clamped Trace's hand.

"Yes, that's right. And you are Nigel …?"

An impish glint flashed in Nigel's eyes. "It's just Nigel and we'll leave it at that."

The young man's grip relaxed leaving, Trace's hand throbbing. Shaking out his hand, Trace wondered, *How did he know my name? Joe hadn't told him.*

Holding the man's gaze, Trace considered him for a moment. Nigel, whose long blondish hair, pulled back in a ponytail and poking out from under a dirty bandana, resembled a gang-banger rather than a freedom fighter. Trace was just glad he was on their side.

In all of Trace's years of police work, he'd never killed a man without just cause. Killing those men in cold blood was against everything he'd stood for. But this was war, and in war, people die.

Trace finished checking his weapon, cinched the serrated Army knife tighter on his shoulder and prepared to face the enemy.

Chapter Thirty-Three

"The preservation of peace and the guaranteeing of man's basic freedoms require courage and eternal vigilance: that the least transgression of international morality shall not go undetected."
Haile Selassie

The barren stretch of road between Wheatfield and Sheridan was an ideal place for an ambush.

Using a military grade drone as over-watch, Joe and his men could see for miles in both directions. If anyone tried to approach them they would scatter and disappear in the nearby foot hills before the enemy arrived. The only break in the monotonous road was one fuel station sporting two gas pumps and a rusting sign which boasted they had the coldest beer in California. It was there, Joe and his men planned to make their move.

Once his men were concealed, Joe, wearing the only International Guard uniform not riddled with holes, stood with the APC's hood raised, looking into the engine compartment. A frustrated expression masked his real intent. Earlier in the day, one of his men intentionally made a small puncture in a hose. Once the engine had gotten hot, it steamed like an old fashioned locomotive. With their fingers crossed, they hoped the ruse was convincing enough to stop the approaching International Guard convoy.

Joe checked his watch and smiled. "Right on time." In the distance he could see the three Grid Authority vehicles rumbling along the highway in their direction. As they neared, the lead vehicle slowed to a stop. Once the dust settled, it appeared the driver had not moved. They may have been radioing in the change of plan or they may have been preparing to defend themselves. From Joe's position, it was unclear. He had to trust Nigel did his job.

Gazing into the engine compartment, Joe held his Colt 45 in one hand and an oily rag in the other. Sweat beaded on his forehead and rolled down his face, nearly blinding him. It was important that he stand perfectly motionless. Like hunting, he needed to draw his game in close before springing the trap.

Seconds ticked and finally the driver's door swung open. A lean young man wearing an International Guard uniform stepped out and took a step in Joe's direction. Joe guessed the soldier was from somewhere in the middle-east, possibly Afghanistan.

The man hiked up his gun belt and took another step in Joe's direction. A moment later, the passenger side door swung open and another middle-easterner stepped out and joined him.

"What seems to be the problem, sir?" the driver asked, his hand resting on his holster. The two men stood far enough apart that making two kill shots was not an option. Fortunately, Joe had a sharpshooter in position. He was taking no chances, or prisoners.

"Looks like my radiator hose is shot. Would you guys have a spare in the back of your truck?" Joe kept his voice level and an eye on the closest man.

"We got word an APC was stolen a few days ago. We were wondering if this might be it. Step down and identify yourself," the driver asked, unsnapping his weapon strap.

"It just might be. Why don't you ask the guys I took it from?" Joe lifted his Colt and squeezed off one round, striking the driver in the forehead, blowing off the back of his skull. A beat later, a soft pop sounded and the other man jolted backward. His head nearly ripped from his shoulders.

All at once, the rear doors of the other two vehicles flew open and a dozen soldiers poured out like angry hornets.

Pop, pop, pop!

The sharpshooter picked off three before they took a dozen steps.

A moment later, the air blazed with bullets from both sides. Trace and the others, lying belly down in the desert camouflaged with scrub bushes, opened fire. Caught in the open, one by one the International Guardsmen were cut down where they stood. Within sixty seconds, the noxious air cleared, revealing twelve bloody corpses.

Relieved he wasn't forced to kill an unarmed man; Trace shouldered his weapon and joined the others as they began to off-load the crates of uniforms. It was then he realized his friend, Joe Franklin had been wounded.

"Sir, you're bleeding," he said, just as the man collapsed.

"It's just a graze."

By the amount of blood soaking the ground, Trace knew it was more than just a flesh wound.

"Joe, you gotta lie down." Turning, he called for a medic.

As he waited and watched, he prayed he'd get an opportunity to speak to his friend about his spiritual condition. Something he'd been avoiding since he'd been rescued.

As it turned out, the bullet, which had hit him in the shoulder, had missed an artery by a millimeter, but clipped a major vein. Once he was patched up and with the morphine controlling the pain, Trace slid closer to where Joe lay.

"You're one lucky man," he said, patting his friend's good arm.

Joe turned and looked at Trace. "Yeah, I s'pose."

Trace peered down. "Actually, luck has little to do with it. God still has something for you to do."

He smirked. "Me and God ain't on speaking terms. If you know what I mean."

Trace smiled. "So I've noticed. That's what I mean. But He still has something for you to do."

Confusion marked Joe's face. "Trace, what are you talking about?"

"I mean, God wants you to trust Him … to believe in Him."

Another smirk.

"Don't laugh. I've been down that road. I've tried work, alcohol, everything, and believe me; it's a dead end. Now God spared your life for a reason and that's so you could hear His offer of forgiveness one more time."

"Now you're sounding like my wife. God rest her soul. Where was God the day those thugs killed my family and nearly killed me?"

Trace knew that question was coming. He shook his head. "I don't claim to have all the answers. But I do know, just going to church doesn't save anyone. Neither does knowing God keep us from having trouble. Jesus said, 'in this world you will have trouble, but be of good cheer, I have overcome the world.'"

Joe grew somber. "I hear ya, but that doesn't explain—"

"No it doesn't, but it does give us hope. God didn't spare His Son but delivered Him up for our redemption. If He would do that for your and my sorry rear-ends, how would He not give us all things we need for life and godliness."

"Now you've gone to preachin'"

Trace smiled at Joe's honesty. It was refreshing. "I'm not preachin, just telling one thirsty man here to find water … the water of life."

A moment stretched as Joe contemplated what Trace told him. Finally, Joe lifted his hand. "Pray with me."

Trace took his hand and listened to Joe's simple prayer. When he'd finished, he opened his tear-soaked eyes. Releasing a peaceful breath, he whispered, "Thanks, man."

Trace leaned down and gently hugged his new brother in the faith. "When you get to feeling better, I've got some verses to go over with you. They've meant a lot to me, maybe they'll encourage you too."

He nodded. "I look forward to that." Looking at Nigel, he said, "Have the men collect all the ID's off the bodies."

Pushing himself up on stiff legs, Trace waited for the blood to reach his head. "I'd better lend a hand."

Then he began rifling through the dead soldier's pockets looking for wallets, ID's, keys, anything they could use to their advantage. As he finished with the last man, a hand reached out and closed around his wrist. Two angry eyes peered up at him as he pointed his gun at Trace's head. Trace saw his life flash before him.

Bang!

Time held its breath and Trace wasn't sure if it was him or the other guy who'd been shot. A beat later the hand quivered, then relaxed.

Breathing in gulps, Trace began to shake violently. He doubled over and emptied the contents of his stomach on the dead bodies.

"Here, take this," Nigel said, handing him a plastic water jug. "Haven't you even seen a man die before?"

Trace took a swig and washed his mouth out, then poured the rest down his parched throat. "I have. Just not like that. For a moment, I thought I was a dead man."

Nigel jammed his pistol in his holster and smiled. "Get used to it. Before this war is over, you're going to see a lot of men die. Maybe even some of us."

Joe leaned up on his side and patted Trace on the back. "You did good today. Now let's collect all the body armor, weapons and uniforms from these men and bury the bodies in that shallow riverbed." He pointed with his nose toward a dried creek.

The men followed his orders and soon the prairie looked as desolate as it did before they arrived. "Okay men, listen up. I need six volunteers to put on those new uniforms and take the rest of the crates to Corcoran. You are going to infiltrate the guards in the prison." Six hands went up including Trace's. "Not you, Trace, I've got another job for you."

***

A buzzer sounded somewhere in the Corcoran State Penitentiary complex announcing the end of one shift and the beginning of another. As the guards filed out a delivery truck appeared at the front gate.

"Why so late?" The guard asked.

Vance, one of the volunteers, a clean shaven man with tats on his forearms handed him a clipboard.

"Had a leaky hose. We stopped at the station between Wheatfield and Sheridan to get it fixed." Shaking his head, he peppered his sentence with an ample amount of expletives to convince anyone he was a sailor. "All's that pathetic attendant at the fueling station could offer us was a roll of duct tape."

Giving one of his fellow guards a nod, he handed the clipboard back. "Pop your hood."

Thankful he'd covered every detail, Vance complied with a huff.

After a quick inspection of the duct taped hose, the guard slammed the hood back down. Mopping his brow, he gave a thumbs up to his commander.

"Hey, I'm just doing my job. Take your vehicle around to the back. There will be one more security inspection and then you'll be good to go."

Relieved the man didn't ask any more questions, he put the truck in gear and pulled slowly around to the rear of the facility. The next inspection went smoothly and he backed the truck up to the loading dock.

Fat Louie stood with a clipboard against his hip and a wad of tobacco in his jaw. He'd been reassigned to the loading dock as punishment for his part in the cafeteria debacle. He aimed and spit at a roach crawling across the loading dock, then smiled. "You boys are late." His rotund gut jiggled as he spoke.

"Yeah, what of it?" Vance huffed. He was in no mood for small talk.

Louie shrugged off the rebuff as the guards from the first shift strode past. Joe's men held their positions inside the APC waiting until the old guard cleared the area. Once the last of them left, Vance gave the signal for his men to move out.

"You men," Fat Louie said, eyeing them warily.

Vance froze, fingering the butt of his sidearm.

"Yeah?"

"Are those the new unies?"

Vance relaxed his hand. "Yep, fresh from the tailor. We got crates of them. I just hope there is one for your fat butt." The other men surrounding him burst into laughter.

Louie stood and brushed off some crumbs from a box of cookies he'd been eating before his nap. "I don't appreciate your disrespect, newbie. If I were you, I'd watch my back. These prisoners can get rather rowdy sometimes. Wouldn't want you to get caught in the middle of a brawl."

Vance let the comment slide and handed him a clipboard with the manifest clipped to the top. "We have to report to our posts, so I'm going to leave this with you to sort out. C'mon men. Let's get a move on."

Having been given the guard assignments, Vance and his men began to infiltrate the prison. Whenever there was a shift change, when the old guards left, Joe sent a team of men to kill them and take their uniforms and ID's.

By the end of the week, everyone was in place.

It was time.

Chapter Thirty-Four

"I appreciate you arranging for this trip," Cami said, eyeing the familiar skyline from the Lear jet as it made its final approach.

"But I am curious why Sacramento was never included on our itinerary."

The creases in Amanda's forehead deepened. "It just never seemed to work out."

Cami returned her gaze through the porthole window, but in its reflection she caught a glimpse of Amanda's expression. The moment Cami's head turned, her lips went from a smile to a sneer.

The real reason for not including Sacramento on the unification tour was the same reason they used shock treatments on her ... to shatter all memories of the place.

"Fasten your seatbelts. We're going to make a rapid descent to avoid a big thundercloud to our west. I want to get this plane down before it hits." The captain's voice interrupted Cami's thoughts. She settled back in her seat and closed her eyes. Would she find Trace? Would she discover her condo had been ransacked? Was it taken over by squatters? A dozen questions swirled around in her head like flakes in a water-ball. After months of being gone, she was finally home.

Once they touched down, a cavalcade of official vehicles roared up to the descending staircase. A lieutenant in a crisp clean uniform leapt from the first vehicle and helped Cami and Amanda get in.

"Why the entourage?"

Amanda turned to face Cami, innocence painted across her features. "It's standard operating procedure. You should be used to it my now. We wouldn't want some overly zealous paparazzi-type nosing around, asking a lot of stupid questions." Her cackle was just another thing that grated on Cami's nerves, that and her whiny voice.

After months of being shadowed by the woman, Cami was ready to scream. She'd listen in on every personal conversation, read every email, and tried to eavesdrop on every phone call. Cami counted it a small miracle she didn't get caught making the one phone call that might change her future. The thought of outsmarting the woman brought a smile to Cami's face.

***

"Hungry?" Amanda's question interrupted her thoughts.

"Famished."

"Know of any good places to eat?"

Having been prompted by Millie to make their first stop at the Firehouse Restaurant, Cami offered her a smile and gave the driver the directions.

"Yes, ma'am."

After helping the ladies get inside, the driver ran around the limo and got in. Then he pointed the car in the direction of downtown Sacramento. The ride to 2nd Street took only forty-five minutes, but with the tension between the two women being wire tight. It was all Cami could do to hide her jitters. Her only consolation was that she had the hometown advantage. Why not exert some control over her life? After all, it wasn't everyday they had the President's spokesperson drop in for a casual lunch.

The tension was broken as Amanda texted someone a private message. When she'd finished, she set her phone aside and smiled smugly causing Cami to wonder what that was all about.

"You can park right in front of the restaurant," Cami told the driver. Looking at Amanda, she spoke to her for the first time since getting in the limo. "This place is one of the anchors in this part of town. It's a bit swanky for my taste, but I figured if the Grid Authority is footing the bill, why not go all out." Her smile was a bit too broad, but she didn't care. She had hit Amanda right on her control-freak button.

Amanda crossed her arms and huffed. "Whatever, but I do hope you won't mind a little company."

Cami's pulse quickened.

"Yes, you see, I happen to be good friends with the mayor. So I just texted her and asked if she would mind joining us."

Feeling a cold chill form in the pit of her stomach, Cami tried to calm her breathing. That's one for Amanda, Cami thought. Let's see what Millie has up her sleeve.

Before she could comment, the driver swung the door open. Outside, the manager and his entire crew stood, broad grins on their faces.

"Greetings ladies." The manager said with a slight Italian lilt in his voice. "My name is Armando. My staff and I are here to serve your every need."

Cami didn't remember him from the last time she'd been there, but then again, it had been over a year and a lot had changed since then.

A lot.

"May I show you to your seats? We have you overlooking the river. It's a spectacular view. I'm sure you will love it." His self-adulation made Cami wonder if he was applying for White House chief cook position.

After weaving through a nearly empty dining room, they arrived at their table.

"Thank you, Mr. Armando. This is wonderful." Cami said, patting him on the forearm familiarly. Then she stepped aside to allow him to pull her chair out and took her seat. The same courtesy was not offered to Amanda which only made the meeting that much sweeter.

As they were getting settled, two women approached them. "Ah, Mayor Gonzalez and Chief Councilwoman Dietz. How nice of you to join us." Amanda said, asserting herself.

Cami smiled and extended her hand. "Oh yes, I was hoping you'd come. I would have been so disappointed to have come all this way and not see you again. If I remember correctly, it was nearly a year ago that we had lunch in this very spot just before I left for Washington. My, my, how time flies. Isn't that right, Amanda? Oh you do know Miss Borden, my personal assistant."

Heads nodded. Cami smiled, enjoying the moment.

That's one up on the little twit, Cami thought. This is going to be so sweet. It was so much better than hearing Amanda go on and on about her brother.

Returning her thoughts to the banter between the other three women, Cami let her eyes scan the restaurant. There were at least a dozen secret service personnel situated throughout the room. How many outside, she didn't know. All she knew was her instructions were to get them to the restaurant. Millie would do the rest.

Laughter broke Cami's concentration as Amanda tried to dominate the conversation with one of her personal anecdotes about the President.

Someone cleared their throat interrupting the chatter.

"Ladies, would you like to place your drink order? We have an excellent wine selection as well as martinis."

Cami feigned scanning the list, having never gotten used to the taste of alcohol. She ordered water with a touch of lime. While Amanda ordered a Strawberry Rhubarb Spritz and the others ordered wine.

It took only minutes for the drinks to arrive along with their menus. The waiter took special care to hand Cami's menu to her, giving Amanda a quick glance.

Cami opened to the first of several pages and began to scan the offerings. As her finger traced the items, it suddenly stopped. A sticky note bearing two words held her gaze. 'Second stall.' Cami's breath froze in her throat. Hoping no one saw her reaction, she slowly closed the menu.

Handing it back, she caught the waiter's eye. "I'll have the Smoked Tenderloin Carpaccio and the

Butterscotch Pudding for dessert. Its drag'ee pretzel, toffee bits and vanilla anglaise, is to die for."

The waiter gave a slight bow and backed away.

Amanda huffed and handed the menu back. "I'll have the same thing. Thank you very much."

She's definitely not a foodie, Cami decided.

As soon as the waiter left, the chatter resumed. It was all Cami could do to keep up. The few times she tried to engage the mayor or city councilwoman, Amanda marginalized her comments and took over the conversation. This was becoming a power grab, but Cami didn't care. The game was afoot.

The chatter paused only long enough for their meal to arrive, then rushed ahead. To Cami, it seemed all too planned, too controlled and she wondered if this was Amanda's way of saying, 'Don't mess with me.'

She let the women prattle on and began to scan the crowd. Since the outbreak, the staff and customer base had been greatly reduced. She recognized no one with the exception of one woman who kept eyeing her. She wasn't sure if she knew the woman, or if the woman recognized her from the many interviews she'd done, or if she were a part of her security detail. But her constant glances kept Cami distracted causing her to miss much of the conversation. It mattered little, however. She wasn't interested in their gossip.

"Amanda, while we are waiting for our dessert to arrive, I need to use the powder room."

Mirroring her action, Amanda stood. "You know, I was thinking the same thing. Let's go together."

Frustrated, she couldn't lose her that easily, Cami gathered her purse and headed straight to the back of the restaurant where the nostalgic rest rooms were located.

The door swung open easily revealing half a dozen stalls. Taking the lead, Cami stepped to the second stall before Amanda had a chance to inspect it. "I've got to go so bad," she said shutting the door in one smooth motion.

Amanda systematically checked the remaining stalls for any unwanted guests before choosing the last one.

Once inside, Cami scanned the small cubical for any reason why she was instructed to use this one rather than any of the other stalls. Pulling out a length of toilet paper, she saw her answer. A short note read, 'Stand on the seat and be very quiet.'

Her heart pounded against her ribs as she followed the instructions. After she'd finished the original reason for her visit, she stood on the rim of the toilet and held her breath.

"Are you finished? I didn't even hear you come out." It was Amanda.

"Oh, this bladder of mine. I really do need to see my doctor when I get back." Cami heard someone say. It was her voice, but clearly it was not her.

Peeking between the narrow gap in the stall door, Cami's breath caught in her throat. A woman matching her exact description stood, dabbing her lips with a new layer of lipstick. "I should have ordered coffee, too. I love their vanilla bean." She chattered on as if she were Cami herself.

Amanda's smile shifted and she grabbed Cami's look-a-like by the arm. "Don't try that again. I've got every door, every window under surveillance. If you try to give me the slip, I'll have you stopped before you get three steps."

The woman returned Amanda's steely gaze. "The only slip I'll give you is the one with the price of my meal on it." Then she smiled wickedly.

The door closed with a gentle bump and Cami began to breathe again. *Who was that woman? How did she know I love vanilla bean coffee?*

She remained in her crouched position until her legs burned. Finally, she took a cautious step down, and eased the stall door open. Footsteps scuffed in the hall outside the ladies room and she ducked back inside the stall and resumed her former position.

"You can come out now, Miss Stetson." The voice was unfamiliar.

Who was this woman? How did she know she was there? Did she have a gun? Cami slid the lock open and peeked out. Her palms slicked when she saw the same woman who'd been eyeing her.

The woman stood against the ladies room door, a pert smile tweaked the corners of her mouth and the impish twinkle danced in her eye.

Knowing it was useless to continue the charade; Cami opened the stall door and stepped out.

"We have only a few minutes, so let's go," the woman whispered.

"But what about—"

"Shush, shush. Explanations and introductions will come later. We must hurry."

The woman took Cami by the arm and swung the restroom door open. With a quick glance to her left, she led her through the kitchen, passed the walk-in freezer, and out the rear of the restaurant where a Lincoln Navigator waited. "Get in. Don't ask questions. I'll meet you in a few minutes."

Cami's heart sputtered at the fast-paced exit. Looking back, her eyes strained at the silhouetted figure standing in the shadows as her driver pulled into the alley. Within five minutes of entering the ladies room, Cami's life had taken an abrupt turn. Still trying to slow her pounding heart, she forced her lungs to work.

"Where are you taking—"

The driver lifted his hand, cutting her off.

Cami resigned herself to the fact that she was not going to extract any information from her driver. She crossed her arms over her chest, leaned back and tried to enjoy the ride.

Navigating the streets like a pro, the driver guided the big vehicle from old town into urban sprawl. Familiar buildings passed in review like the relics of the Red Army on parade. With each turn, memories began to flood back. The capitol dome appeared between buildings and she saw herself running up the steps for an appointment. The police station where Trace worked brought back additional painful memories. One last turn and the driver brought his vehicle to a gentle stop in front of an apartment building.

"We're here," his cheery tone sounded vaguely familiar.

"Here where?" she asked, trying to clear her mind.

Chapter Thirty-Five

"You may temporarily find a safe distance to travel undetected, but eventually, you will be found and dealt with."   **A. Nonymous**

A truck packed with explosives raced through the streets headed for the front gate of Corcoran State Penitentiary.

Unable to stop, the unmanned vehicle endured a withering assault by machine gunfire and sniper bullets. Finally, when all else failed, the guards protecting the entrance, pointed a rocket propelled grenade launcher at it and fired. The RPG exploded from its tube and slammed into the cab of the vehicle. A nanosecond later, the rear compartment ignited blasting a hole in the concrete barrier. Debris shot in all directions sending guards diving for cover.

The diversionary action sent the prison facility into lock down.

Klaxons sounded sending every guard, with the exception of Fat Louie who'd been drugged earlier, on high alert.

"Okay boys, this is it," Joe said. "We take them out one by one. No guns, no shooting. Once we've killed the regular prison guards we'll link up with our boys on the inside. Using their IDs, we'll breach Cell Block 9B."

Glancing at his watch, he clicked the corner of his mouth. "The guards should be moving our people from the 'Yard' as we speak. We need to hurry."

Heads nodded.

"Nigel."

"Yes, sir?"

"You take two men to the security hub. Give me two clicks in my headset when you've gained control of the video feed. I want to know who's around the next corner before we go walking into a trap."

Patting his commander on the shoulder, he gave him a broad grin. "They'll never know what hit 'em. See you in five mics."

Taking two other men with him, Nigel climbed the steps to the loading dock and entered the prison facility.

Five minutes later, two clicks crackled in Joe's ear piece. "Okay, let's do this by the numbers."

***

With Klaxon's blaring from the attack on the front gate, Joe and his men began to leap-frog through the corridors.

Moving from one hall to the next, they took out guard after guard. In sixty seconds they had cleared the area of threats and began making their way to Cell Block 9B.

"Hold it chief," Nigel's voice crackled in his headset. "You've got a line of prisoners moving in your direction. I see one guard in the lead and one bringing up the rear."

Joe hadn't counted on the guards moving a group of prisoners through this section of the prison. It was time to think outside the box. Shooting it out with the guards would cost him the mission. Instead, he stepped around the corner, his chest swelled, his eyes aflame. Taking a quick glance at the name plate on the guard's uniform, he jabbed his finger into his chest.

"Corporal Morrison, what in blazes are you doing marching these people through this restricted area?" Thanks to Nigel's quick thinking, he knew this was not the usual route the guards took.

"Sir, I, I—"

"Do you know what the penalty is for breaking protocol not to mention, stupidity?"

The young guard, obviously stunned by the threat of demotion, stammered a weak response.

'Sir, it's—"

"Enough of your excuses, I want you to turn these prisoners around and march them back to their cells."

The shaken guard gulped, his throat constricted with every shallow breath. "But sir, it's these inmates—"

"Do it now!" Joe barked.

"Hurry, more guards are moving in your vector," Nigel's voice was laced with tension.

Joe knew he had to act fast. He couldn't afford to draw the attention of the incoming guards. "Corporal, you and your men are relieved of your duty. Report to the front gate and assist in defending it. I am taking command of this detail. Now get your tail outta here and forget you ever met me."

The color had drained from the young guard's face. Giving Joe a crisp salute, he glanced at the other guard, who returned a quizzical shrug. It was obvious these men were not required to think independently. They understood one thing . . . the chain of command. If the man addressing you out ranked you, you said 'yes, sir,' and jumped at their command, no questions asked.

Joe returned his salute and accepted the clipboard from him. The surprised inmates knew to keep their mouths shut. Silently, they waited to see how it would turn out.

It suddenly dawned on Joe that he'd just inherited an extra dozen inmates besides the four he'd planned on helping to escape. With time running down to the last grain of sand in the hour-glass, he made a snap decision.

He turned to his men. "You two, take these people to the trucks." Handing one of them the clipboard, he turned to his remaining team. "Let's find our guys and get out of here." His wide-eyed men checked their weapons and lined up behind their leader.

With Nigel's guidance, Joe and the others avoided any other encounters with the old guard. They arrived at what looked like Cell Block 9B. The guards wearing the new uniforms offered their password and Joe countered with his own. After exchanged handshakes, they assembled for a quick conference. "Let's get your people lined up. The clock is ticking."

Joe's men took their positions while Nigel, in the control room, hit the electronic release button which controlled the cell doors. Without speaking, the inmates assembled in the main corridor and formed a straight line, their eyes fixed on the person's head directly in front of them."

No one spoke. It all depended on how normal this routine looked.

Giving his men a nod Joe began a controlled march through the hall leading to the loading dock. With Nigel's help, they avoided any more unfriendlies.

When they reached the loading docks, the rest of his men were ready. They helped the prisoners get into the trucks all while Fat Louie remained unconscious.

With phase one completed, Joe focused on phase two … escaping without having to shoot their way out.

His com crackled to life. It was Nigel. "Sir, I've informed the gate guards not to detain you for an exit inspection. I told them your supervisor is demanding your immediate return to the central hub or heads will roll. Anyone charged with delaying you will be shot."

"And you, my friend?"

Nigel's voice turned somber. "Sir, the boys and I have talked about it and we've decided to stay behind and cover your six. It looks like we're about to become a permanent member of the Corcoran State Prison System."

"Oh no you don't. We'll wait for you."

"No can do, sir. You know as well as I do, that's not an option. You need us to cover your lousy tails until you're clear of this place. We'll cause enough havoc to keep the guards occupied, but you better get a move on. The clock is ticking." He choked out the rest of his words with a grunt.

Knowing he was right, Joe cleared his throat, "You're a good man, Nigel. We owe you our lives. Now don't let them take you without a fight."

"You got it, chief."

Chapter Thirty-Six

"Home," the driver said, as he tugged his ball cap further over his eyes.

As Cami stepped out, she caught a whiff of her driver's cologne. The scent triggered a distant memory, one that had been numbed by too many shock treatments. As her mind cleared, the familiar fragrance took the shape of her driver.

"Trace?" her voice quivered.

Forgetting they were vulnerable to unwanted eyes, Cami threw her arms around his neck and squeezed. "I thought I'd lost you," she sputtered.

Trace settled his lips on hers, silencing her next question and sending her heart into high gear. She let the kiss linger, wishing it would never end.

Finally, he pulled back. Holding her gaze, he spoke in a raspy tone. "That's what I was going to say. That missile must have barely missed us. I blacked out before I could reach you."

Cami felt her world shift beneath her feet. "I, I don't remember a missile. I don't remember anything."

Tears glazed Trace's eyes. "My gracious, what have they done to you? You don't remember us driving to Santa Vern when someone fired a missile from a drone?"

"No, no. It was a car accident. Amanda told me I was involved in a car accident on the Washington beltway. I was unconscious for weeks. That's when the pandemic struck. They told me you, Lily and Will were dead." Cami's body went rigid, her eyes wide with confusion.

"Well, as you can see, it's not true," Trace said. "Let me help you get inside. We can talk there. Also, I have a surprise waiting for you."

Cami tilted her head back. The pressure behind her eyes mounted until she couldn't hold back any longer. "All those speeches, those interviews, those cocktail parties, they were part of a well-crafted deception which I believed." The edge in her voice caught Trace by surprise.

"We've all been lied to. Now it's our turn to get the truth out."

Reaching into the Lincoln Towncar, Cami retrieved her purse which sat on the far side of the vehicle. He extended his arm and they fell in step with each other as they walked to her front door.

"Do you have a key?" she asked, reaching inside her purse.

"You won't find it there. I'm positive your handlers made sure you had nothing that would remind you of your past." As Trace spoke, he pulled a key from his pocket, shoved it in the slot and turned the knob. He swung the door open and Wag bounded through the hall to greet them.

"Where did he come from?" Cami sputtered.

The woman who'd ushered her from the restaurant appeared behind Wag. She looked at Cami. "He just appeared a few days ago. I figured he belonged to you so I let him in and fed him. He was badly undernourished.

Cami buried her face in his mane. "I thought I'd never see him again."

Wag began to inspect Cami's coat and let out a low growl. As he sniffed her purse, he bared his teeth and snarled. "Wag, what's wrong?" she asked, lifting it so he couldn't reach it.

The woman inspected its contents. "Shoot!" she withdrew a listening device in her hand. Finger to her lips, she indicated that they remain quiet until she deactivated it.

"Your dog may have just saved you from a whole lot of trouble."

Wag growled again as she moved the device from out of his reach. "Now, let's get down to business. We don't have much time."

As they moved to the living room, Wag trailed close behind. There was something familiar in the woman's walk and Cami cocked her head.

"Millie?" Cami sputtered.

"Yes, it's me," Removing her wig and facial implants, she looked at Trace. "You don't know me, but I know you. My name is Millie. We have a lot of catching up to do."

Chapter Thirty-Seven

"Addicts can gamble uninterrupted and undetected for unlimited periods of time." **A. Nonymous**

T he moment Joe and his men had cleared the prison facility, Nigel began to see movement in the monitors in front of him.

The switchboard lit up with requests from unit supervisors demanding to know why there were no guards at their usual posts.

"Sir, I diverted as many men as possible to the front gate including the guards from Cell Block 5C since all the prisoners were in lock-down. They should be back in position within minutes."

Another call came in followed by two others. Nigel relayed the same message, holding off the inevitable. As he scanned the monitors, he recognized the guards in Cell Block 9B. His heart jackhammered. *Why were they still there? They should have left fifteen minutes ago.* It suddenly dawned on him. Joe had taken the wrong set of prisoners. His fingers twitched over the control knobs as he focused in on the grainy picture of Lily, Troy and a small group of detainees being ushered from their cells. *If Joe didn't get Lily and Troy, who did they get?*

"Sergeant Barnes, are you there? Come in. Over?" It was the unit supervisor and he didn't sound too happy.

With Sergeant Barnes lying on the floor with a bullet in his head, Nigel knew it wouldn't be long before the unit supervisor would realize something was wrong. With few options left, and time running out, Nigel looked at his men, sweat gathered on his upper lip and he wiped it with the back of his hand. "Okay, it's show time." He pushed a button.

Immediately, the doors of every cell within the correctional institution swung open. Within seconds, angry detainees stormed the corridors overwhelming the guards.

Why hadn't I thought of this sooner?

Nigel fingered his weapon and sprang from the observation unit, his two men following close behind. Together, they sprinted down the hall leading to Cell Block 9B. With a little luck, he could round up Lily and the others before they were either shot or trampled by the rampaging inmates.

As he turned the last corner, a spray of lead ripped through the air, barely missing him. It was one of the guard units. They had set up a blockade between Cell Block 9 and one of the exits. Anyone crazy enough to step into the corridor was cut down. A number of inmates had already been shot and lay in bloody, contorted positions on the floor.

Nigel assessed the scene looking for a familiar face. His breath froze in his throat as he caught a glimpse of John Conner's body among the fallen. Frantically, Nigel scanned the floor for Lily or Troy. They were not among the dead, and he released a long-held breath.

Waving a handkerchief, Nigel flagged down the guards manning the blockade. "Hold your fire. I'm coming in to help. I've got more ammunition."

One of the guards hollered, "Hold your fire. He's one of us."

That was all Nigel needed. He dove behind the overturned table while the rest of his team held their positions.

"This place is a madhouse. The inmates have taken over the command center and are letting the lifers out," he said.

The nervous guards turned to see a mass of angry men gathering at the far end of the hall.

Pop, pop, pop!

Nigel used up the remainder of his magazine on the surprised guards. He snapped up a weapon from one of the men he'd just shot and yelled, "Rick, Lonnie."

His teammates joined him, their eyes wide with terror.

"What, you've never seen a man die before?"

They exchanged fearful expressions. "Not this close," Rick said.

"Get over it. Now let's go. We've got friendlies to help."

Down the corridor they rushed with reckless abandonment. "Lily, Troy, Olivia stop!" he hollered, before they walked into another trap. Using a mirror, he glanced around the corner. Another 50 caliber machine gun unit was set up waiting for anyone to cross their path.

"This way," he ordered.

Taking Lily and Olivia by the wrists, he tugged the two women behind him and ran in the direction of the loading dock.

Not being used to running, Troy soon fell behind. He stopped, his lungs screaming for oxygen.

"Troy, keep up." Nigel yelled over his shoulder.

Despite his discomfort, he forced his legs to push himself to the limit. All at once, Nigel held up a hand. Troy stopped short of plowing into him and caught Lily from tripping. He doubled over, panting.

"Can you handle a gun?" Nigel asked.

Troy took a few breaths and nodded. "Yes," he choked out.

Nigel pulled an extra gun from his belt and shoved it into his hands. "Good, get ready. We may have to shoot our way out of here."

Nodding to Rick, he said, "Cover our six. Lonnie, take point." The two men nodded and took their positions. Like a line of ducklings, they moved in unison until they reached the loading dock.

Chapter Thirty-Eight

"Take a seat while I get you the dessert you missed at the restaurant." Millie said, closing the front door and locking it.

Cami gave her a quizzical look as Trace helped her from her coat. He shrugged his off and hung both over the back of a chair. Seeing Cami wobble, he grabbed her by the elbow and steadied her. "Careful," he said, guiding her to the living room. "Can I get you anything?"

Cami reached up and touched his face. Her hand felt ice cold. "You've aged," she said, her eyes remained unfocused.

A coarse chuckle bubbled up in his chest. "Thanks, you don't look a day over thirty-two."

She smiled. "Thirty-three," she corrected. "I can't believe it's been nearly a year."

"Believe it," Millie said as she reemerged from the kitchen. Wag followed her in and took a seat next to Cami, listening to every word.

"She is actually quite good at her job," Millie continued, "Cami is most convincing when she puts her mind to it."

Trace nodded and took a seat next to Cami. She clutched his hands trying to warm her fingers.

"I feel so used," she sputtered. "How could I let myself be so deceived?"

Trace placed his arm around her shoulder in an attempt to console her. "Cami, listen, you've been traumatized. It's going to take a little while to sort things out, but let me assure you of this, I love you and I want to marry you."

Blinking away the fuzz in her mind, she locked her eyes on him. "I believe you, but how do I get my life back?"

Millie set the tray on the coffee stand and took a seat across from them. "That's what we all want, Cami."

Cami eyed the array of desserts.

"I believe you ordered Butterscotch Pudding. I, myself am preferable to the Espresso Torte. Their dark chocolate with espresso crème fraiche is to die for. And you, Mr. O'Reilly, I figured you as a Grand Marnier Soufflé man. It's not only the most expensive dessert on the menu, but it's the largest. Dig in. We've got a lot to cover and not a long time to do so."

Trace handed Cami her dessert and filled the cups with the most aromatic coffee he'd smelled since visiting the Green Mountain Beanery.

Millie munched in between questions and answers.

"First of all Cami, you were not in an accident, at least not the kind Amanda told you that you were in."

She stabbed a fork full of torte as Trace took her through the afternoon of their arrival in Sacramento and subsequent missile attack. Cami sat rigid, listening. Her eyebrows knit as if trying to visualize the events.

Hand to her forehead, Cami slumped back on the couch. "It all seems so, surreal."

"I wouldn't have believed it myself had I not been there. I really thought I'd lost you," Trace added.

"Actually," Millie continued, "having the Secretary of State come to your aid was a miracle. That alone saved your life. For that you can be thankful. It was only after he purged the government of all loyalists and established the Grid Authority as the rule of law that we realized the two edged sword we were dealing with." Millie crossed her legs and eyed the two sitting across from her.

Wag's eyes twitched as he watched the conversation bounce around the room.

"You said, 'We.' Who are we talking about?" Cami asked, her body suddenly growing tense.

"Cami, as I told you, I'm with the former CIA. Now I'm a part of an underground movement called the NRA, the National Resistance Army." She chuckled. "Interestingly we chose the same letters as the National Rifle Association and for good reason. We believe in the Bill of Rights, the Constitution and the Bible, not in that particular order, I might add. My fellow patriots and I are committed to the overthrow of this regime. It is corrupt and gained power by lying to the public and taking advantage of a crisis. Even as we speak, we have people in key positions ready to move into action as soon as we give them the word."

Cami laced her fingers into Trace's, still shivering. It was obvious she was not quite up to speed yet. "Where do I, or should I say, 'we' come in?"

Trace sat back and let Millie continue. She took the last sip of her coffee and set her cup down. "I thought you'd never ask. As you know, we pulled a bait and switch with you back at the restaurant. But your double can only play the ruse so long before Amanda discovers what we've done." Standing, she snagged our coats. "Put these on. I'll tell you the plan on the way back."

"But, but I thought you were here to help me escape." Cami's eyes switched between Millie and Trace.

Reaching out, Millie took her hand. "Cami, listen to me. We're going to get you out as quickly as possible, but first, we need you to find the release codes which control the national grids. Only after we've got our hands on them, can we destroy the grid fields separating our partisan forces. Once that's done, we can move in mass and attack the command and control units, blind them, and let the rest of our military forces move in and retake our government."

Cami's face paled. "You're talking about a civil war."

Trace shrugged his coat on. "Ain't nothin' civil about it. This is all out war! And there are more of us than them."

"I don't know what to say," Cami sputtered. "I wouldn't know where to begin looking for those codes. And what about POTUS? He'll kill me if he catches me trying to get the codes."

Millie continued, "We need to get you inside the Oval Office. As you know, I occupy the desk just outside, but I am forbidden to ever enter his office without him being there. So I listen. There is not one word spoken in his private sanctuary that I don't hear."

"Why can't you get the codes?" Cami asked, her eyes wide with trepidation.

Millie dipped her head. "He never speaks about the codes, at least not in plain language. He refers to them as protocols and necessary means, but I know he keeps them close at hand. I've heard him talking with one of the Grid Commanders about an anomaly that occurs every once in a while. He took them from a secret location in the Oval Office and made reference to some numbers. I wasn't able to make any sense of them."

"An anomaly? What kind of anomaly?" Trace asked, surprised that he'd not heard about this development.

The dimple between Millie's eyes deepened and she paused. He couldn't tell if it was indecision or an unwillingness to be completely open.

"Well, we can't know for sure, but we believe there may be one other person who can cross the grids without setting off an alarm. It caused an anomaly every time he does it, however."

Trace sat up straighter. "Wait, you said, 'him,' do you know who he is?"

Nodding, Millie continued, "Actually, yes, but I cannot reveal his identity. Not at this time. As far as we know, you, Lily and Troy and this unidentified individual are the only ones who can cross the grid borders without triggering an alarm. There is a mission happening as we speak to get Troy and Lily out of prison."

Cami exchanged shocked expressions with Trace. "Now?"

Millie nodded. "Yes, in your case, you don't have an ID chip either. Since you are the Grid Authority's spokeswoman, you're immune to the virus. You can move about freely. That's another reason why we need to get you back in the custody of Amanda. If your lookalike is on that plane when it takes off, the moment they cross the grid, the virus will reactivate, she'll go nuts and probably kill everyone on board including herself."

Trace's heart broke as memories of Cami's last day in the capitol returned.

Hand to her mouth. She gasped, "The plane crash . . . all those people . . . those birds."

Patting her on the arm, Millie held her gaze. The warmth in her eyes told her she felt the same sense of loss. "Yes and a lot more have died and will die if we don't get our government back. I know firsthand that people, especially people of faith, are being systematically hunted down and sent to special holding camps. From what I've been able to glean, it's a chilling picture."

Chapter Thirty-Nine

"Stress can often times go undetected in those who feel they have a good control over life."   **A. Nonymous**

T he doors to the loading dock appeared to be unguarded, but Nigel was taking no chances.

He raised a clutched fist and the line stopped. Using his mirror again, he caught the reflection of the overweight guard. He had roused from the drug and leaned heavily against the wall. Now he stood as the lone sentinel between certain death and their freedom.

"Drop your weapon or I'll shoot you where you stand," Nigel ordered, holding his gun with two hands and stepping from behind the door.

The surprised guard sucked in a sharp breath, raised his hands and began to back away.

"I said, drop your weapon."

The gun fell to the concrete with a heavy thud. "Now kick it over to me."

Gunfire echoed from deep within the building. Nigel couldn't tell if it came from the guards or the inmates. He just knew danger was near.

The whites of the guard's eyes rounded as the sound of gunfire grew louder. He kicked the gun in Nigel's direction. "Olivia, pick it up and be ready to use it."

She staggered forward and picked it up.

"That vehicle, are the keys in it?" Nigel motioned to an International Guard utility van parked at the end of the dock. Fat Louie nodded. "Okay, if you want to live, you will do exactly what I say. Understand?" The guard gulped and nodded as large rings of sweat formed under his arms.

"Good, now you are going to take that clipboard, sign out and leisurely drive us out of this facility."

"But—"

"No buts. You're going to take us out of here and if anyone asks what you're doing, you're going to convince them you're on official business. My gun will be inches away from your head, just to ensure you don't do anything stupid. Got it?"

The shaken guard eased his stance. "Yes, but you'll never get away with it."

"You'd better hope we do. The other alternative is for me to leave you here to be abused and killed by the inmates. You up for that?"

"No, but first I want to make one thing very clear. I didn't agree with the things they were doing here. I was just—"

"Shut it," Lily spat as she and the others emerged from the doorway. "You're just as bad as the rest of them … worse."

Fat Louie's eyes rounded as recognition struck him.

"You don't deserve to live you piece of human trash," Lily seethed.

Troy grabbed the man by his throat and pressed the gun against Louie's head. "You're lucky I don't kill you."

"Let him go! We need him." Nigel ordered.

"But you don't know what he did to me," Lily argued.

"Doesn't matter. Right now he's our best hope for getting out of here. Now let's go."

Lily bristled, but obeyed.

Still clutching Fat Louie's throat, Troy shoved him into the driver's seat. "We'll deal with you later." He felt bad for Conner getting shot, but he didn't care if this man lived or died.

By the time they'd convinced Fat Louie to comply, Rick had Lily tucked away in the back under a tarp. He turned to Olivia who stood back.

"You guys will never make it if someone doesn't cover your back. I'm not much use to the underground now anyway. So give me another gun. I'll hold them off as long as possible."

Nigel exchanged glances with his men. He knew he might need backup, but he was loath to leaving anyone behind. "No, I think my plan will work. You're coming with us and we'll see how much more you can contribute to the movement. I know from experience, you've got a lot of pull, so hop in."

Olivia's eye teared. "Nigel! And I thought you didn't care."

He winked and helped her get in. Once he was situated behind Fat Louie, he shoved the gun in his ribs.

"Drive."

Fat Louie wiped the sweat from his eyes and pulled forward as far as the first guard shack.

"Going somewhere, Fat Louie?" the guard at the crossing gate asked.

Handing him the signed clipboard, he nodded. "Yeah, me and the boys are going to celebrate. They sent me for the beer."

"What are you celebrating?"

Louie cocked his head. "After the truck bomb, a few of the detainees in the 'Yard' got rowdy and we had to take them out. That calls for a celebration, in my book."

"What do you mean, 'we'? I doubt you've ever drawn your weapon once in anger. If an inmate ever threatened you, you'd probably hand him your gun and offer to drive him out of here."

Nigel could barely keep from laughing.

"Very funny. Maybe next time I'll do just that. Now give me the clipboard and I'll be on my way." His angry outburst took the guard by surprise.

"Hey, I was just kidding. Here," handing him the clipboard. "And don't forget the pretzels."

Putting the vehicle in gear, Louie stomped the gas pedal and raced away. Once they cleared the area, Nigel and the others began to breathe easier. "Okay Louie, slow down. Follow my directions and you may live another day," Nigel said as he climbed into the passenger seat.

Once they'd gotten far enough away, Nigel took over the driving and had Louie bound and blindfolded. His continued curses ended with Troy clobbering him on the head with the butt of his gun.

"That felt good," Troy said as Fat Louie slumped down. "Now throw that tarp over him. Maybe he'll suffocate."

"Troy!" Lily couldn't hide her shock.

"Just kidding … sorta."

Chapter Forty

Trace sat quietly as Millie finished giving an overview of their plan.

When she twisted her wrist and glanced at her watch, he knew it was time to go.

"We'd better get going. I still have a lot to cover and we don't have much time," she said.

"But what about Wag? Will he be okay?"

Millie peered down at the sleeping animal. "He can't stay. I've arranged for your lookalike to be here in fifteen minutes and they can't find him here."

Cami's eyes glazed.

"Honey, Wag is the least of our worries," Trace said, trying to sound conciliatory. "I'll come back for him after I've dropped you off. Now let's go."

She knelt one last time and gave Wag a big hug. Standing again, she wiped the tears from her eyes. "This is so hard," she said, her lower lip quivering. "Just about the time I think I've got my life back together, I have to give it all up." Her voice trembled.

Millie tugged her into a tight embrace. "It'll be all right. We've all had to sacrifice, but it will be worth it when we see them frog marching Bleakly and his gang to prison."

Cami inhaled a shuttering breath as Millie brushed a few dog hairs from her coat. "I wouldn't want any of these to give away our little secret."

As they loaded in the Lincoln, Wag sat on the stoop and watched. It was as if he knew his masters were heading into harm's way. The moment the taillights of the Lincoln disappeared around the corner, Wag sprang into action.

He was on a mission

***

Millie touched her ear piece as the news of the successful NRA mission was relayed to her.

She smiled and let out a nervous breath.

"Something funny?" Cami asked as Trace weaved the big vehicle through the deserted streets of Sacramento. She and Millie had been rehearsing their plan ever since they left the condo.

"No, not funny. I just got some very good news."

"Care to share it?" Trace asked as he swerved to miss a pedestrian.

Millie glanced into the rear view mirror and met Trace's eyes. "Not at this time. We need to stay focused. Cami, can you do this?"

She nodded. "Yes, I'm ready."

"Good, because our lives depend on it."

The parking lot surrounding the private airstrip was deserted making it easy for Trace to guide the Towncar to a secluded section out of sight.

"I'm thinking about trading in my Renault for one of these after this mess is over."

Cami eyed him narrowly. "You've got to be kidding."

"I'm just saying."

"Yeah right."

Millie smiled. "We could arrange it."

"Millie, don't encourage him."

"What'd I say?" he said, his shoulders hiking up.

"Forget it," Cami said with a chuckle.

The Lear jet's engines purred like a couple of well-fed leopards. The night pressed in all around them, and the open bay held an ominous welcome as if some evil lurked in the shadows.

"So you understand the plan?" Millie's question brought Cami's attention into focus. "Yes, hide in the ladies room just like my look-alike did. She'll take the stall next to me and I'll count to sixty, flush and come out."

"And don't act surprised if a cleaning lady steps in and makes a lot of noise. She's one of us. Follow her lead."

Millie pointed. "Park over there, in the shadows."

Trace did so and flipped the headlights off.

After extracting himself from the car, he helped Cami get ready to leave. He placed his arms around her and held her close. "God has gotten us this far, He will get us through this. We can do all things through Christ who gives us strength."

Cami gave his hand a final squeeze. "I'll miss you. Pray that I'll be brave and complete my mission."

"I already have and will continue." He drew her close and kissed her deeply. For a brief moment, he felt the world stop spinning and time hold its breath.

After he released her, she stepped back and followed Millie into the building. With one last glance over her shoulder, she disappeared. Their early arrival gave them the advantage of moving around without being seen.

***

As the loneliness of night closed in around him, Trace suddenly felt the demon of self-condemnation drape its leathery cape over him.

He hated himself for doubting God when things got so dark. He should have been stronger. He knew better. His relapse into alcohol made him feel dirty. Falling to his knees, he sobbed out a throaty prayer asking for his Heavenly Father's forgiveness. In the silence, he felt so unclean before the throne of grace, so unworthy. Finally, the words of Jesus pressed into his heart. *I died for those sins, my blood covered them and I remember them no more. Go and sin no more.*

After pushing himself up on wobbly legs, he gazed up at the canvas sky. His eyes fogged making the stars glitter like ice crystals. He took in a cleansing breath and let it out more determined to trust God in the good times and the bad times.

Sensing the need to do something other than stand around, he made a snap decision. He began to move along in the shadows behind Millie and Cami. When he reached the door to the hanger, he slipped inside. To one side, was an office where the pilot and co-pilot and a few guards lounged.

A door opened and the co-pilot, a man about his size, stepped out. He reached into his pocket and pulled out a pack of cigarettes. An orange glow illuminated the man's angular face as he ignited the cigarette. When he stepped further from the hanger, Trace made his move.

Having found a fist size rock, he slugged the man, then caught him before he hit the ground.

Adrenaline surged through his blood as he quickly exchanged clothes with the co-pilot. Knowing he couldn't afford to let the man be discovered, he popped the trunk of the Lincoln open, then tied and gagged him before dropping him inside.

Still breathing hard, he waited until his breath calmed before climbing the steps and taking the copilot's seat. He hoped the pilot wouldn't discover what happened until it was too late. To insure his cooperated, Trace stuffed the co-pilot's 45 caliber Taurus, in his belt, tugged his jacket down and strapped in.

***

Once inside the hanger, the two women avoided the office and disappeared around the corner.

After checking the area and making sure the coast was clear, Millie gave Cami a quick nod. Cami gulped and slipped onto the ladies room. Inside, she checked her lipstick and hair while Millie kept watch.

"You know what to do once you get back?" Millie whispered in a breathy tone.

The whites of Cami's eyes glowed like beacons. "Yes, but how will I get the codes to you?"

Giving her a coy smile, Millie said, "I'll be sitting right outside. Once you're in the Oval Office my operatives will cause a diversion. That's your signal. If POTUS tips his hand, you be ready. You may need to think on your feet. Just remember, I've got your back. Get in, get the codes and get out. I'll do the rest."

Cami gave her an acknowledging nod before pulling her close. "Thank you for all you've done, for giving me my life back."

"Just don't overplay it. I don't want Amanda to get suspicious."

Cami released her hold and stepped into the stall. "Okay, I'm ready."

With one final hug, Millie backed away.

Chapter Forty-One

"Sir, that's a lot more detainees than we expected."

It was Joe's second in command, Len Walker, a retired policeman. He was checking the ID's of the newly freed prisoners against the list of personnel they came to get. "How are we supposed to feed, house and treat the medical needs of so many people?"

"How many are there?" Joe asked, his hand pressing against his chest.

"Fifteen, sir. And there's another thing. I don't think we got the people we went after."

A bolder appeared in the middle of the road and Joe swerved to miss it.

The truck jostled and Len gripped the door frame, an expletive escaped his lips.

Joe shot him a glance. "Sorry, I didn't see that until it was too late."

Peering at his commander, Len lowered his voice, "Sir, are you all right? You don't look so good."

The color had leaked from Joe's face and he mopped his brow with the back of his hand. "It's nothing." Pressing his hand to his chest, he tried to take a breath, but cringed. "I think . . . I'm having a . . . heart attack."

Gasping for air, he let the steering wheel go. The vehicle swerved off the road. It hit the soft shoulder and plowed into an outcropping sending the occupants in the delivery truck sprawling. Joe slumped over the steering wheel barely conscious.

"Help me get him out of here," Len ordered. Two of his men climbed forward and slid the side door open. "Take his shoulders, I'll get his legs."

"What happened to him?" One of the detainees asked. His salt and pepper hair, strong jawline and piercing black eyes commanded Len's full attention.

"He said he was having a heart attack, and then he collapsed. We can't stay here. It won't be long before this whole place will be crawling with the International Guard. We gotta get moving."

The man looked at Len and extended his hand. "We are in your debt. Is there is anything we can do?"

Taken aback at the man's commanding presence, he narrowed his eyes. "Do I know you?"

He smiled and glanced around. The men surrounding him fought back grins. "You might, I'm James F. Richardson, the former President of the United States."

"Current President, sir," his acting chief of staff interjected.

Richardson's expression softened into a smile. "President in absentia. We've been arguing this point ever since Bleakly wrest the government from us. This is what remains of my cabinet," nodding to a dozen somber looking men.

Overhearing the two men's exchange, the eight man squad of NRA partisans formed a tight circle around the President. Len squared his shoulders and gave the Commander-in-Chief a crisp salute. "Sir, with your permission, we need to get Joe back to our hide out. Would your people mind lending a hand? We need to get this truck back on the road and get the heck outta here."

The President returned his salute and nodded to his men. "Do whatever he says." With a quick move, he took a position on the front bumper and helped lift it up. After some heavy breathing, the men maneuvered the truck back on the road.

"Thank you men," Len said as he and the others took their places. Once Joe was placed in the back, he put the truck in gear and resumed their journey.

"Where are you taking us?" Richardson asked, wiping sweat from his brow with a handkerchief bearing his initials.

"Have you ever heard of the Santa Vern Uranium Mine?"

The President gave his men a quizzical look. Heads shook. "No, we haven't."

"It's good you haven't. We'll be there in about a half hour. Once we get there, we'll reassemble and plan our next move."

Chapter Forty-Two

It had only been a few hours since Amanda and Cami had taken off for Sacramento and already Norman felt at a loss.

He depended so much on Amanda for advice, that when she was out of his presence for any amount of time, he couldn't focus. Feeling jittery, he poured himself a large glass of Jim Bean and tipped it up to his lips. The combination of psychotic drugs and alcohol sent him careening over the edge. Confused and disorientated, he stumbled from the Oval Office.

"Millie?"

The woman sitting behind the desk of secretaries stood to attention. "Sir, Millie asked for the day off. You signed her papers yesterday."

"And you are—"

"—Miss Johnson, sir. I've worked for you—"

"I don't care. Where's Amanda!?" His voice carried throughout the West Wing. Staffers stopped mid-stride, secretaries froze. They'd seen the President lose his temper before and dreaded these outbursts.

"Sir, don't you remember? Cami and Amanda flew to Sacramento. It was part of the unification tour. You authorized it."

"I did no such thing. All of you ... get out. You're all conspiring against me. And don't deny it. I can hear you whispering behind my back. You all hate me and want me dead."

Hearing the President's rantings, his security detail had moved into position. Their weapons close at hand.

As staffers and secretaries began to move away, the phone rang on Miss Johnson desk. Carefully she lifted the receiver. "Office of Secretaries."

Her voice remained calm despite the electrically charged atmosphere. It was the commandant of Corcoran State Prison and he didn't sound happy. "Sir, I don't think this is a good time—"

Bleakly swiveled around. "See, this is exactly what I'm talking about. Everyone is keeping secrets from me. Everyone!"

He grabbed the phone from the shaken woman's hand, demanded to take control.

"This is Hector Ortega, commandant of Corcoran State Prison, sir."

"What do you want? I'm a busy man."

The head of his protective detail looked at the others. It was clear, they didn't like the President conducting official business where everyone could hear. Leaning close, he whispered, "Mr. President, don't you think you should take the call inside your office?"

POTUS glared back at the man. His glassy eyes remained unfocused. "I'll determine where I should take a phone call and right now, I'm talking to… what did you say your name was … is?"

Confused, Commander Ortega repeated his name.

"Yes, you were saying?"

"Sir, there has been an incident."

"An incident? What kind of incident?"

Ortega cleared his throat nervously. "Sir, someone detonated a truck bomb directly in front of the prison. At the same time, there was a coordinated effort on the part of the NRA. They breached our security system and helped fifteen political prisoners escape."

Bleakly turned the air a deep color of blue. "Ortega, I put you in charge of that prison because I knew you were tough. Now you're telling me you couldn't defend your pathetic jail against a few shotgun toting Bible thumpers!" He raged.

The shaken man stuttered out a weak, "Yes, but—"

"I don't care a rat's tail about your excuses. Call out the National Guard. Find those escapees or by Zeus your head will roll." Then he slammed the phone down.

Mrs. Johnson's face had paled to the color of milk as she replaced the phone to its cradle. "Mr. President, do you want me to send a message to the governor declaring grid twenty-six in a state of emergency?"

Bleakly glanced at the head of security. "Wesley, what do you think?"

He had never addressed his security detail by their first name and never asked them for advice. It was obvious the President was not in his right mind.

In an effort to defuse the situation, he said, "Sir, why don't we discuss your options back in your office."

Like a tottering old man, Bleakly let him guide him back to the seclusion of the Oval Office. As the door quietly closed, staffers and secretaries exchanged worried looks before returning to work.

Still unsteady on his feet, Bleakly made his way to the wet bar, filled a shot glass with the strongest whiskey he had and downed it. "Care for a drink?" he said to the head of security detail.

"No, sir. I'm on the clock and I don't think it's a good idea for you to be drinking, too."

Bleakly wobbled to the Resolute Desk and plopped down behind it. "I don't care what you think. I'm the Pres … I'm the Presa …"

"Sir, maybe you should lie down. I'll see to it no one disturbs you." As he moved to help the President to the couch, Bleakly reached inside the man's suit coat and drew his weapon. Pointing it at his face, he blurted, "You're just trying to get me in a position where you can strangle me."

His eyes were wild, his hair disheveled and the alcohol he'd consumed had loosened all restraints.

"Sir, I assure you—"

The gun discharged, sending parts of skull, brains and blood all over the wall behind him. Before his body hit the floor, the security detail stationed outside the Oval Office rushed in. Shocked, they stopped short of stumbling over their fallen comrade's body. A pool of blood formed and spread to the national seal embedded in the carpet.

"He tried to kill me," the President muttered. "Now I'm going to lie down and rest. I'm very tired."

The astonished agents gaped at each other. Bleakly, still clutching the gun, stretched out on the couch next to the quivering corpse and closed his eyes.

Chapter Forty-Three

"Of course, the liar often imagines that he does no harm as long as his lies go undetected." **Sam Harris**

News of the prisoner escape reached Amanda as their Lear jet disappeared into the inky sky over Sacramento.

She threw her tumbler of Bourbon across the plane nearly smashing out one of the portholes. Seething, she paced the aisle like a caged animal. "How dare those despicables. They have no right to barge into one of our prison facilities, kill our people and make off with the former President. Who do they think they are? If they think for one minute they can get on national television and reinstate the man they have another thing coming. We have proof that it was Richardson who created the mess we're in. If it weren't for my brother, this country would have completely drifted into anarchy."

Cami sat back and enjoyed the spectacle. She knew the truth. Bleakly, Scott Wan and Dr. Jovanovich were to blame for the country's troubles, not President Richardson. It was they and their lapdog media co-conspirators who engineered the coup, and they did it without firing a shot. They even turned public opinion against Bible-believing Christians blaming them for backing a faulty political system.

And most recently, the Grid Authority had begun shutting down unauthorized churches, radio stations and hunting down Christians. The world outside Cami's artificial bubble had changed drastically in the last year.

***

Amanda lifted her phone and speed dialed the White House. "Let me speak to Norman," she demanded.

A long pause.

"What do you mean he can't be disturbed? I'm his sister! I demand you put me through to Norman immediately."

The wait took longer than normal. While she waited, she filled another shot glass with the first bottle she could find and splashed it down her throat.

"Norman, what took you so long? You sound terrible."

The one sided conversation was loud enough for Cami to hear without eavesdropping.

"Where are you?"

"Norman, you know where I am."

"Have you heard about Corcoran?"

"Yes, but not from you. How could this happen?"

Another long pause.

"Norman, are you there?"

"Yes, but I'm not feeling so well."

Amanda let an expletive fly. "Have you taken your meds?"

The President mumbled something incoherent.

"Norman, focus. Have you taken your meds!?"

His drunken sobs filled the connection. "Norman, give the phone to Millie."

A cold chill shot through Cami.

After a protracted wait, a voice came on the line.

"Millie, what's going on? Is Norman going to be all right?"

By now, Cami had bitten her thumb nail to the quick. She wondered how in heaven's name Millie could be on the phone.

"As a matter of fact, he's not. I think he got his meds mixed up." Her contact within the White House had patched Amanda's phone call to her remote location after informing her about the President shooting his security agent.

"Look, Millie, give him a couple Advil and tell him to lie down. I'll be back by eleven tonight. I'll handle whatever mess he made then."

Amanda ended the phone call with a curse. She finished her third shot of Jack Daniels and stared out the window dully. After a few minutes, she turned to Cami. "You're awfully quiet. Didn't you enjoy your visit to Sacramento?"

Cami grabbed a cushion and clutched it against her midsection. "Oh, yes. It was great. I especially enjoyed seeing my apartment, too.

Amanda relaxed in the seat next to Cami and cocked her head. "You know, it took nearly an act of congress to get the manager to let us in."

"It was nice of him to do so, but I guess I'll just have to sell all my furniture and stuff though."

"Does that mean you're going to accept the Norman's proposal?" Amanda asked, her eyes rounding.

A cold chill formed in Cami's stomach. She took a deep breath and let it out slowly. It was all about timing, building the anticipation and delivering the punchline. "Yes, but—"

"But what?" Amanda was clearly hooked.

"I have a few conditions."

Taken aback by Cami's assertiveness, Amanda crossed her legs and leaned closer. "Oh, and what are they? A long honeymoon? Pre-nuptials?"

Finger to her chin, Cami ticked off her requirements. "No. Nothing like that. First, I get to plan my own wedding, with Norman, of course. Two, I seem to remember Norman having a full-length, three dimensional portrait of himself standing in front of a raging fire. I love that picture."

"So you want it hung over your bed?" Amanda asked, an impish twinkle in her eyes.

Cami waved the comment aside. "No, silly. I want one of myself, in front of the same fireplace."

The color of Amanda's face darkened. "But the Norman doesn't allow anyone to enter the Oval Office. Not even his first secretary, what's her name? Millie. Not even Millie is permitted to enter without him being there."

"Well, I'm not just anybody. If he expects me to be open and transparent with him then he needs to do the same. Now about that portrait I want to be standing opposite Norman as if I'm looking in his direction. I want it to be in front of that same gorgeous fireplace." Her hands waved animatedly.

Sitting back in her seat, Amanda laced her fingers over her knees. Cami could see the wheels in her conniving head whirling. If she said no to her requirements, she'd be off the hook. If she agreed, she'd get her chance at finding the codes.

Amanda unlaced her fingers and turned to face Cami. "You have a deal."

Cami wasn't sure if the plane was bugged, or if Amanda had good instincts, but for whatever reason, she'd agreed. Now it was up to her.

With a little diversion and a lot of luck, she just might succeed.

Chapter Forty-Four

A ir turbulence and a strong headwind forced the pilot of the Lear jet carrying Amanda and Cami to alter his flight plan.

He was redirected to another DOD airfield. Once he got the aircraft down, he taxied to one of the private hangers where the women deplaned.

After waiting thirty minutes, Amanda grew inpatient. "Why is it taking so long?" she seethed.

Cami stifled a yawn. "I don't know. Did you call ahead?"

"Of course I did."

When the security detail finally arrived, it comprised of only one vehicle. It would have required another thirty minutes to secure a second vehicle. Rather than risk the wait, Amanda decided to drop Cami off at her condo and head directly to the White House. It was nearly two a.m. when she entered the West Wing and found it in total meltdown.

"What's happened?" she demanded.

The skeleton crew was clearly shaken by her presence. It was Miss Johnson who had the courage to step up. "Your brother shot one of his security agents."

"He didn't!"

"He did, and most of the White House staff has either been fired or quit."

The news hit Amanda like a tsunami. In a rage, she demanded to speak with the chief of staff.

"He was the first to quit," Miss Johnson added.

"And the President's security detail? Have they been replaced?"

She glanced nervously from side to side. Lowering her voice, she said, "Ma'am, they are refusing to protect POTUS for fear of being shot."

Amanda colored the air. "How dare them. Call General Haggerty. Order him to send his personal body guards to protect the him."

"I, I don't have the authority—"

Amanda cursed. "Give me the phone. I'll do it. And don't breathe a word of this outside this room. Do you understand? If the press gets wind of this, your head is on the chopping block."

Miss Johnson's face turned the pallor of death. "Yes, ma'am."

As she scurried off, Amanda stepped into the Oval Office where her brother snored soundly. Not caring about his unstable condition, she flipped on the lights and bellowed, "Norman, what have you done?"

POTUS jolted to life and gazed around, his red eyes unfocused.

"I, I—"

"Shut up, you boob. I was only gone one day and you managed to kill a man and drive half your staff into hiding. It will be a miracle if we can contain this before your blasted wedding."

Norman's eyes slowly began to focus. "My what?"

"Your wedding, marriage … matrimony, whatever."

"You mean Cami accepted my proposal?"

Amanda huffed. "Yes, you big dummy. Of course she did." Her voice took on a dreamy tone. "It took a little persuading on my part, but I think I made her understand it was for the good of the nation."

"I can't believe it." His hangdog face brightened.

"Don't get too excited. She doesn't love you and I know for certain you don't love her." Amanda plopped down on a seat next to her brother.

He leaned his elbows heavily on his knees. "If only she did. Love me that is."

Amanda eyed him with disdain. "That's not going to happen. You're unlovable. Daddy said so."

Norman's jaw tightened, tears welled in his eyes. After his mother died, his father remarried. The second marriage produced Amanda. That's when the abuse began. His jealous step-mother falsely accused him of setting the house on fire. The accusation landed him in juvenile detention. After six months, he returned home to face a steady diet of insults and mistreatment. His drunken father and hateful step-mother made living in the Bleakly home a veritable hell. While in his preteen years he spent long hours locked inside a dog pen.

It was only natural for him to react the way he did when Wag attacked him. His fear of dogs was as deeply rooted as was his hatred of them. However, the infection he'd gotten from Wag's bite, proved to be far worse than anyone expected.

If he didn't get the liver transplant soon, he would die.

"Cami had just a couple of small requests." Amanda said, setting her musings aside.

Norman took a shaky breath. "What are they?"

Holding up a finger, she began, "first, she wants to plan her own wedding."

"And?"

"And she wants to have a portrait painted of herself mirroring your image in the Oval Office."

Stroking his chin, he smiled wickedly. "So she's got an ego. We can use that against her if necessary."

"Believe me, it will be necessary. Cami is proving too much of an independent thinker for my taste. At the restaurant, she had the audacity of ordering the most expensive meal on the menu."

Norman waved the complaint aside. He eyed the portrait of himself admiringly. "Yes, I think I can arrange that. It will be nice to have a real woman by my side—"

"Norman! I can't believe you said that. After all I've done for you."

A devilish chuckle percolated in his throat. Then he pulled her into a passionate embrace and kissed her.

"It'll be our little secret."

Chapter Forty-Five

"What is originality? It is undetected plagiarism!"

illiam Ralph Inge

"**K**eep your hands where I can see them," warned Nigel.

Troy was driving and had just turned off the main highway and entered the twisting road leading deep into the mountainous region of Santa Vern and he was taking no chances. Fat Louie kept licking his upper lip as sweat ran down his face, burning his eyes.

"Can I at least use a handkerchief to wipe the sweat from my face?" he asked.

Nigel pulled his bandana from his head and handed it to him.

Fat Louie recoiled. "Thanks, but I'd rather use the back of my hand."

Nigel laughed and replaced it, covering a matted mass of hair. "That's okay, I wouldn't want your filthy sweat soiling my nice new bandana anyway. Now hold still while I blindfold you."

The fat man clamped his mouth shut.

"Where are you taking me?"

Troy swerved to miss a boulder. "I should shoot you for what you did to Lily."

Lily laid her hand on Troy's arm. "It's okay, Troy, really. I have forgiven him in my heart and so should you."

He flashed an angry glance at Lily. "But he took something precious from you."

Her hand still resting on his arm, she continued. "Yes, yes he did. And I can't blame you for being angry. But wouldn't taking his life be the same thing? I can live with myself knowing what he did to me was wrong. Can you live with yourself if you blew his brains out? I'm alive and on my way to Heaven. Louie is just a sinner doing what sinners do. If you kill him, he'll end up in Hell, not that he doesn't deserve it."

Nigel watched the exchange in silence. Finally he spoke up, still aiming the gun at Fat Louie's head. "She's got a point. Maybe I should shoot him."

Lily nearly pounded on him. "No, no one is going to shoot him. Don't you understand? I've forgiven him and that settles it!"

"But I haven't!" Troy protested.

Nigel started to say something, but didn't.

Finally, Olivia, who'd heard the conversation, but remained detached, got everyone's attention. "You know, truth be known, we all have done things we're not proud of. I've come from a long line of drug dealers, liars and murderers. I've got blood on my hands, too. There isn't a day that goes by that I don't pray to God and ask him to forgive me for what I've done."

Lily's jaw fell open. "Miss Olivia, I didn't know you were a Christian. Why haven't you said something?"

The woman shifted her weight from one hip to the other. It was obvious, she was in pain. "I'm not, at least not in the strictest definition. You might consider me a recovering sinner. As far as Fat Louie is concerned, I think he should suffer for what he did. He can't go around abusing defenseless women with impunity, but shooting him? Nay, why waste a bullet on him? I'd say, put him in a cave with a candle and a Bible. That should cure him." An impish twinkle sparkled in her eyes.

Nigel nudged Troy. "Turn left and slow down. When you get to a boxed canyon, stop the van. We'll go the rest of the way on foot."

The rest of the journey was spent in silence with each person considering Olivia's last comment.

As they entered the uranium mine compound, a cheer filled the night air. The foot-weary escapees found their way to a circle of wooden chairs surrounding a campfire and accepted a belated dinner.

"Take this man into custody," Nigel ordered. "Put him in the stockade, give him something to eat and drink. Oh, and give him a Bible." Looking at Troy and Lily, he continued, "I'll inform the President you're here. In the meantime, eat up. I'll find a few empty bunks for you guys so you can get some shut-eye. We've got a lot to do and not a lot of time to do it." With a nod, he disappeared into the mine in search of his Commander and Chief.

***

The following morning, Lily and Troy woke up to the sound of men marching in cadence and the aroma of stale coffee.

They followed the smoke and found the mess tent where groups of men and women in various uniforms gathered.

"Where's Nigel?" Lily asked the first person she saw.

"Nigel?"

"Yeah, you know … the guy with long hair and a bandana. The guy who helped us escape from Corcoran. Has anyone seen him?"

Heads shook.

After a few beats, someone spoke up. "Rumor has it, he had a falling out with the President over the way he handled your rescue."

"Nah," someone else said, "I heard he was sent out on a secret mission."

Others had their opinion, but it was obvious, no one knew where he was, or they weren't telling.

***

As evening returned, the canyons surrounding the uranium mine compound whispered softly as sleeping soldiers rested from their duties.

Long shadows stretched across the rugged landscape like a curtain waiting to rise. The next scene for the nation's future was about to be played out.

Sitting as still as a wooden Indian, Lily studied the heavens in search of a drone. She'd been assigned guard duty two weeks ago, but she didn't mind. Despite the chill, she loved watching the stars glide silently across the sea of ebony. It was a drastic change from the noisy prison with its curses and moans. Now she listened to new sounds; a lone wolf's cry, an owl asking who, low voices emanating up the canyon.

She tugged the army blanket tighter around her shoulders and breathed. A long stream of condensation clouded her view of the distant horizon before dissipating. As she peered through the moonless night, a figure, like a specter, moved between sentinel cacti. She lifted her NVG's to her eyes and suddenly the prairie glowed an eerie green. The figure moved again. With the stealth of a mountain lion, it moved from point to point until it reached the outer perimeter.

"Halt or I'll shoot," Lily ordered, her carbine pointed in the intruder's direction.

The figure stopped midstride. Lifting his hands, he said, "Blackbirds." It was the code word.

"Brewer," Lily countered.

The figure lowered his hands. "Permission to enter?"

Lily breathed a sigh of relief and lowered her weapon. "Permission granted. Step into the light and identify yourself." flipping on a low level flashlight.

The man stepped into the ring of light and saluted. "It's me, Nigel. I've got information for the President."

Lily's heart sputtered. "Oh, hi. I didn't recognize you," returning his salute. "You've been gone for weeks. I thought you were fired or something."

He shrugged. "I know. He has me running all over the country."

"What are you, some kind of spy or assassin?" she asked half kidding.

Nigel adjusted the pack on his back. His tattered uniform was stained with what appeared to be dried blood. Lily couldn't tell if it was human or animal. All she knew was, Nigel was not someone to be trifled with. His presence didn't frighten her; it brought a sense of peace.

She inhaled the night air. It carried a mixture of manly sweat, gun smoke and the great outdoors. She let it linger for a moment before exhaling.

"Care to sit with me? It gets mighty lonely out here."

Nigel hesitated for a moment before taking a step. "I'm sorry, but they're is expecting me at headquarters."

"At this hour?"

He glanced over his shoulder and their eyes met. For a moment, it seemed he wanted to say something. Then, like a breath of condensation, it vanished.

"I've gotta go." He turned abruptly and disappeared as silently as he came.

Retaking her seat, Lily tried to unravel the knot of emotions his presence stirred. What was it about Nigel that caused her heart to slam against her chest? She tried to focus on the distant horizon, but all she saw was his eyes probing hers. As the hours slipped past, his voice still echoed in her ears.

Chapter Forty-Six

T he following two weeks were a flurry of activity. President Bleakly's call for a nationwide manhunt for any members of the former administration had the country in a frenzy. With a bounty of $500.000 on Richardson's head, the search become a national past time. If found they were to be executed without the benefit of a trial.

Reports of sightings of the former President and those responsible for his escape had the Bleakly administration stretched to the limit.

Cami held daily press conferences fielding questions from the media and holding interviews. Despite the leaks about the White House shooting, the media chose to ignore it. Rather, they focused on the attack on Corcoran and the subsequent prisoner escape.

As President Bleakly's psychological condition worsened, his tirades lasted for hours. It was nearly impossible to replace staffers as fast as they quit. Only Millie remained, and that was because she was the only person who knew where everything was.

Cami split her time between interviews and wedding plans. She found it difficult to steal even a few minutes of the President's time, let alone his attention. *Hopefully this nightmare will end soon and I won't have to steal codes. Maybe I'll just wake up and find it was all a dream.*

When Cami was not sitting in front of a teleprompter and camera, she sat huddled in her condo trying not to worry over the safety of her loved ones. A sharp rap on her front door sent a shot of adrenaline through her veins.

Fearing it was Amanda coming to micromanage her wedding plans, she peered through the peephole.

"May I come in?" It was President Bleakly.

Cami's blood ran cold. Had he discovered the ruse? Had one of the grid commanders shot Trace? Had someone uncovered her part in the conspiracy? She knew she was ready to die for the cause of Christ, but she dreaded the torture she would endure in the process.

She sent up a flare prayer. After taking a quick look at her reflection in the mirror, she smoothed out the wrinkles in her skirt and turned the door knob.

"Mr. President, to what do I owe this pleasure?" Cami pushed out a tight smile and hoped he didn't recognize the slight tremble in her voice.

He nodded to his new security detail and they backed away. Pulling his hand from behind his back, he presented her with a vase of long-stemmed roses. "For you, my Dear, I have been far too preoccupied of late. I wanted to make it up to you." His eyes bore a warm glow and the corners of his mouth angled down. "I don't want our marriage to be merely perfunctory. I need a wife that is as devoted to this marriage as me."

It didn't escape Cami the number of 'I's' he used in his poorly constructed apology, if it was an apology. But seeing his contrite demeanor and his sacrificial offering did much to throw off her math. Setting aside her misgivings, she lifted her gaze until their eyes met.

"How thoughtful, it's been a long time since I've received flowers. Come to think of it, I don't ever remember getting any. Then again, my memory hasn't been what it should be of late."

Being near such a powerful man always caused her heart to stumble. It was all she could do to keep her breathing at a normal rate. She closed the gap between them and accepted the vase, but as her fingers folded around its smooth surface, they brushed over his. A jolt of electricity snapped between them. Shocked by her unexpected response, she drew back nearly dropping the expensive vase. The action caused some water to splash on his sleeve. "Oh, I'm so sorry. How clumsy of me. Let me get something to clean it off."

With the vase firmly clasped between her hands, she rushed to the kitchen and set it down. *Cami, get a grip. You know this is not real. Why are you acting so strangely?* She took a few calming breathes and set the vase on the marble counter. The scent of rose pedals filled the air causing her to inhale deeply. *Cami,* she chided herself. Frustrated at how easily her emotions could be swayed, she snagged a towel and rushed back to where the Norman stood. "Here, let me take care of this," she muttered and began to dab the water from his hand-sewn, Italian silk suit-coat.

Glancing up, she caught a flash of anger before it evaporated. *If he got angry over such a minor infraction, what would he do it he discovered his wife-to-be was a traitor?* She shuddered at the thought.

"There, good as new." Cami tried to keep her tone conversational. "But I'm sure you've got more important things to do than stand in my foyer."

She stepped back, allowing him to enter. Before she closed the door, Cami took a quick glance up and down the wide hall. There were no less than a dozen secret service agents standing guard. Their taut stance, bulging neck and shoulders, their shielded eyes didn't bring a sense of calm to her racing heart.

As she closed the door, she turned and slammed into him. "Oh, Mr. President, you startled me." Hand to her chest, she forced air into her lungs. "Come in. Can I get you something to drink?"

Norman followed her to the living room and lowered himself into one of the plush chairs, not taking his eyes off of her. His silence was disconcerting, yet she knew enough about him, not to push.

Leaning forward, he placed his arms on his knees. "I understand you have a few conditions before our marriage."

Cami let her shoulders relax slightly. Tilting her head, she tucked a few strands of hair behind her ear and offered him a coy smile. "I guess Amanda told you."

He shifted his weight. "Yes, she mentioned it. Something about a hand painted portrait of you next to me? Why so vain?"

The absurdity of his question almost gave her a laugh-out-loud moment.

Almost.

Taking a calming breath, she pushed ahead. "It would bring a balance to your own auspicious portrait, don't you think?"

Bleakly's back arched. The veins in his neck pulsated. Lifting a finger he opened his mouth, then clamped it shut.

"I want it in front of the same fireplace. That way, anyone who questions our relationship will know it is based on mutual trust and commitment." Cami knew from experience how he thought and how to wield her influence over him.

He held her gaze for longer than she'd expected. For a moment, she wondered if she'd overstepped her bounds. Standing, he arranged his coat and folded his hands behind his back. "I'll arrange to have the same artist come for an initial setting. Can you come tomorrow? Would three in the afternoon work for you? That way after we are through, you might consider joining me and a few guests for a private celebration."

"Celebration? What are we celebrating?"

"Our engagement, of course. In a few weeks we will be man and wife." His eyes bore a sinister glow, primitive, primordial, evil.

"So you're moving up the date? I thought we'd decided on a fall wedding."

"Yes, we did, but—"

"What about the invitations? They've already been printed. I'll have to inform the florist, the guests, the baker and the seamstress of the change. That's a lot to ask. Why the rush?"

"I've got several trips planned and I would like to get our wedding out of the way."

His poorly phrased excuse made Cami's breath turn cold.

Cami stood and walked to the large paned window overlooking the skyline. Crossing her arms over her chest, she huffed. "We agreed on a fall wedding and I'm not changing it. So tell whoever you were planning on visiting they can just go pound sand."

Norman's shoulders slumped. "All right, but—"

"No buts, Norman." She knew she had the upper hand and used it to her advantage.

He steadied himself on the arm of the couch. "I'll tell Amanda. We'll keep the date we'd agreed on. I'll let myself out."

As his shadow receded, Cami thought. *You'll rot in Hell before you lay a hand on me.*

Chapter Forty-Seven

"In the more speculate tragic kingdom, the religious subtext will go undetected by many." **A. Nonymous**

A yellow glow illuminated the faces of a half-dozen men as they gathered around a rustic wooden table.

President Richardson and his war cabinet had been in deep consultation all day and into the night. He had sent out a number of scouts to organize the partisan groups into one fighting unit and establish a secure communications link after the one set up by Olivia was destroyed. All but one scout had returned.

And he was late.

Troy had just returned from guard duty and had just taken a seat nearby to eat his dinner when a stir sounded outside. A rustle of voices echoed at the entrance of the uranium mine as Nigel was greeted by his fellow scouts. Trace stopped eating long enough to see the President glance up.

"Nigel my boy, good to see you. I was getting worried. Any trouble?"

Nigel's rugged face brightened. "No, sir. Nothing my Bowie couldn't handle," he said, pointing to the twelve inch serrated blade strapped to his shoulder.

He eyed him for a moment. "Whose blood?"

Looking down at his stained clothes, Nigel smiled. "It's a mix of wolf, deer and human."

Members of the President's cabinet grew somber. "Has anyone followed you?" Joe asked. He'd recovered from his heart attack enough to be the commander of the Army.

Nigel shook his head. "No. I made sure of that. Now can we get down to business? I'm tired and hungry and we've got a lot to go over."

By now, Troy had finished his meal and was interested to know what Nigel had learned. The men parted letting Nigel join their tight circle.

"Okay, what do you have?" the President asked.

Using the tip of his Bowie knife, Nigel stabbed the center of the map directly over St. Louis. "That's where Hub Central is located. But that's not all. The place is heavily guarded and there are redundancies to the system. To top that, the entire grid system is linked to a military grade satellite. In order to shut the system down we'll have to hack into their main frame, temporarily take it off line and then cause a power surge."

Fred Woodbury, the head of communications, cocked his head. "And you know this from …?"

"From crawling through the sewer system and listening and learning everything there is to know about the enemy's computers, sir. I have actually penetrated their security protocols and got down to the fifth level below ground where their primary power source is located. And I've seen firsthand, the brain which links their computers to the satellite."

The lines in the Richardson's face deepened. "Son, if you got that close, why didn't you just go ahead and shut the darned thing down?"

Troy wondered the same thing.

Nigel straightened and leveled his gaze. "Because, sir, this isn't a one man job. I'll require at least two other people on my team—"

"Wait one cotton-pickin' minute! Who said anything about it being your mission? You're a scout, not some rogue saboteur," the President said.

"No, I'm not a lone saboteur ... there'll be three of us."

"You're out of line," Richardson said with an edge to his voice.

"And we're out of time, sir. I know how to get in and get out. I know their protocols and where the enemy's weaknesses are. So if you don't mind, this *is* my mission and I'm calling the shots."

For a moment, Troy thought he might punch the young man in the mouth for insubordination, but then, seeing the bloody Bowie knife, thought better of it.

Joe raised a finger, interrupting a further escalation of tension. "Sir, he has a point. We don't have time to send in another scout. Our people are in place, ready to steal the codes. Once that is done, we'll have to act fast or we'll lose the initiative."

Troy, who'd taken a keen interest in the outcome of the conversation, had to agree.

President Richardson softened his tone. "Okay, but it will take time to train your two accomplices."

"It won't take that much training and I'll oversee it."

"Do you have someone in mind?"

Nigel paused. "Yes, yes I do. Troy Ashcroft and Lily O'Reilly. They can move across the boarders without detection. They're smart and eager. We'll make a great team."

This time it was Troy's turn to get riled up. He stood and inserted himself into the group. "I hope you're not thinking about a suicide mission. This is my fiancée and me you're talking about."

Nigel cocked his head. "Trust me. This is no suicide mission."

"And how do you know we'd be willing to volunteer, let alone, fulfill this *mission*?" Troy asked, ready to pound this guy into next week.

Nigel's eyes warmed slightly. He certainly didn't want this to escalate. He needed these two people and wanted them on his side. "Believe me, I have every confidence that together we can complete the mission." Turning to the others, he continued. "Now are we going to stand around and flap-jaw or are we going to take this country back?"

Joe Franklin cleared his throat. "The guy's got a point."

Again, heads nodded in agreement and Troy felt out maneuvered and out voted.

"Okay, let's do it. Nigel, start training your people at first light. If all goes as planned, we should have the codes within the next two weeks. You need to be ready to move out by Friday. I want to hit them on the following Sunday." Glancing at a bank of clocks he continued. "It is 0100 hours on Monday. You've got six days. By the way, once you've disabled the grids controlling the borders, how do you propose knocking out the satellite?"

A wicked smile parted Nigel's lips. "That's where the fun begins. The computers function the same way our computers do. They have surge protectors. Part of our job will be to deactivate the surge protectors long enough for us to disable the border grids. Then I'll reboot the main energy source and send a giant electrical surge into the main frame. That will fry the link between the computers and the satellite."

Troy had taken his seat again and considered the plan. "That's a lot of steps. Are you sure the three of us can handle it? I mean, you're dealing with a lot of systems at the same time."

"True, but once we've hacked into the main frame we can navigate between systems pretty easily."

The President straightened. "Okay, let's get some shut-eye. You can brief us on your mission later."

As Nigel and the others parted, Troy grabbed his arm. "I'm sorry for the way I acted in there. It's just … that's my fiancée we're talking about."

Nigel stopped walking and faced him. "Don't worry. I wouldn't do anything that would put you or Lily in any unnecessary danger."

"I think you already have."

Nigel placed his calloused hand on Troy's shoulder. "I get it, but I need you. Believe me, by God's grace, we can do it."

It was the first time Troy heard the man mention God. He just hoped he knew the Lord, not just talked about Him.

Chapter Forty-Eight

"I wonder why Nigel keeps disappearing and reappearing." Lily wondered out loud.

She'd spent the night on guard duty and had returned with just enough time to wolf down a scant breakfast before meeting Troy. He, on the other hand, had worried all night how he was going to break the news about their upcoming mission.

Now was not the time.

Standing in the center of a makeshift boxing ring, they bobbed and weaved in their weekly sparring match. Sweat dripped from her face and slicked her body, but she kept moving just out of reach of Troy's gloved fists.

"I don't know. He's kind of a rogue warrior, if you ask me."

"Yeah, one with an ego the size of Stone Mountain."

Nigel had just finished washing his upper torso and was drying himself off with an old towel. His bare back and chest showed evidence of close combat and Lily wondered how many times he'd been shot. As he turned to face her, she noticed an ugly wound on his right arm. He quickly threw a towel across himself and turned but the action made Lily's heart flutter.

Troy took advantage of her wandering eyes to land a few solid punches to Lily's abs. She countered with a right hook to his jaw, sending his spinning.

"Keep your fists up," their trainer hollered.

Troy spit.

Lily grinned.

The match continued for another ten minutes before Nigel stepped next to their trainer. He whispered something and he rang the bell. "You two, hit the showers."

Troy helped Lily climb from the ring and gave her a hug.

"Eww, you're sweaty," Lily said.

"And you're not? I'll see you in a few minutes."

As Lily headed to the women's section, Nigel sauntered up. He picked up a towel and tossed it to Lily. "Nice job. You've got talent."

"I hardly thought you'd noticed. You're hardly ever around," she said, wiping the sweat from her face.

His rugged features, long beard, shaggy hair were still wet.

"Oh, I noticed. I also noticed your sparring partner. He's a keeper."

Lily felt the heat creep up her neck. *What did he mean by that? Did everyone know they were a thing? Were they the subject of camp speculation? Were the others betting on how long it would be before Troy sprang the big question?*

The lines around Nigel's eyes wrinkled into a smile. "What I meant was, he handled himself pretty well back in the prison facility. I'd trust him to cover my six anytime."

The complement, though a little rough around the edges seemed heart-felt.

"Thanks, I think." Lily said. Turning, she started to walk away.

"Look, you and Troy have a special gift. Do you have any computer science or hacking skills?"

Lily stared at him like he'd spoken in a foreign language. "What do you mean, hacking?"

The way Nigel rubbed the back of his neck reminded her of someone, but a lot of people had familiar quirks. His was pretty common.

"The President has authorized a secret mission. It involves you, me and Troy."

Before Lily could drill him with another question, he'd turned and strode outside, leaving Lily to wonder what he had in mind. By the time she recovered, he'd stepped outside and had vanished.

Still questioning his cryptic statement about learning how to hack, Lily quickly showered and met Troy at the entrance of the mine.

"Did you hear what Nigel said?"

Troy's shoulders rose and fell. Feigning ignorance, he smiled sheepishly. Thanks to Nigel, he didn't have to break the news to Lily. "No what?"

A figure stepped from around an outcropping. It was Nigel. "What I said was, you're about to take a crash course in computer hacking. Now follow me."

Lily's heart skipped a beat.

Grudgingly, Troy stood. "C'mon, this ought to be fun."

Nigel winked. "Oh, it will be." As he spoke, he led them into a cove where a number of computers sat on metal tables. "How's your computer skills Troy?"

Troy took a seat and ran his fingers over the keys. "Not bad, what did you have in mind?"

Nigel brought up a program. "Let's see if you can get past this security protocol and we'll talk."

To both Lily's and Nigel's surprise, Troy broke through the first layer and had gotten to the second within two minutes.

"Not bad." He reset the program and offered the chair to Lily. "Now you try."

A conspiratorial smile stretched across Lily's face. "Game on."

In less than sixty seconds, she'd hacked to the third level. Sitting back, she crossed her arms over her chest. "Is that the best you can offer?"

Nigel slid his chair next to Lily and reprogrammed the computer. For the next four days, the three of them practiced their hacking skills. By Friday, they were ready for the next challenge ... breaking into the Grid Authority's main hub.

Later, after dinner, Lily and Troy went outside to walk off their dinner. The rugged hills surrounding their compound had already begun to turn a variegated hue of purple. Long shadows stretched across the canyon like a curtain. It wouldn't be long before the stars appeared and began their nightly silent dance.

It was the first time they both were free from any responsibility in a long time and Lily wanted to take advantage of it. She pulled Troy's arm around her slender waist and walked in silence.

All at once, one of the lookouts sounded the warning.

"Drone, get everyone inside."

Troy grabbed Lily by the hand and raced back to the entrance of the mine. After everyone had gathered inside, Nigel helped Troy pull the canvas down making the entrance look like a rock wall.

A minute later, the low hum of a drone grew louder. Everyone held their breath hoping it didn't fire one of its heat-seeking missiles. As the sound grew fainter, a common sigh of relief echoed throughout the open space. The "all clear" sounded and they pulled the canvas back.

***

"I don't know how much more of this I can stand."

The whites of Lily's eyes reflected the flickering glow of candles located along the mine's walls.

Troy drew her close. "I know. This waiting is getting to me, too. At least we're together, that's more than we can say for your dad."

Lily shifted in his arms and glanced around. "Come to think of it, I've not seen him since he and Joe's team returned from stealing those uniforms."

Troy led her to an outcropping and patted it. It was cold but offered a rest from standing. "I'll have to ask Joe about that the next time I see him."

Snuggling next to him, Lily laced her fingers in his. "Troy, a few days ago Nigel came by."

Troy's back stiffened. They'd worked closely all week, but every time Nigel got close, Lily got flustered. He wondered if he was trying to steal her affections. Sooner or later, he would have to deal with him.

"Oh? What did he say? That you really look good when you're all sweaty?"

"Troy!? Do I detect a tinge of jealousy in your voice?"

Hands held in surrender. "I plead the fifth."

"The fifth doesn't count any more, remember?"

"Okay, okay, guilty as charged. I just don't like the guy. He's a pompous—"

"Troy, that's enough. He didn't hit on me. Actually, he paid you a very high compliment."

"He did?" feeling slightly ashamed for his outburst.

"Yes. As a matter of fact, he said you handled yourself rather well the day we escaped and that he'd gladly have you watch his back."

"His back, hmm. You sure he wasn't talking about your backside?"

Lily's jaw fell open, then snapped shut. Crossing her arms, she let out a huff. "I can't believe you said that. After all, he was just being nice."

"Nice hmm. I'll show him nice."

"Troy!"

"Okay, I'm sorry."

The moment stretched in silence. Finally, Lily broke the tension.

"Nigel said something curious."

"He did?" Troy avoided making a snide remark about Nigel's obvious mental shortcomings. "What did he say?"

"Just before he left on another secret mission, I overheard him and Joe talking."

"About what?"

Lily's forehead wrinkled. "About someone high up in the Grid Authority stealing the codes which control all the grids. If we could find that person, we could hack into the system and shut it down."

"I thought that was what they were training us to do."

Troy stood and began to pace. "It is, but who knows when they're going to send us out. I for one am tired of waiting."

She sighed deeply. "Don't you think we should talk it over with the President?"

Troy shook his head. "He's so busy organizing the various partisan groups that he hasn't taken time to plan how he's going to get them across the grids. Olivia is in no condition to be much help and Joe is involved with training the troops.

A beat passed and Lily's head bobbed. "You're right, but it won't be easy or quick. If the big shots find out what we're planning to do, they'll try to talk us out of it."

"I think we should gather as much money as we can, pack our bags with as many supplies as we can carry and get going. With any luck we could contact Cami and enlist her help."

"What about the border crossings? You know they'll be heavily guarded." Lily asked.

"That's just it; we don't have to cross at the checkpoints. We can go around them. They'll never know because we are undetectable."

Lily stood and brushed off the dirt from her bottom. "What about the bridges? Aren't they guarded?"

"Nope, not within each grid. You see, that's the beauty of this system, they are confident no one can cross a grid border, but they forget one thing."

"What's that?"

"Us."

Chapter Forty-Nine

"The aim in the game is to go undetected." **A. Nonymous**

"Good, no moon." Nigel whispered.

His nightly reconnaissance missions had gone undetected by the International Guard units and their drones which constantly swept the area. Wearing night vision goggles he scanned the road ahead looking for any unfriendly faces.

There were none.

He shifted his backpack higher on his shoulders and began to make his way to the last rendezvous point.

With the President's backing, he had established a virtual underground railroad connecting the east coast militia with the west coast. He had just one more contact to make and the mission would be a go.

Once they had the grid codes in their possession, they would insert Troy and Lily into hub central where they would hack into the computer's main frames and shut down the border grids.

Under the cover of darkness, the militia would gather at the borders ready to attack the moment the grid borders went down. It was a bold plan, one that required a great deal of coordination, stealth, and speed …

And a lot of luck.

As Nigel climbed the last ridge, movement caught his attention. His heart jackhammered. Had he been seen? Were they about to shoot him? Or would he have to fight it out with a lone gunman?

He crouched low and drew his Bowie knife. A gleam of moonlight danced on its razor sharp edge. As he waited, his nostrils were assaulted by his body odor. He'd been out in the field so long that he hoped it wasn't his scent that had given away his position. Taking a prone position, every muscle grew tense, ready to pounce upon whoever was out there.

A bush shivered and a shadow emerged from behind it. The figure growled deeply, then sprang at him with demonic ferocity. Nigel slashed the air open, missing the creature by a hairs breadth. It snarled wildly and sprang again. It landed solidly on him, sending him tumbling backward. His knife hand struck a rock, sending the blade clattering into a crevice beyond his reach. The two thrashed in the scrub bush making a huge ruckus. It was a miracle no one heard the commotion.

Skittering backward, Nigel tried to pull his .45 from its holster, but his hand got caught by an ornery vine. The beast's jaws snapped fiercely, inches from his throat. It was all he could do to keep the animal from sinking its teeth into his exposed flesh.

Suddenly, his eyes focused on his attacker.

"Wag?"

The dog's throat released a guttural rumble. The whites of his eyes glowed with a primordial rage.

"Relax, old buddy. It's—"Wag snarled and leapt over Nigel like he wasn't there. A moment later, someone yelled in pain as the dog's teeth tore into him.

In an instant, Nigel was on his feet. He snatched up his knife and dove for the man. It was Fat Louie. He had escaped and was on the lam. Nigel knew if he didn't silence the man, it wouldn't be long before the entire International Guard would descend upon them.

In one powerful move, he placed his left hand over Fat Louie's mouth and plunged the knife into his chest. The man's eyes widened then grew dull. He ceased struggling and began to quiver. Once his body became still, Nigel removed the knife, and wiped the crimson stain on Louie's uniform. Looking around, he scanned the area to see if they'd been detected.

Silence had retaken its place across the prairie.

"Thanks Wag," he said massaging the dog's neck.

Had Wag not shown up when he did, the outcome might have been different. The sound of rustling in the bushes brought the hair on the back of Nigel's neck to attention. Wag yipped and a half dog, half wolf emerged followed by a pack.

"Well, well, well. What have we here?" Nigel said, eyeing Wag's family.

The female growled slightly as Nigel reached to pet her on the head. "It's okay. I'm a friend."

Wag lifted his paw as if to introduce himself. Nigel took it and gave it a gentle shake. "Nice to meet you. My name is—"

Heavy footfalls interrupted him.

Chapter Fifty

"It was a miraculous thing to be able to watch the person you love undetected."   **Ann Patchett**

*S*nap!
　　"What was that?" Lily's tense whisper was the first word she'd said since she and Troy struck out on their own three hours earlier. They had made good progress having navigated by dead reckoning from point A to point B. But Lily was beginning to feel the weight of her heavy combat boots. The chilled night air nipped at her exposed flesh and she brushed away the goosebumps.

Troy chuckled. "I think it was a twig you stepped on."

"Me!? You're making just as much noise."

He chuckled.

"Do you want to take a short break? My feet are killing me," he said.

"I sure do. I thought we were going to use a truck."

"I did too, but the vehicle compound was heavily guarded and I didn't want to knock out one of our buddies just to steal a vehicle."

Taking a seat on a rounded bolder, Troy lowered his backpack to the ground and began rubbing the kinks out of his neck and back. Then he unclipped his canteen, took a swig and handed it to Lily. His eyes widened as she nearly emptied the container. "Hey, slow down. We've got to make it stretch till we reach a stream."

"But I was thirsty."

Troy shook the last drop out and let it slide down his throat. "If we run across a car or truck we'll take it for sure, but out here in the middle of the desert I doubt we'll find one."

Releasing a heavy sigh, she plopped next to him and crossed her arms. She tilted her head up and scanned the heavens. She'd been so focused on not tripping over a rock or outcropping, that she failed to see the spectacular velvet sky overhead. "Aren't those stars beautiful?"

Troy paused and gazed up. "Kinda reminds me of a diamond studded canvas portraying wild and wondrous creatures."

Lily slid closer, wrapped her arms around his waist and tugged him close. "Wow, that was eloquent. You should write these things down. One day, when we have a house full of grandchildren you can read your stories to them."

"Ah hum. Aren't you skipping a few things? Like marriage, a honeymoon, a home, children and then grandchildren?"

With a huff, Lily released her hold on him and crossed her chest. "I was just projecting into the future. Can't a girl dream?"

Sensing the half grin behind her shaded face, Troy tilted her chin up with his two fingers. "I was too, especially the marriage and honeymoon part."

A soft chuckle percolated in her chest.

***

Crunch!

Lily leaped into his arms and clung to his neck like an octopus. "That wasn't me this time." Her eyes stabbed the blackness.

"Going someplace?" a familiar voice sliced through the darkness. "Don't shoot, I'm heavily armed."

"Nigel? Is that you?" Lily's voice wavered.

"Yeah, it's me. Where are you two going?"

Nigel stepped closer. The light of a slivered moon illuminated a wry smile.

Troy released his hand from the butt of his weapon. "We're going to find Miss Cami and get her to help us steal the grid codes. Where'd you come from?"

Nigel lowered his backpack and sat on it. "I guess this is as good a time as any to let you in on a little secret. Actually, it's a top secret, but since it involves you, I think it's safe.

"Us?" Lily and Troy said in unison.

Pulling a jug of water from his pack, he took a long pull, replaced the cap and set it on the ground. "Have you guys eaten?"

They shook their heads. "No, we've been so busy hiking across this God-forsaken desert we haven't thought about eating."

"You forgot rule number one in the hiking book."

"What's that?" Lily and Troy said in unison.

"Eat when you're not hungry, drink when you're not thirsty." He unsnapped his backpack and withdrew three energy bars. "Here, eat them slowly."

While they munched, Lily asked, "So what's the big top secret thingy you and the Richardson cooked up?" Her fingers forming air quotes.

Keeping his voice to a whisper, Nigel began, "President Richardson and his men have been planning this for weeks. Before you two set out on your own, we were going to take you to Grid Eighteen where hub central is located. That's why I was training you." He ran his hand across the back of his neck.

Something snagged a memory in Lily's mind. "Grid Eighteen? Where is that?"

Nigel relaxed his stance, knelt on the ground Indian style and began drawing a map with a twig. "It's near St. Louis." Using a stick, he sliced the sand until he stopped at a rock. "We'll travel east until we reach the Colorado River, cross it here, then turn south," pointing at a wiggly line he'd drawn. "We have people at each major crossing point waiting for us."

Troy knelt next to him. "Where is that?" He asked, pointing to an X.

Nigel continued. "That's Emigrant Gap. It's the gateway to the Rockies. If you don't have a good vehicle, the war will be over before you two get across them."

"And where do you propose we get a good vehicle?" Arms wrapped around her waist, Lily's chilled voice cut through the brisk night air.

As she spoke, the soft hum of an engine rose and fell in the distance. "That's our ride now." Nigel pointed in the direction from where they'd come.

He stood and helped Troy and Lily to their feet. "It's fully stocked and has a full tank of fuel. I've set up rendezvous points all along the way. At each border crossing, we'll have people waiting for us. They'll guide you across the grids until we reach our destination. Let's go, we're burning precious hours."

The Land Rover sat idling on the shoulder of the black strip of highway, Troy called out to Nigel. "How did you know we left and how did you find us?"

He stifled a laugh. "Oh, it wasn't that hard. You two walk like a couple of elephants. It's a wonder the entire International Guard hadn't descended on you."

Lily stopped mid-stride and turned sharply, her fists in tight knots. "I know that laugh. Who are you and what have you done with my brother?"

***

Before Lily pounced on him, Troy grabbed her.

His hands held up, Nigel backed up. "I, I don't know what you're talking about, *Lil.*"

"Will? Is that you?" Lily's voice echoed across the open plains.

"Hush! Do you want to wake up the dead? Of course it's me. Who else do you think it is?"

Lily leaped into his arms and embraced him for the first time in nearly a year. "Oh, Will, I didn't recognize you. Your beard, your long hair and that filthy bandana, I thought I'd never see you again."

"Never, I've been keeping an eye out for you ever since we got separated, but I had to wait for the right moment to spring it on you."

"Why? You had the chance several times."

"I couldn't. I'd been sworn to secrecy, plus, there are informants in our ranks. If word got out that there was someone like me around, well..."

"Someone like you? What's that mean?" Troy asked.

Will drew Troy in a manly hug. "I'm sorta like you guys. I'm immune from the virus. The only difference is, I don't have an ID chip. I've been crossing in and out of the grids for months undetected. They've got a big bounty on my head if I'm ever captured."

Hand to her chest, Lily's eyes glistened. "Oh Will. I'm just so happy."

Troy extended his hand. "Man, am I glad it's you and not some stud named Nigel. Where'd you come up with a name like that, anyway?"

He struggled. "I don't know. It just came to me."

Troy shook his head and eyed him for a moment.

Will continued, "You don't know how many times I wanted to tell you guy, but as I said, I was sworn to secrecy. By the way, did you know Fat Louie was on your trail?"

Lily's jaw fell open. "I had no idea."

"Yep, had Wag not heard him, he might have killed you both."

"Wag?" Lily and Troy asked.

Looking around, "Yes, he's somewhere around here." He whistled, "Wag."

Wag and his pack of friends appeared. The female snarled protectively as Lily embraced Wag for the first time since he'd been taken. "Oh, Wag. I've been so worried about you." As if the dog could understand what she said. "I thought he'd been killed by those birds." She said, looking up at Troy and Will.

"No, that didn't happen. He somehow found his way back to the uranium mine. Olivia didn't take too kindly to him, so she chained him up. I guess he didn't like being incarcerated any more than you and Troy."

Lily's lip pouched.

"Anyway, you and Troy sneaking out of camp nearly blew it."

Clutching Troy's arm, Lily stood and headed to the extended van which sat along the deserted highway. She opened the door and climbed in. "Can we take Wag with us?"

Will shook his head. "Not a good idea."

Tears rimmed Lily's eyes. She got back out and knelt in front of Wag. "Look, Wag, you can't go where we're going and I wouldn't make you even if I could. But we have to do this. I promise, after this is all over, I'll find you, Cami and Dad, and we'll be a family again. Do you understand?"

Wag glanced over his shoulder at his companions, then back to Lily. With a sharp yip, he backed away and disappeared into the night followed by the pack."

She stood. "I don't know, was that a yes bark or a no bark?"

Troy chuckled and wiped the tears from her eyes. "I'm not sure, but he's pretty smart."

Will checked his watch. "Okay, the clock is ticking. Hop in and I'll fill in the details."

Her nose wrinkling, Lily climbed in first. "Will, when was the last time you took a bath?"

After sucking in a breath of fresh air, Troy climbed in and closed the door.

Will sniffed his armpit. "I don't know. It's been a while. I'll get one when I get back that's for sure." He flipped the dome light on, his shirt was covered in fresh blood and his hands were skinned and bloody. He gave Troy an apologetic smile. "Sorry about the shirt. It's yours you know. I had to break into your apartment a few weeks ago to get a change of clothes."

Acknowledgment raised Troy's eyebrows. "I thought I'd seen that shirt before." With a quick nod, he said, "Okay. Driver, take us to the border."

Lily glanced at the driver. "Miss Olivia! What are you doing here?"

She cocked her head and peered at them in the rear view mirror. "Oh, I'm not out of fight just yet. I talked Nigel, uh, Will into letting me get you from here to St. Louie, Louie." A wide smile crinkled her forehead and deepened the lines around her mouth.

Will patted her arm. "You want the short or the long version? I've got time."

Lily laced her fingers through Troy's as they bumped along the highway ascending to a height of fifty-two hundred feet.

"I'll take the long version."

Chapter Fifty-One

"A love for the world begins in the soul, and often undetected by people who are slowly succumbing to its lies."   **C. J. Mahaney**

"**A**nd so that's my story," Will said after explaining how he was rescued by Olivia and Conner.

"While I was stuck in the back of the Garda truck I got to thinking. I remembered a verse you told me, Lily. You said, 'what would it profit if a man gained the whole world and lost his own soul.' I sat there with bags of money all around me, and feared I would die and go to Hell."

Eyes rounding, Lily leaned forward and touched his arm. "Will, what did you do?"

"I did what you said; I prayed and asked Jesus into my heart, to come into my life. I put my trust in Him to take me to Heaven when I die."

Lily shifted so she could look her brother square in the eyes. "Tell me you didn't do it only because you thought you were going to die."

Will's eyes swelled with tears. "Lily, I did it because I knew it was true. I knew you were right about me being a sinner and all. And, well, I didn't like myself very much and I knew God didn't either."

Lily placed her hand on his. It was trembling. "On the contrary, God knows you and loves you very much."

Nodding, he wiped his eyes. "I know that now. I did as you said and prayed. God has filled my heart with his peace and now I'm ready to face him or whatever awaits us."

Lily's smile warmed his heart and he pulled her close. They were family … part of the family of God.

After a long hug, Lily pulled back. "So tell us how you got out of the truck."

***

Three hours later, Olivia peered over her shoulder.

"Nigel, I, mean, Will. We are approaching our first check-point." She kept her eyes locked on the rapidly approaching border crossing.

Will looked up. "Okay, just act normal. The border guards are our people."

The van slowed and pulled to a stop in a parking area overlooking a wide vista. Stepping out of the van, Lily's breath froze. Hand to her chest, she scanned the horizon bathed in moonlight. "This is breath-taking," she sputtered. "If I didn't know better, you would think all was well with the world."

Troy took his place next to her and wormed his arm around her. The wide mountain range, shimmered under a domed blanket of sackcloth studded with stars, extended as far as the eye could see. A brisk wind rustled through the alpines, freshening the crisp air.

Pointing to the east, Lily held out her arm. "Look Troy, Jupiter and Venus, they're almost totally in line with each other. And look, that other star." Moving her index finger up and a little to the left. "That's Regulus, the brightest star in the constellation Leo."

Will followed their gaze. "Yes, that's the first time they converged since Jesus was born. It could have spiritual significance of biblical proportions."

Troy patted his shoulder. "Not bad. Sounds like you've been keeping up with the signs of the times."

Offering him a wry smile, Will winked. "Hey, better to be ready. The Lord may come as a thief in the night and catch us all away."

As they waited for their papers to be approved, Olivia stepped into the tight circle. "Well, this is as far as I go. From here, you guys are on your own."

Will extended his arms and drew her into a tender hug. "Olivia, thanks for everything. When this is over, I'm going to take you out for the biggest steak."

She patted his shoulder. "Will, you're like the son I never had." The pressure behind her eyes built and she sucked in a shaky breath. "I'll be praying for you ... for all of you." As she spoke, another vehicle pulled behind theirs.

"Looks like that's my ride. I'd better be going." After a tearful exchange of hugs and kisses, Olivia climbed in the car and headed back down the mountain while Lily, Troy and Will loaded into the van. They had a mission to carry out and many miles to cover before they could really celebrate.

Chapter Fifty-Two

Cami had Norman Bleakly wrapped around her finger.

Over Amanda's protests, she'd wormed her way into the Oval Office. Not knowing when the diversion would take place, she took her place in front of the fireplace and stood while a sketch artist did his work. He planned to finish the portrait in the privacy of his studio and create a stunning three dimensional masterpiece for which he was famous. After hours of holding her position, all Cami wanted to do was to sit in a hot tub and relax.

From Cami's position she could see President Bleakly's gaze. It never left her, never faded, never lost interest. It seemed, he was either deeply in love, or highly suspicious.

She couldn't tell.

While the artist quietly worked, the President received several phone calls and entertained several international guests. Each time, he had to dismiss Cami and the artist rather than allow them to overhear any high level discussions.

When they resumed, POTUS appeared nervous. His bouts with depression had worsened as well as his fits of anger. It was Amanda who often came to his rescue, offering him a pill and some calming words.

Glancing up, Cami caught him staring. She tried to focus on the real reason for her being inside the oval office, but her mind kept returning to Trace and then Bleakly's malevolent gaze.

Focus, Cami, focus.

You must remain calm and get the codes, she told herself. The chimes doled out twelve noon and POTUS stood. "Let's take a break and get lunch. I can either have the White House staff bring something up from the kitchen or we can go out." He was not addressing the artist.

Cami rubbed the kink in her neck. "I think I'll just find a quiet spot someplace and lie down."

"You can use one of the beds in my private residence." He offered her a mirthless smile.

"No thanks. I think the Lincoln Bedroom will do nicely." With that, she sauntered off, leaving the artist and the President standing with their mouths hanging open.

An hour later, Cami met the artist in front of Millie's desk. They were discussing his progress. "How are you holding up?" Millie asked Cami as she drew closer.

Cami cut her eyes in the direction of Amanda who sat at a nearby desk, typing an executive order.

"As well as could be expected. I had no idea it would take so long to sketch a picture."

The artist huffed.

Millie smiled. "What can I say, this man's an artist. Don't you agree, Ramon?"

He accepted the compliment with grace and gave her a slight bow. "Yes indeed. But I should be finished by day's end."

The two women exchanged glances. Millie lifted the phone to her ear and spoke to the President.

"POTUS will see you now."

Cami had just resumed her position when Ramon grabbed his stomach and moaned. "Sir, if you will excuse me I'm not feeling very well."

Bleakly stood, clearly annoyed at his sudden outburst. "Okay, but hurry back, I don't have all day."

Ramon clutched his lower abdomen and scurried out.

The moment the door closed an alarm sounded.

The chief of security stepped through the paneled door. "Sir, we have an emergency. You and Ms. Stetson need to come with me."

This was it. The diversion she'd been waiting for!

Cami glanced in the President's direction. In an instant, he glanced at the cigar box on his desk and looked up. Their eyes met momentarily and Cami blinked.

She had discovered his secret.

Although she'd never seen him smoke, he occasionally offered his guests a cigar. The codes had to be hidden in plain sight. And why not? If he felt his office was impenetrable, why go through the trouble of having them under lock and key, especially if he needed to get to them quickly.

Bleakly bristled and stood. "Come with me. It's probably a false alarm. Let's go." His grip tightened on her elbow as he led her from the Oval Office.

As they passed Millie's desk, Cami's ankle twisted and she tumbled to her knees. In a heartbeat, Millie was at her side, catching her before she hit her head.

"Cigar box," Cami whispered in her ear before Bleakly yanked her to her feet.

With Millie's help, Cami limped to the elevator. As the elevator door began to close, POTUS motioned for Amanda to join them. Her icy stare turned deadly, but she obeyed. A moment later the elevator doors closed and the carriage began its rapid descent.

***

The instant the elevator doors closed, Millie slipped into the Oval Office.

The small piece of paper Cami jammed into the locking system kept the door from locking. *How clever,* Millie thought. *That Cami is one sharp girl.*

Three quick steps and she crossed the Oval Office and was standing by the Resolute Desk. A mahogany box with an ornately carved lid occupied its corner. She withdrew a pair of latex gloves and slipped them on before lifting the lid. Inside were rows of Cohiba Esplendido cigars. Being careful not to disturb them, Millie lifted the first tray and smiled. There it was, a credit card shaped piece of plastic. On it were imprinted the codes to the Twenty-Six Grids. Her breath turned to ice as a security man marched by one of the windows. She froze, but he kept his eyes straight, not noticing her. With seconds ticking, she opened the ink blotter. It was a small card duplicator. She placed the coded credit card inside and closed the lid. Ten seconds later, it beeped and she lifted the lid again. The device had made an exact duplicate. Taking a calming breath, she replaced the original in the exact position as she found it, then returned the tray. With her job complete, she knew she had only seconds to spare. Being careful not to leave any footprints, she backed out of the Oval Office. Just before the door closed, she removed the wad of paper from the lock and retreated to a secluded corner.

A moment later the all clear was sounded.

***

Half way down to the bunker, the alarm shut off.

The head of the security detail pressed his finger to his ear where a listening device fed him a constant flow of information. He nodded. "We're clear. The threat has been neutralized."

With one exception, all the occupants on the elevator breathed easier. An icy chill ran down Cami's back. *I wonder who sacrificed their life for the cause.*

The agent pushed the 'Up' button and the carriage reversed its direction. A few minutes later, the doors slid open and the agent glanced around. He lifted his wrist to his mouth and spoke softly.

"Sir, the Oval Office has been cleared. You're free to enter."

POTUS let out a curse and swept passed the man holding the door.

As Cami retook her position, Norman ogled her lustfully. He licked his lips sending a knot into the pit of her stomach. *What does this man have on his mind?*

The intercom crackled with Millie's voice breaking the wire tight moment. "Sir, I'm afraid the artist is too ill to finish today. He would like to reschedule."

This was her cue to get out ... fast.

Bleakly stood abruptly sending his cushioned chair flying backward. "No, that's impossible. Tell him to work with what he has and make it fast. I want to get this #$@&!% wedding over." His sudden outburst sent chills over Cami's body. Their eyes met again and the color drained from his face.

Her heart pounding, Cami stood. "Norman! I thought you loved me." She turned sharply. "You and I are finished. This wedding is off!"

With a huff, she pivoted and marched out leaving the most powerful man in the world standing helpless.

As she stomped passed Millie's desk, she gave her a pert smile and a wink. The elevator doors were still open and she marched inside. Fingers quaking, she pressed the down button. She had just become enemy number one.

Still breathing hard, she reached the parking level, got off the elevator and looked around. The parking deck had several security guards posted at each exit. Hand to her chest, she tried to calm her pounding heart. *Was it really over? She had succeeded.* Her elation lasted for only a few seconds before doubts arose. *Did POTUS suspect the alarm was a ruse? Did Millie act quickly enough?* She couldn't bear the thought of Millie getting caught. Would the President send his thugs to kill her or Millie? Others had died for the cause of freedom. What if she was called to pay the ultimate price for freedom? She thought about her Savior. He'd given His all to purchase her redemption. How could she expect less of herself.

Getting into her car, she started the engine and put it in gear. With a little luck, she would get to her condo, pack and get out of town.

Her phone chirped. It was Millie.

Chapter Fifty-Three

"Professor Moriarty is the organizer of half that is evil and of nearly all that is undetected in this great city."

Arthur Conan Doyle

T he moment the elevator doors closed, Millie heard the Bleakly erupt in a volley of expletives.

"How dare that ungrateful gold-digger call off the wedding. And walk out on me. No one walks out on me," he bellowed.

Amanda, who had been sitting at a desk, jumped to her feet and rushed into the Oval Office.

"Norman, what happened?"

"That conniving, manipulating, slut just called off the wedding!"

"Why?"

"How should I know." It was obvious, he was either clueless or chose not to acknowledge his outburst caused her to walk out.

"Norman, maybe it was just a misunder—"

"No, it was no misunderstanding. She meant what she said. I don't care what you have to do. Stop her! Cut off all her funds, her checking account, her credit cards. Send my secret service agents after her and get her back!"

Millie picked up two tubes of lipstick, the red one and the pink one. If she applied red, all heck would break loose. If she applied the pink, she'd get a phone call instructing her to meet her contact in the cafeteria.

It was imperative she pass the codes to her counterpart, but Millie knew she couldn't leave, not with things spinning out of control in the West Wing. She had to watch Cami's back and her own. At the risk of her phone call being traced, she dialed Cami's number. She had less than two minutes to tell her what kind of danger she was in. She hoped with Amanda being distracted she could do this without being caught.

Fingers trembling, she dialed Cami's number.

***

"Millie, thank God you called," Cami breathed into the phone. "I'm so scared."

"Cami, listen. I don't have long, so pay attention. You've got to get off the grid. Now!"

"I'm on my way to my condo—"

"No! Don't go there."

"Why, I've got to get a few things—"

"It's not safe. I overheard Amanda and the President discussing the whole alarm scenario. I think they've figured out that it was a ruse. My life may be in danger and I haven't had time to get the codes out yet." Millie's usual calm tone sounded rattled. "Look, they've closed your bank account, canceled all your credit cards and have a tracking device on your car. They can triangulate your phones and pinpoint your exact location. You've got to ditch your car. Use public transit or walk. Also, you've got to change the way you look. But under no circumstance are you to return to your condo. You must get out of town. Do you understand?"

"Yes," Cami's voice broke. "Thanks."

The line went dead and Cami gazed at her phone. She hated leaving the few things she'd acquired behind. Her mind raced, she had no money, and no way of getting her hands on some. Her jewelry, she thought. It's worth thousands of dollars. *If I could pawn it, I'd have enough to get far from here.*

She skidded to a stop at a gas station, pushed herself out of her car and set her cell phone on the seat of a parked car. Moments later, the owner came out with a six-pack of beer, got in his car and took off. Knowing her car wouldn't last thirty minutes on that side of town; she jammed the key into the ignition and left the door standing open.

With what little cash she had in her purse, she flagged down a cab and told the driver to take her to her condo.

Chapter Fifty-Four

The moment Cami stepped inside her condo she knew something was wrong.

Taking a calming breath she stepped deeper into the living room. Movement caught attention and she turned. "Is anybody there?"

A figure emerged from the bedroom. "You little sneak," Amanda hissed as she stepped from around a corner. "We took you in, gave you all the money you could want, a condo, a name, a life and this is how you repay us?" Her voice ratcheted up an octave as she continued her diatribe.

"Amanda." Fear clawed up Cami's throat. "Whatever are you talking about?"

"You know exactly what I'm talking about," she growled. "That little stunt you pulled in front of Millie's desk. You said something to her. What was it?"

Cami felt the blood drain from her face. "I thanked her. That's all."

"No, you said something else. What was it? I demand you tell me, or so help me."

"Or what? You'll use shock treatments on me like you did to wipe my memory out? Is that what you had in mind? Or would you rather just rip my liver from my body and give it to Norman to eat?" She couldn't believe she was saying such things. But she'd had it with their little game.

Amanda took a step in her direction.

Cami stepped back.

"You know, Norman was actually falling for you."

Cami's mouth fell open. "He what?"

"I said, he was falling in love with you, over my protests, but not anymore."

"I, I don't know what you're talking about. I thought you wanted me to marry Norman. Why the change?"

She fisted her hip and cocked her head. "We did, that was before this." Amanda tossed a local tabloid into her shaking hands.

Cami scanned the headlines. 'UNNAMED SOURCE LINKS GRID SPOKESWOMAN CAMI STETSON TO THE UNDERGROUND.'

The muscles in Cami's throat constricted. *At least she wasn't accusing me of spying.* Letting the paper fall to the floor, Cami adjusted the shoulder strap of her purse and released an exasperated sigh. "Since when did you start believing the tabloids? Their stock and trade is lies and distortions. This is no different." Cami stepped around the kitchen island to put some distance between her and Amanda.

"I know something's going on," she seethed. "I think you and Millie are working for the underground."

"Amanda! How can you say that? Millie is one of your most loyal staff members. She stuck it out even after Norman shot the head of security."

It was Amanda's turn to look shocked. "How did you know about that?"

"Amanda, I'm not stupid."

"Did Millie tell you? I know she eavesdrops. I caught her listening to Norman's conversations once."

"Amanda, leave her out of this. She's got nothing to do with why I stomped out." She had to keep Amanda from suspecting Millie. Her mind raced. "You're just jealous that Norman started liking me. First you set me up with him, then when he shows me real interest, you get all testy. Was this all just a big game to you?"

Her tactic worked. Amanda's face twisted into a cruel smile. A guttural chuckle percolated from her chest. "Norman is mine. We were just using you until we could get your liver. Once the transplant was successful you would mysteriously contract an incurable disease and, well … The nation would mourn your passing. We all would. But in the end, it's me Norman loves."

It was clear Norman wasn't the only one suffering from schizophrenia.

It was time for Cami to run.

Amanda pulled a pistol from the small of her back and aimed it at Cami. "Now tell me what you said to Millie."

Cami let her purse slide from her shoulder. She reached inside and found her 9 mm Colt. Keeping her hands below the counter, she gripped the weapon and moved to her right. Amanda countered. Her eyes bore the look of a shark about to attack.

As they moved around the marble island, the vase containing a dozen roses cut from the Rose Garden, blocked Cami's view. Suddenly, Amanda squeezed the trigger. The blast struck the vase sending glass, rose petals and water in all directions.

"Next time, I won't miss."

Cami kept moving in round-robin fashion.

"Now tell me what you said to Millie?"

Keys jangled in the front door.

Amanda's eyes shifted.

Bang!

Bang!

Two shots rang out.

One ricocheted off a frying pan. The other hit its mark.

Stunned, Amanda fell back, a crimson circle blossoming from a wound in her chest. She slumped to the floor, gasping for air.

The door flew open and Cami stood frozen in place. In an instant, her look-a-like stepped around the corner, her two hands gripping the butt of her weapon. A wisp of smoke drifted from its barrel.

"Cami, what are you doing here?" her look-a-like spat.

"I, I."

"Never mind. We suspected you'd return to get your jewelry. That's why I got here first. We knew Amanda would be waiting for you." As she spoke, she knelt and felt Amanda' neck. "She's still alive, but she's fading fast."

Amanda's breathing became shallow and her body started to shake violently.

"I can't look," Cami said, averting her eyes.

After a moment, Cami's look-a-like stood. "They suspect Millie. I need to get a message to her right now, and you need to get out of here. When Amanda doesn't check in with POTUS, he'll know something isn't right. He'll send others. If they find you—" She didn't have to finish her statement. "I'll have our people clean up the mess. In the meantime, you've got to go." Tossing her a set of keys, she said. "Drive my car. Go as fast as the law allows and get out of Washington, D.C. Get to a small radio station in Point Pleasant, West Virginia called, WBGS. The station manager is one of us. He'll know what to do. Now go."

Cami cracked the door open an inch and peered in both directions. It was clear. As she swung the door open, her look-a-like tossed a wad of money in her direction. She caught it and stuffed it inside her coat.

"That should get you as far as West Virginia. And don't attempt to use your credit cards."

Cami nodded and dashed down the corridor.

Chapter Fifty-Five

"If left undetected, sin, like a cancer, can eat you alive."
The Author

The atmosphere inside the White House scintillated with electricity.

While the President ranted and raved about Cami, news of Amanda's death reached the Oval Office making matters worse. His aides were too frightened to give him any details. It was left up to his chief of staff to deliver the bad news. In a rage, he shot the man.

If Millie didn't escape now, she never would. She reached into her purse and pulled out the tube of red lipstick and started to apply a layer. Suddenly, a security agent stepped in front of her desk. With her contact blocked, he couldn't see her signal. She knew any move out of the ordinary would spell disaster. Counting the seconds, she waited for the man to move, but it seemed he was in no hurry.

"Millie!" the President demanded. "Get in here."

"Yes, sir." Standing on shaky legs, she entered the Oval Office.

"Care for a smoke?" His eyes bulged.

Millie took a dry swallow. "No, sir." Her voice wavered.

Bleakly slid around the Resolute Desk like a lizard. His hand clamped her throat. All it would take was seven pounds of pressure and he would snuff her life out. Lifting her off her feet, he swung her around and threw her head down on the desk. Streaks of bright colors flashed across her sight. If she defended herself, she'd be shot for attacking the President. If she didn't, he'd kill her.

His grip relaxed enough for her to snatch a breath. Her feet caught a hold of the posh carpet and she pivoted from his grasp. Her survival instincts kicked in. Before he could grab her again, she launched a volley of debilitating punches, leaving him gasping for air. Another quick punch to his throat silenced him before he could call for his security detail.

She eased his limp body to the couch and lifted his feet to make it look like he was napping. Silent as a spirit, she slipped through the private exit and dashed down the hall.

Suddenly, she stopped. From where she stood, she could see her contact. But he couldn't see her. Having lost her lipstick in the Oval Office, she knew she had to improvise. Using the blood from her head wound, she swiped it across her lips and peered in his direction. A moment later, the first of three explosions rocked the capital.

Alarms sounded.

The President's security detail would be in the Oval Office in mere seconds. Her actions would be discovered and she would be shot on sight. Gulping oxygen, she ran down the hall. She knew the emergency exit doors would lock down at any moment, but she kept going. She made it through the first three. The fourth one closed a split second before she reached it. She slammed into it with a thud. Feeling trapped, she headed for the stairs leading to the White House kitchen.

Cooks stood, their aprons stained with a mixture of powder, icing, batter and juices. Eyes widening, they leaped aside as she plowed through the center of the kitchen.

"Emergency! Let me through." As she motored past a cutting board, she grabbed a large butcher knife and kept going. She smashed into a door and bounced off it. Her muffled cry was interrupted by the approach of a large man wearing a chef hat and sporting a meat cleaver.

She turned and slashed the air between them.

"Hold it, ma'am. I'm not going to hurt you. Now step aside," he grinned.

Taking a deep breath, Millie let it out and stepped a distance away.

The big man placed his meaty shoulder against the steel frame, he heaved once.

Nothing.

With time at a premium, he hurled himself into the door like a linebacker. It splinted and flew open.

Millie barely had time to thank the man before heavy footsteps echoed throughout the food preparation area. The big man shoved her through the door and slammed it shut. A moment later, she heard a heavy freezer unit being dragged across the floor. "That should buy me a few minutes," she muttered breathlessly.

As police units and first responders swarmed the area, Millie had few choices of transportation. Her car was not an option. Using her cell phone wasn't either. She removed the battery and tossed it one direction and stomped the rest to splinters. Then she began in a low run through the parking deck. She recognized some of her coworker's cars and knew if she stole one of them they'd report her in a heartbeat.

The visitor's VIP parking was her next source of options. As she rounded a corner, she noticed an elderly man leaving his car. It was of the age that it didn't need a computer scientist to work on the engine.

"Good, no *On Star* tracking system," she said as the man limped to the elevator doors.

While she waited, she removed the license plate from the vehicle and replaced it with the one next to her. The instant he disappeared, she was under the dashboard hot wiring the starter. The car sputtered, then started. Being careful, she backed the car from its slot.

The next obstacle was getting out of the parking deck without being recognized. She needed a disguise. She glanced around inside the car for something she could use to hide her identity; a hat, a pair of glasses … anything. Fortunately, the elderly man left his sports coat and a ball cap. She quickly tugged them on and pointed the car in the direction of the exit. A number of guards manned the exit. Sweat beaded on her brow and she swiped them aside.

"This isn't working," she told herself.

She slid the car into an empty slot, got out and climbed over the concrete support wall. She was out of one bad situation, but found herself in a worse pickle. Armed men combed the area. They were looking for one person.

Her.

Chapter Fifty-Six

I t had been three days since Olivia returned from delivering Will, Troy and Lily to their first rendezvous point.

Since then, neither President Richardson nor his team had heard anything from their sources inside the White House or from Nigel. As a precaution, the President's team had maintained radio silence with his operatives, but the wait was getting to him … to everyone. Finally, out of desperation he called his advisers together for a war council meeting.

Standing with his hand on his hips, he viewed the taught faces of the men he trusted most. "Men, I fear the mission has failed. The media is reporting a shakeup of the White House staff. That could mean only one thing. Millie and Cami failed to get the codes."

The air in the small enclave where they were meeting grew thick. "Sir, give it another day. If we don't hear from our people, we'll have to pull the plug on the grid assaults. We'll need to step back and reassess the situation. Rome didn't fall in a day, and neither will the Republic of North America," his chief adviser said.

The President nodded and listened. "Have you men heard the story about General Patton?"

"Which one?" the head of communications asked. "There are many."

"Yes, there are. The one I'm referring to is the time when they needed clear weather for a big bombing run. But it had been raining for days and the forecast was for more rain. He called for the Chaplin of the Army to draft a prayer and have it sent to all the troops. Within a matter of days, the weather cleared and the mission was a go. That's what we need to do."

"What, pray for clear weather?" one of the men asked.

After a round of good natured laugher subsided, President Richardson squared himself in front of the conference table. "No, I was thinking more like having my good friend Joe Franklin do the honor."

Joe, who'd been sitting quietly by, jumped to his feet.

Not having time for his protest, Richardson silenced him with a wave. "Joe, since your encounter with God, I've watched the change that has taken place in your life. I've seen you pray. It reminded me of General Washington kneeling in the snow at Gettysburg, praying for his frozen men. I'd trust your prayer any day."

Joe gave a slight bow. "I'd be honored, sir."

***

Two hours later, a hush settled on the cavernous junction where three mine shafts converged.

Lights from dozens of candles and oil based lanterns flickered off the moist walls as all but the most essential personnel assembled. Men in rugged overalls, soldiers with their weapons slung over their shoulders, and women in various attire gathered, their heads bowed, shoulders bent.

The cool air hung heavy throughout the mine, but it didn't dampen Joe's spirit. He rose to his feet and addressed the assembly with confidence in an all-powerful God.

"Ladies and gentlemen, during a national radio broadcast on June 5, 1944, President Roosevelt addressed the nation and spoke about the Allied liberation of Rome. He said nothing about the Normandy operation, already underway. The following evening he again addressed the nation and led it in this eloquent prayer, which I have adopted for this hour. 'Almighty God: Our sons and our daughters, pride of our Nation, this day have set upon a mighty endeavor, a struggle to preserve our Republic, our religion, and our civilization, and to set free a suffering humanity. Lead them straight and true; give strength to their arms, stoutness to their hearts, steadfastness in their faith.

They need Thy blessings. Their road is long and hard and the enemy is strong. But we know by Thy grace, and by the righteousness of our cause, they will not rest-until the victory is won. The darkness will be rent by noise and flame. Men's souls will be shaken with the violence of war. For these men are lately drawn from the ways of peace. They fight not for the lust of conquest. They fight to end conquest. They fight to liberate. They fight to let justice arise, and tolerance and good will among all Thy people. They yearn, not for the end of battle, but for their return to the haven of home.

Some may never return. Embrace these, Father, and receive them, Thy heroic servants, into Thy kingdom. And for us at home – fathers, mothers, children, wives, sisters, and brothers of brave men overseas – whose thoughts and prayers are ever with them—help us, Almighty God, to rededicate ourselves in renewed faith in Thee in this hour of great sacrifice. I ask that our people devote themselves in a continuance of prayer. As we rise to each new day, and again when each day is spent, let words of prayer be on our lips, invoking Thy help to our efforts.

And, O Lord, give us Faith. Give us Faith in Thee; Faith in our sons and daughters; Faith in each other; Faith in our united crusade. Let not the keenness of our spirit ever be dulled. Let not the impacts of temporary events or temporal matters deter us in our unconquerable purpose.

With Thy blessing, we shall prevail over the unholy forces of our enemy. Help us to conquer the apostles of greed and racial arrogances. Lead us to the saving of our country, a peace that will let all of men live in freedom, reaping the just rewards of their honest toil.

Thy will be done, Almighty God. Amen."

Chapter Fifty-Seven

"You may temporarily find a safe distance to travel undetected, but eventually, you will be found and dealt with." **A. Nonymous**

When Cami reached the parking deck, she noticed a black Ford Escalade sitting not far from where she'd parked.

She wondered why she hadn't noticed it when she arrived, but then, she wasn't paying attention to such details. Now she was.

Still breathing hard, she scanned the area looking for her look-a-like's car. *There, that's got to be it.*

It took her a minute but she was sure it was. Fingers shaking uncontrollably, she grabbed the door handle and yanked. The car door swung open and she quickly got in. She tried to calm her breathing but with all she'd been through, it wasn't working. After a minute of fumbling with the keys, she finally found the right one and jammed it into the ignition.

Thankfully, the engine turned over. After a quick glance over her shoulder, she put the car in gear and pulled out of the parking deck. As she rounded the corner, an Escalade approached her from the opposite direction. A chill ran the length of her back. Gripping the wheel, she steeled her nerves and pressed the gas pedal.

As the big vehicle rolled past, she tried to get a look at the driver but its windows were shaded. It had to be some of the President's men.

She accelerated trying to put distance between her and the Escalade. Two blocks later, she noticed they had turned around and were following her. She sped up, running a red light in the process. She just hoped she didn't draw the attention of a DC cop. Her hands slicked. Her heart pounded so hard she thought it would leap from her chest. With the Escalade rapidly closing the distance, she knew she would never lose them in this traffic. A slow moving city transit bus pulled out in front of her and she swerved to miss it. As it crossed the lane to the left, she mashed the brake and let the bus shield her from the passing Escalade. The move let her get behind the Ford and she shadowed the bus for a few blocks until she reached the intersection leading to the highway.

In a daring move, she swung the wheel to the right and ramped up on the highway. The action took the driver of the Escalade by surprise. They had just passed the ramp and it would require them going several blocks before they could turn around.

Breathing hard, she glanced into the rear view mirror. Another vehicle was trailing her five cars back. She returned her attention to the road ahead moments before she rear-ended a van full of children. She yanked the wheel to the left barely missing the van. The wide-eyed children gaped at her as she zoomed past them.

She was running out of moves.

Another entrance ramp later and the big Escalade reappeared. This time, she got a glimpse of the driver. He was one of the secret service agents and he didn't look very pleased to be chasing her.

Once the secret service men caught a glimpse of Cami's vehicle, the race was on again. In a matter of seconds, they were on her tail. She knew what was coming. They would attempt a PIT maneuver. If they succeeded, it would be all over for her.

She sent up a quick prayer and bore down on the accelerator. Swerving between trucks and cars, she kept her pursuers at bay while she looked for a way out of her predicament.

Suddenly, her car jolted forward, nearly causing her to lose control. She blinked into her rear view mirror. The grill of the big Ford filled her view and she nearly lost control of her bladder.

"Oh, Lord, help me."

She yanked the wheel to the left avoiding another rear-end collision. The action wasn't expected and the Escalade slammed into the rear of an SUV. The unsuspecting driver lost control of his vehicle and went into a roll. Cars, trucks, and busses scattered like a bevy of quail, but Cami and her pursuers kept moving.

Just as the Ford struck her car, its rear tires lost their grip on the pavement and it began a slow-motion spin. Its left rear panel struck the concrete median causing it to flip. In an instant, the bodies of the men inside were flung out as the big vehicle careened out of control. It was obvious they weren't wearing their seatbelts.

Cami watched in horror as other vehicles struck the men who lay strung along the highway. Tears blurred her vision at the carnage caused by the high speed chase.

But she knew she wasn't out of danger yet. The car that had pulled the PIT maneuver on the Escalade was still following her. It had dropped back several cars and was following her at a safe, non-threatening distance, but still there.

As the miles clicked by, Cami's breathing returned to normal. Maybe her tail was there to report where she was headed and there would be a roadblock waiting just around the next bend. She considered ramping off, but not having a phone or GPS, she wasn't sure where she'd end up. Determined not to give up, she kept one eye on the road and the other on the cars five lengths back.

All at once, she remembered why the doctor told her not to drink so much iced tea. Her overly small bladder had a way of deciding it was full at the worst of times. Instinctively, she gnawed on her thumbnail. She needed to get off and relieve herself and she realized her fuel tank was registering empty.

If she ramped off, the car would follow her. She sent up another flare prayer and took her chances. After taking the next exit, she pointed her car to the first gas station she could find. Fortunately, a busy RaceTrac appeared a quarter mile ahead. Crossing her fingers, she pulled into a parking slot, slammed the car in park and dove for the front door.

As she'd reached the door two large truck drivers emerged. "'Scuse me, little lady," one of them said. "You look like you've seen a ghost."

Still breathing in short gulps, she eyed them with concern. "There's a man following me. He's right over there." She nodded in the direction of the car that had been following her. Its door hung open and there was no one in the front seat.

"Ma'am, I don't see no one following you. But if you'd like me to accompany you to the—"

"Shut up, Mike," the other man said, punching the man's arm in a friendly manner. "He's just running his mouth. Look, if you want, we'll watch that car and if the driver tries anything funny, he'll have to deal with us."

Cami tried to smile but her lips refused to cooperate. Needing to relieve her bladder, she thanked the men and raced to the Ladies room.

Chapter Fifty-Eight

Millie quickly analyzed her situation.

She was wearing a man's sports coat and ball cap. The police were looking for a woman. With any luck, they might overlook her. Taking a calming breath, she tried to make her heart stop pounding. It felt like it was going to break her ribs. Talk about a telltale heart, she chided herself.

Finally, the moment came. A pair of patrolmen had passed her position without noticing her. The two others were talking to some pedestrians who were asking why the White House tour was canceled. While they were distracted, she crept from behind the wall and casually crossed the street.

Standing among a group of tourists, she glanced at her watch.

It had been ten minutes since she'd left the White House. Her window to get out of Washington was rapidly closing. If she couldn't get outside the first perimeter soon, she probably wouldn't ever get out. She made a snap decision. Rather than run the risk of being caught in the open, she ducked inside a movie theater. To her left was a line of movie goers. To her right, was a coffee shop.

A number of men sat at their computers viewing various sites. One man had his coffee dangerously close to the edge of the counter. It took only one small bump to send it all over his lap. In an instant, he was on his feet yelping about how hot the liquid was. With him distracted, Millie snatched the laptop and made for the theater. She paid for a ticket and chose a movie which was in progress. Bounding up the steps to the back row, she excused herself and parted a few lovebirds who were certainly not interested in the movie.

Once seated, she logged onto the internet and found the secure link to the NRA. She slid the duplicate copy of the codes into the port and waited for them to download. While she waited, she noticed the movie. It was The Secret Life of Pets, her favorite. Despite the theater being dark, she hoped no one would report her. The lovers a few seats down certainly wouldn't.

The computer pinged indicating the file had been sent and she smiled.

An immediate response appeared indicating they'd received the encrypted code. Relief washed over her like a flood and she breathed easier.

For the next fifty minutes she sat and stared at the big screen. Finally, the flick came to an end. As the lights gradually grew brighter, she realized how ridiculous she looked. The old man's sports coat was in desperate need of repair and she still had the ball cap on. Standing, she followed the movie goers out the exit and found the street much quieter than they were when she entered.

As if on cue, a cab rolled to a stop directly in front of her. Before someone else grabbed it, she jumped in and slammed the door.

"Where to?" The driver, a transplant from the Middle -East, asked.

"Anywhere but here." The driver nodded.

As they moved into traffic the driver peered into the mirror, he asked, "Are you a man who wants to be a woman, a woman who wants to be a man or are you a woman who wants to look like a man?"

Millie glanced down at her clothes. "Umm, my boyfriend loaned me his coat and baseball cap because it was chilly inside the theater."

"Where is your boyfriend, now?"

With a huff, she continued, "Oh, he's a first responder. When the call went out after the explosions, he left me sitting in the theater."

Her fabrication seemed to satisfy the driver. "Tell you what. I'll take you anywhere you want. The fare's on me."

Guilt stabbed her conscience. With limited funds, she thought it best to continue the ruse, thank the man and leave it there.

She was sure by now that all the bridges would be closed and most major thoroughfares under heavy surveillance. Her only chance was to head east into Maryland. There was a safe house located in Pepper Mill Village she could use. That was, if US 295 wasn't closed.

She made a snap decision. "Could you take me to Pepper Mill Village without having to use any major highways?"

His eyes widened. "I think I understand. Sure thing, ma'am."

The driver adjusted his hat and weaved through the maze of traffic. Thirty minutes later, they cruised to a stop in front of a Dunkin Donut shop.

"I can make it from here," Millie said, routing through her purse.

The driver's hand flew up. "No need to pay. As I said, the fare's on me. Go in peace and may Allah the merciful grant you safe passage."

Millie was in no position to argue with the man.

"Thank you, kind sir … God bless you."

The driver waved, made a U-turn and sped off leaving Millie standing on the curb. It took a few moments for her to get her bearings. The safe house was a few blocks away. With nightfall fast approaching, she hoped to make it without anyone noticing.

She set off at a comfortable pace and by nine o'clock entered the foyer of the Central Garden II Apartments. A set of car keys hung on a hook. A safe, located behind a picture, held several credit cards and a new ID.

Under the bathroom sink were a number of boxes displaying various shades of hair color along with skin treatment. She chose honey blond. With the skin treatment, she gave herself a good suntan. When she emerged from the bathroom, she was a different woman.

Her stomach growled reminding her that she'd not eaten since this morning. Perusing the pantry, she found a box of macaroni and a can of tuna. *Hmm, tuna fish casserole sounds good.* While the noodles cooked, she booted up the stolen computer and fired off an email requesting further instructions. By the time her dinner was ready, she had her instructions.

Chapter Fifty-Nine

"Look and you will find it – what is unsought will go undetected."   **Sophocles**

Will, Troy and Lily had been traveling on foot all night and Lily's stomach grumbled.

Lifting his hand, Will slapped a mosquito. "Bloody things," he muttered.

It was the first time anyone had spoken in hours. "Let's take a break. If we don't feed Lily, her stomach will give away our position."

"Very funny, Nigel, I mean, Will. I'm not sure I'll ever get used to calling you Will."

Troy pulled off his back pack and dug through its contents. "Ah, Three Musketeers, my favorite."

Lily gaped at him. "Is that the most nutritious thing you have?"

He shook his head. "No, but it's the tastiest."

She began digging through her backpack. After a few minutes, she produced an energy bar and tore open the wrapper.

While they ate, Will studied a map. "We're not far. I figure the hub is about five klicks."

Lily's face contorted. "Klicks?"

He smiled sending Lily's heart into overdrive. "Yeah, that's about three miles." All at once, his cell phone vibrated. He unclipped it and peered at the screen. A broad smile parted his parched lips. "We got the codes," he whispered. "The mission's a go."

Troy and Lily gave each other a high five.

"Let's take a rest and we'll make the final push at midnight. The guards will be in their routine by then." Will checked his watch and marked the time.

Lily had just drifted off when she heard Will and Troy talking. She roused and sat up. "You boys talking about me?"

"Now why would you ask that?" Will asked.

"Because, the moment I sat up you stopped talking."

The two men grinned at each other like two Cheshire cats. Hands raised in surrender, Troy said, "Guilty as charged. You are always the center of my thoughts and conversation. So get used to it."

Impressed with his eloquence, Lily smiled. "Troy, that's the nicest thing you've said all day."

He lifted her pack and snugged it on her slender shoulders. "The day is yet young. I'll probably say something dumb before it's all over."

Lily gave him a friendly punch in the arm.

By midnight they'd reached the edge of the thick stand of trees. Crickets screamed to one another. In the distance, a lone bullfrog croaked out a warning. Halfway through the journey, they stopped at a paved road which divided the forest. Crouching low, they watched a number of International Guard vehicles rumble by.

Will checked his watch and counted the seconds. The vehicles came at two minute intervals. "Okay, just as soon as the vehicle rounds the corner, Lily you go. Once you're across, Troy will go. Then I'll go once the coast is clear. We'll reassemble and go as far as we can."

She gulped and counted the seconds.

"Go," Will whispered.

Lily's legs churned up dirt and gravel as she sprinted across the two lanes. Once there, she dove behind a large tree and peered out just as another vehicle rumbled by.

After a few beats, Troy dashed from his hidden position and took his place next to Lily. He waited for his breathing to settle before giving Will the okay.

Seconds ticked and Will didn't appear. "I wonder where he is," Lily whispered. Troy strained his eyes. "I don't know. He was right behind me."

A shoe scraped against a rock and they turned.

Troy reached for his weapon.

Lily gasped. "Will, how did you—"

"Keep your voice down. It's what I do."

"What, sneak around scaring people?"

He shifted his backpack, and peered over his shoulder. "We're being followed."

Lily's hand covered her gaping mouth. "How did you know?"

He smiled. "Like I said, it's what I do. Stay low and quiet. There's a village up ahead. Once we get there, we'll plan our next move," he said, his voice laced with concern.

"How long have we been followed?" Troy asked as they continued their journey.

"About two hours ago. I think whoever it is, picked up on our trail and it tracking us to see where we are going."

"What are you going to do?" Troy asked.

Will tried to peer through the heavy fog which coated the trees, making the forest a maze of ghastly shapes. As the night sounds closed in around them, Lily moved instinctively closer to Troy.

Suddenly, a large droplet of condensation fell from a leaf and plopped Lily's forehead. Gasping, she nearly jumped out of her skin.

"Be careful," Will admonished.

"It scared me," she whispered through tight lips.

Troy pulled her close.

"You two keep moving. I'm going to circle back around and see if I can get the drop on whoever it is. That's if it's not the whole International Guard unit."

"Will, be careful." Lily said, her eyes round as saucers.

He checked his Glock. "Oh, I'll be careful."

As he moved away, the fog enclosed around him and soon he disappeared.

Lily shivered. "I wish I'd never volunteered for this mission." Her teeth chattered as they made their way through the woods.

Troy placed his arm around her. "It'll be okay. Will can take care of himself."

"It's not Will I'm worried about. It's us. Can we really sneak into hub central, hack into the main servers and dismantle it before getting caught?"

"Only the Lord knows, but we gotta try. Everyone is counting on us to succeed."

The whites of Lily's eyes glowed in the darkness. "Thanks, no pressure."

Chapter Sixty

When Cami emerged from the Ladies room, she found the two truck drivers standing where she'd left them.

"You sure you don't need a shower, little lady?" the first truck driver asked with a toothy grin.

"No, thank you. However, to show you gentlemen my appreciation … " She tossed them a box of donuts. "Here, maybe these will keep your mind off me and on your tummies." She smiled as the men each grabbed the first donut they could find.

"Thanks lady. You can count on us to watch your car anytime."

Cami waved at them as she climbed back into her car. She started the engine and was on the ramp when she heard movement.

***

Trace, who had been hiding behind her seat, suddenly got a leg cramped.

Fearing he might frighten her, he slowly raised his head. "Trace, where did you come from?" She blurted, nearly running the car off the road.

It was all he could do to keep a straight face. "I've been shadowing you ever since you arrived back in town."

Cami cocked her head. "You have? Why didn't you call me, or signal me instead of popping up out of nowhere."

Trace climbed over the seat and clicked the seatbelt. "I couldn't. With Amanda breathing down your neck, I couldn't risk it. I tried to stop you when you went to your condo, but I lost you in traffic. Then when you left, I caught a glimpse of those goons following you. I knew they'd never expect someone pulling a PIT maneuver on them."

Cami's breathing came easier, but the hives on her neck bespoke her nervous condition. "Tell me how you got inside my car without those two lover boys seeing you?"

Trace grinned. "Oh, that was easy. I told them I was your fiancée and I had a big surprise waiting for you. I sweetened the pot with a box of donuts."

Cami's jaw fell open. Stifling a belly laugh, she glared at him. "I'm not available. I'm engaged to the President."

"Yeah, right. And I'm going to marry the Queen of England."

Her fingers found Trace's and closed into a tight grip. "Do you know where we're headed?" she asked.

He pulled a map from his pocket. "No, but I have a hunch you're about to tell me."

Cami pointed to a spot on the map. "Point Pleasant, West Virginia. They have a radio station there and its manager is a member of the underground."

"That's another five hours driving. Would you like me to take over for a while?"

Cami slowed. "I thought you'd never ask."

As they exchanged places, Trace drew her into a deep embrace.

"We need to get married ... soon," Cami's breath tickled the hairs on his neck sending his heart skittering.

"Maybe Point Pleasant has a Justice of the Peace," he said with a grin.

"Not so fast. You're not getting off that easily."

Feigning defeat, he climbed in behind the steering wheel and nosed the car back on to highway I-68 west.

Five hours later, the car swerved and hit the shoulder of the road. Trace's eyes snapped open and he jerked the car back on the highway.

Cami sat upright and peered at him through bleary eyes.

"Sorry, I nodded off."

"Do you want me to take over?"

"Yeah, I'm blinking out."

After they exchanged places, Trace curled up in a ball and drifted off.

***

In the predawn light, the two lane road twisted like a snake.

It offered Cami the best chance of not being stopped by Homeland Security or the International Guard. As she pulled to a stop at an intersection, she checked her map. Point Pleasant, West Virginia, lay just a few miles ahead.

Her fuel light blinked on telling her she had about forty miles before she ran out of gas. Rather than risk it, she decided to stop at the next gas station. She'd have to use some of the cash the other woman had given her. She just hoped the station was open and took cash. Many didn't.

Rounding a sharp turn, the road widened to reveal a gas station, a diner and a seedy hotel. She released a tired sigh and rolled to a stop by the first pump. The engine stalled just as she pulled in.

"Not a minute too soon," she told herself. "Trace, wake up."

His continued snoring was her answer.

A red light spelling the word Open, blinked intermittently in the grungy window and Cami wondered if the owners ever turned it off. After prying herself out of the car, she stretched, and trudged up the steps to the front door. To her surprise, it wasn't locked. She paused before opening the door all the way.

"Hello, anybody here?"

A cat sprang from a cooler and dashed between her legs sending her heart into overdrive. She screamed and gasped for air. *Where was Trace when you needed him?*

Hand slicking, she gripped the handle and swung the door the rest of the way open. A bell chimed deep in the quaint little store and an elderly shopkeeper hobbled to the front. His kindly eyes and weary smile brightened his face, chasing away the years of sorrow that first greeted her. "Can I help you, young lady?" His soft spoken words warmed Cami's chilled spirit.

"Hello, I need a tank of gas." Handing the elderly gentleman a fifty dollar bill, she smiled.

"Oh, my, I don't think I have that much change. It's been kinda slow here of late."

Smiling back at him, Cami relaxed her stance. "It will probably take all of it to fill my tank, I was down to fumes."

Cutting his eyes toward the door, he lowered his voice. "Where did you come from to be way out here in the boonies?"

Heat crept up her neck and she knew he could see her discomfort.

"It's all right young lady. My name is Jed Lawson and you're among friends. I believe you're headed to the radio station. Is that about right?"

Cami couldn't hide her surprise. It was obvious that he'd pegged her correctly. "How did you know?"

Coming around the counter, he laid a gentle hand on her shoulder and pushed the money back in her direction. "Well, that's our little secret. Suffice it to say, your face is all over the media. You're quite the popular person."

"More like, most wanted," an elderly woman added, wiping her hands on a soiled apron and waddling from somewhere in the back of the store.

"Wanted?"

"Yep, seems like they're looking for you in connection with the death of a Miss Amanda Borden something or other . . . couldn't pronounce her name.

Also, the *President* wants to speak with you on a matter of *national security*." Her words were punctuated with sarcastic emphasis.

"I see. Well then I guess I'd better tank up, drive right back and line up for the firing squad." A smile tickled her lips.

Patting Cami's arm, the elderly woman harrumphed. "Now, now. There's no need for such talk like that 'round-cher."

"I will have to admit, they've even got a few spotters here in our little holler," the elderly man said. "I wouldn't be surprised if they don't have our fillin' station watched. It's best you wait here while I check around. Ma, take Miss Stetson to the back and fix her up a mess a beans and corn bread. I'm gonna park her car outta sight."

As he spoke, Trace staggered in.

"Who's he?" Mr. Lawson asked.

"Oh, he's my … I mean, he's with me."

The two elderly folks gave her a knowing expression.

"I assure you, it's nothing like that," Cami said as she stuffed the money back in her purse."

"Uh huh," Mr. Lawson muttered.

"How did anybody know Miss Stetson was coming here?" Trace asked, trying to shift the conversation.

The elderly man offered her a gummy smile. "Our son runs the radio station. He's been keeping up with things. Got word you were on the run and to keep a sharp eye for ya."

"Do you think it's safe to stay here? You know they won't rest until they find her. Hiding a fugitive could put your lives in grave danger." Trace added.

The elderly man waved his hand dismissively. "That's all right by us. We've lived a good life. Might as well die doing a good thing."

"Ain't nobody going to do any dyin' if I've got anything to do with it," his wife of sixty-two years chimed in. "Let's get this pretty little woman down in the root cellar before some nosy neighbor goes to shooting off her mouth."

Cami got the distinct impression Mrs. Lawson knew exactly who she was talking about.

"What about me?" Trace asked.

"Humph, you come with me. I'll put you up in the hay loft. No one will look for you there."

Chapter Sixty-One

"The movement of the earth around the sun to often goes undetected by a blind man."   **The Author**

"What time is it?" Lily whispered.

Troy checked his watch. "It's been an hour since we left Will."

Lily glanced over her shoulder. "I hope he's okay. I wonder what's taking him so long."

All at once, a shadowy figure emerged from behind a tree.

"Will!" Lily said in a controlled scream.

He appeared with a dog attached to a chain.

"Wag!" She nearly fell over her feet getting to him. "I don't understand."

"Well, I guess Wag understood better than you'd given him credit. My guess is, he's been following us ever since we left him back on the prairie."

Lily reached down and rubbed him behind the ears. "Well, for what it's worth, I'm glad you're here."

"Look, Lily, I know Wag means a lot to you, but we can't take him with us. It's just too risky. A dog will only get in the way, let alone draw attention to us. You understand, don't you?"

It was clear, she didn't like the idea, but she knew he was right. "Yes, but I don't like it."

"Neither do I, to be honest," Will added. Then he attach Wag's collar to a tree with a rope from his backpack.

When he'd finished, he glanced. "Okay, let's go. There's a town nearby. If we can get there without anyone noticing, we'll blend in with the locals, get some food and plan our next move."

Lily gave Wag one last pat on the head and followed the men across the field in the direction of the village.

Fifteen minutes later, they were sitting in a cafe run by the underground, sipping coffee and munching on the first cooked meal since they'd left. It had been a grueling three days. Lily had lost five pounds and Troy had gained them in muscles. Will looked as lean and mean as ever in his biker outfit.

"We need to get our hands on some fresh duds," Will said, his eyes scanning the street outside the window.

Troy glanced down at his shirt. It was rumbled and stained. Lily's shirt and trousers hung on her like a scarecrow.

"Where do you suppose we get them?" he asked, giving his armpits a sniff.

It wasn't hard for Lily and Troy to guess what Will had in mind. The street was under constant surveillance by International Guard soldiers.

Will nodded toward a group of recruits. Their uniforms were crisp and clean and the young men wearing them looked about as smart as the three stooges.

"I think they're about our size. Don't you?"

"Will, you're not going to—"

His calloused hand waved aside her concerns. "Not to worry, Lil. They won't even know what hit 'em."

"You're not going to kill them. Are you?"

Will lowered his voice. "I'll ask them real nicely. If they agree, they are home free. But if they get a little feisty, I just might have to use other means to convince them that we need those unis more than they do."

Troy leaned in close. "Need any help?"

Shaking his head, Will leaned back. "I think I can handle it. But thanks none the less. It might get messy and I don't want you to have nightmares later on."

Lily's hand reached out and clutched Will's. She hardly recognized her brother anymore. The war had changed him. He was no longer the carefree, irresponsible, millennial she'd known. He was a man, possibly a man with blood on his hands. She longed for the old Will to return but knew that was not to be.

Before Will left, he dropped a twenty dollar bill on the table and disappeared through the rear door leaving Troy and Lily to sit and watch through the window.

Minutes ticked like the gonging of Big Ben. Finally, the three newbies began taunting a scruffy old man who'd hobbled up to then and had asked for a few coins. It was obvious he was an alcoholic and would spend all his money on booze.

"Hey old man," one of the young men said. "Don't you know it's against the law to panhandle?"

"Yeah," another chimed in. "Move along or you'll be sorry."

"Oh? And which one of you tough guys is going to make me?" the panhandler asked, straightening to his full height. It was Will.

His disguise had everyone fooled, including Troy and Lily.

"I am," the largest of the three rookies said.

As he reached out, Will spun around. With a swift kick boxing maneuver, he landed a solid punch to the big guy's midsection. The guy doubled over, groaning.

The next loud mouth guy made his move. Will stopped him dead in his tracks with a punch to the throat. His knees buckled as he gasped for air. In one smooth move, Will had crushed the man's windpipe. His face turned purple as he collapsed to the concrete.

The third guy whipped a seven-inch blade from his belt and slashed the air barely missing Will's chest. The action, however, left the guy vulnerable to a triple punch to the face and gut. The stunned attacker was unprepared for the volley of punches. He dropped the knife and clutched his midsection as Will wheeled around for the coup de grâce. The guy doubled over and slumped in the middle of the sidewalk.

In less than thirty seconds, it was all over.

The few bystanders who'd watched began to cheer. Will, his hands held out, palms held down, quieted them. Then he motioned for Troy and Lily to come help him drag the three men into the alley. A few minutes later, they emerged wearing three, crisp uniforms complete with ID tags.

Confident their disguises would keep them from being suspected, Will led Lily and Troy to the first guard post. He'd learned enough by listening to the three rookies talking to know they were headed to the training facility located inside hub central. With as much hubris as he could muster, Will bluffed his way past the first security check point.

Chapter Sixty-Two

The idea of a root cellar didn't quite translate to the reality of what it actually was.

To Cami's surprise, it was a well furnished apartment buried beneath the house. The only access, however, was through a narrow opening behind a movable shelf loaded with jars of peaches, pickles and mater's, as Mrs. Lawson called them. It wasn't the posh apartment she was accustomed to, but it was clean, bug-free and provided her with a restful place to sleep.

"I can't thank you enough, Mr. and Mrs. Lawson." Cami said, holding the older woman's gnarled hand.

"Deary, in the short time we've known you, you have become like a second daughter to us. We just wish you could have met Jed," the older woman said, referring to their radio broadcaster son.

"Why? What has happened to him?"

Tears welled in Mrs. Lawson's eyes. "Yesterday, they came for him. Seems like they didn't like him speaking out against all the lies they've been feeding the public."

Guilt stabbed Cami's conscience. "I'm sorry to hear that. I wish there was something I could do."

Her eyes clearing, Mrs. Lawson sucked in a halting breath. "Oh there is, Miss Stetson. There certainly is." Her tone hardened. "Tomorrow, we are going to sneak you down to the radio station and you are going set the record straight." It was obvious the woman understood the power of the spoken word.

"Won't the authorities shut the station down before I get the message out?"

"Don't worry about that. You just do your job. Speak the truth in power and authority. And let the rest depend on the good Lord."

"But I don't know the first thing about running a radio station. We need Jed."

"He's been arrested, remember?" Mr. Lawson said, his voice growing thick with emotion.

***

Hearing the discussion, Trace stepped closer.

"Then we'll just have to get him out of jail. I kinda have some experience at doing that."

Cami eyed him with interest. "And how do you propose doing that?"

Trace ran his hand across the back of his neck. "I'm working on it. Tell you what. You go to the station and Mr. Lawson and I will check out the local jail."

Thirty minutes later, Mr. Lawson and Trace rumbled into town in his Ford F150 pickup truck. The police department was guarded by a couple of road-weary, overweight donut pushers. Their sagging holsters held ancient revolvers and they looked about as interested in guarding the front door as a couple of Keystone Cops.

"We could ask them real nicely and they just might let us usher your son outta there," Trace said as they viewed the pair from Mr. Lawson's aging pickup.

He narrowed his gaze and adjusted his cap. "That they might, but I 'spec the sheriff might have other ideas."

Trace pulled a borrowed ball cap lower over his eyes. "Or we could go in, guns blazing."

Mr. Lawson leaned out his window and spit a chaw of tobacco. "That might work, too. But it would get messy."

Trace chuckled. "Messy is my middle name." Grabbing the door handle, he swung the door open.

With his double-barrel shotgun clutched under his bent elbow, Mr. Lawson stepped out and followed him.

Mr. Lawson nodded at the two policemen sitting outside the department. "Gentlemen."

They acknowledged by holding up their hands.

"Gentlemen! Why don't you fellas take a break and get some breakfast. You look like you could use a hearty meal." he said, a broad smile wrinkling the creases around his eyes.

The two men eagerly complied leaving the jail unguarded.

"Shall we?" trace asked, opening the front door.

Together, they weaved their way to the holding cells where a number of political detainees awaited transfer. On the way in, Trace had grabbed a set of keys and began unlocking the cell doors. As the last one swung open, Jed stepped out. After a brief introduction, Jed and his dad made for the exit with Trace bringing up the rear.

Once they were back in the pickup, Mr. Lawson briefed Jed on the plan.

With the prospect of finally getting a chance to make a difference, Jed set his jaw. "Well, let's get moving. The sheriff is expected back any minute."

Mr. Lawson put the truck in gear and sped around the street corner just as the sheriff appeared carrying a cup of coffee and a brown paper bag.

Fortunately, one of the inmates had slashed the police cruiser's tires. By the time he'd gotten them fixed, the mission was over.

***

The email Millie received from the NRA chilled her to the bone.

She was to return to D.C. and set up a press conference between President Richardson and the national media in the Press Room via satellite feed. How that was to be accomplished rested with her and a few technicians. With her fake ID, she knew she could get past security but how to convince the White House correspondents to assemble for a press conference with the ousted President was a bit of a stretch. Especially since her name was at the top of the FBI's most wanted list.

Suddenly, she hit on an idea. She knew Cami had escaped the dragnet around DC and had reached her destination in West Virginia. Using a burner cell phone, she called Cami and explained the plan. It was bold and dangerous, but Cami agreed. She would go on the air and expose the Bleakly Administration's role in the government takeover. With the evidence Millie provided, she would mount an irrefutable argument charging Norman Bleakly with murder, conspiracy, misuse of government funds and a host of high crimes and misdemeanors.

After sending a hot tip to one of the New York Times Washington Bureau editors, Millie knew the other correspondents would smell blood in the water and want to get in on the action. At the same time, her contact in California would be setting up a satellite feed to intercept the feeding frenzy happening in the Press Room. It all depended on split second timing. And it all depended on Lily, Troy and Will shutting down the grid borders.

***

The news of Amanda's death nearly sent President Bleakly over the edge.

His confidant, his chief adviser, his sister and lover were gone, leaving him to wonder whether or not to keep going.

With Millie suspected of being a traitor and on the lam, he suspected the codes had been stolen. A quick inspection of the cigar box confirmed his suspicions. One of the Cohiba Esplendido's was slightly rotated, something he'd never allow. It was one of his idiosyncrasies. A crooked picture, an off-centered flower arrangement, it didn't matter. He'd adjust them because he had to. And a rotated cigar was not acceptable. He concluded the grid codes had either been stolen or copied. There was little he could do from Washington. Any changes would have to be input manually. And since this was his brain child, it would be up to him to make the changes.

"Millie," he bellowed, before realizing she wasn't there. "Anybody."

A fear-stricken aid appeared at the Oval Office door. "Yes, sir."

Not looking up, from his computer, he said, "Call DOD, have them prep my private jet."

"But sir,"

"Don't but sir me. Call the airport. I want to be in the air within the hour."

As the aid turned, he paused. "Can I tell them where you're going, sir?"

POTUS looked up, and pinned the aid with a deadly stare. "Tell them I'm going to St. Louis, to the grid hub."

The aid nodded and disappeared around the corner.

***

By the time the President and his remaining security detail arrived at the DOD airstrip, the Lear jet's engines whined.

Thirty minutes later, they were halfway across the nation with the heartland in their sights.

The acting chief of staff fidgeted nervously while Bleakly brooded. "Sir, tell me again what you plan to do once we hit the ground."

"We are going to the Hub Central and I am personally going to reprogram the grid codes. I told you that."

"Yes, sir, that you did. But don't you think you should inform the head of Homeland Security and the

International Guard before doing that? With the new codes, anyone crossing the borders without the new protocols will set off the ID chips. It will be a blood bath."

POTUS considered him with a malevolent gaze. "I can't risk the border grids going down. If the underground gets wind of that, we'll for sure have a blood bath and it will be my administration's blood we'll be swimming in."

The pilot's voice broke the wire tight moment. "Sir, we are on final approach, please take your seat and be sure your seatbelt is fastened. This is going to be a rough landing."

Bleakly followed the captain's orders and peered out at the blackening sky. It seemed the weather gods were angry with him.

***

President Richardson waited penitently while the makeup specialist finished prepping his face.

It had been nearly a year since he'd appeared on television and his team wanted him to look the same as he did the day he was arrested ... or better.

If politics is all about perception, then this was the time to sway the public with a full-court press. The moment the grid borders went down, he would step behind a podium bearing the seal of the United States of America and address the nation. His image would be linked to a satellite feed which would be displayed a few minutes after Cami finished with her condemnation of the Bleakly Administration.

Minutes ticked by as the eyes of the nation were on Lily, Troy and Will.

Chapter Sixty-Three

"As far as we know, our computer has never had an undetected error."   **Conrad Weisert**

"Okay, this is it," Will said, scanning the sprawling complex.

"I've scouted out this entire facility and have a pretty good idea where everything is." Nodding in the direction of a five story building with dozens of chimneys, he gave Troy and Lily the five-cent tour. "That, over there, is the Electrical Power Production Unit. That other one," he pointed to a glass enclosed multi-storied building which resembled an office complex. "That houses the super computers. See that large satellite dish?" Two heads bobbed. "That's the uplink to the satellite hovering somewhere in outer space."

"And that building?" Troy nodded toward a brick building.

"That's where we're headed, it's the Training Facility. That's where all new recruits report to get their final assignments. We'll act like we just arrived and see where they send us. Then, once we have ID's and pass-cards, we'll be able to move about fairly easily, but first, I need to do something about my hair and beard."

Troy and Lily glanced at each other. "How about Lily and I go inside and wait. I feel rather conspicuous standing out here."

Will nodded. "Good idea. See ya in a few minutes." Then he disappeared though the restroom door. Fifteen minutes later he emerged, his beard shaved, his long hair trimmed.

Lily sucked in a sharp breath. "Will, I barely recognize you."

His smile warmed her spirit.

"I barely recognize myself. C'mon, let's see if we can convince the guy in charge of this training facility to give us some official looking papers."

They arrived at the Training Facility just as a group of recruits were leaving. They entered and found the petty officer sitting behind a desk looking like a carryover from the Cold-War. His Burgundy Beret hat had the insignia of the International Guard, but it was clear, he wasn't from the US. His firm jaw line and straight nose bespoke European … Russian.

He glanced up and said "You're late." His thick Russian accent confirmed Will's suspicions. "I had to give your assignment to other people. If you can't show up on time, I'll be forced to—"

Before he finished, Troy struck him with a loose brick he'd found outside. The man's eyes rolled back in his head and he slumped over his desk.

Will placed two fingers against the man's neck.

"Is he, he dead?" Lily's voice quaked.

"No, but he'll have one heck-of-a headache when he wakes up. Troy, help me get him out of sight."

Lily bit the edge of her lip as Will and Troy dragged the man's limp body around to the back of a set of filing cabinets.

As they did, Lily inspected the papers on his desk, looking at the assignments. A set of rolled papers caught her eyes and she unrolled them. "Look guys," holding up the schematic.

"Bingo, that's our way in." Will pumped the air with his fist. "This is a blueprint of the entire complex." Pulling a page back, he pointed to a system of subterranean tunnels.

Lily's finger followed the lines. "I remember when the inmates took over the jail and Dad and I climbed down into the sewer system in order to escape. If we could find the drain, we could come up through them and gain access to the hub without even raising an alarm."

Will leaned closer. "You're right. Look, here is the main tunnel which leads through the center of the complex and look here," pointing to a circle with an 'X'. Those are ladders leading to the next level. They're probably not guarded. We should be able to go from floor to floor undetected."

Troy pinched his chin between his thumb and index finger. "Let's take this with us so we won't get lost. If we're questioned, we'll tell them we are doing a routine inspection of the electrical system."

The walkie-talkie on the unconscious guard's belt crackled to life and everyone froze. "Captain Ivan Romanov, we have just been informed that President Bleakly is on his way. I need you to send a team to secure the LZ. See to it that he has everything he requires. Over?"

The request for a response meant that someone pick up the walkie-talkie and answer.

Will was the first to move. "I'll do it." With care, he removed the device and squeezed the speaker button. "Roger that sir. Out," he said, using a husky voice.

Lily's face paled. "Will, what are we going to do? We can't stand by and let him change the codes."

"And we can't let him catch us in the middle of hacking into their computers either," Troy added. "We need to get out of here."

Lily took a step in the direction of the door.

"Wait! Why not just tell the guards that we are the President's advance team here to run an analytics test on their computers before he arrives? That way we can get in, do what we came to do and get the heck out of here.

Finger to his chin, Troy smiled. "That sure beats crawling through those nasty sewers."

Hands held in surrender, Lily nodded. "Then we'd better hurry."

"I agree," Will added.

"And the codes Millie sent you?" Troy asked.

Will patted his chest pocket for a copy of the grid codes he'd copied on a notecard. "Here and here," he said, pointing to his head. I've committed them to memory just in case."

"Okay then," Lily said, taking a deep breath, "let's go."

Nodding, Troy led the way to the front door, the roll of blueprints under his arm. "After you."

"Hey wait," Will held up a finger. He snatched a clipboard from the desk and brought up Norman Bleakly's forged signature on his IPhone. "Lily, how's your handwriting?"

She squinted at the screen. "Passable. I think I can do it. Especially since most people have never seen POTUS's real signature."

She found a black narrow point marker and scribbled his signature on the bottom of a memo with the message stating they were the advanced team on official business. "That should get us in."

Will grabbed a hard hat from a rack which lined the wall and tossed two others to Troy and Lily. "Great, you just gave us permission to inspect the electrical and cooling systems of this facility."

Chapter Sixty-Four

Clipboard in hand, Will led Troy and Lily across the expansive Central Hub facility.

Men in International Guard uniforms and young people wearing white lab coats moved about with mixed expressions. Some of them also had clipboards and walked with a purposeful gait, while others ignored the trio and looked past them as if they weren't there.

"Keep walking," Troy whispered, "There's a guard approaching."

His walkie-talkie squawked and he cocked his head to listen and respond. He turned abruptly and headed in the direction of the Training Facility.

"I think someone discovered the guy you slugged," Lily said, glancing over her shoulder.

"Don't look. Stay calm and act normal. With any luck the guards will be distracted and let us pass." Will said, confidently. As they neared the second security checkpoint a guard stepped directly in front of them. "Let me do the talking," Will whispered.

Lily's eyes widened at her brother's assertiveness.

Will squared himself in front of the guard and handed the clipboard bearing President Bleakly's signature. "As you probably heard, President Bleakly is on his way here as we speak. We are his advanced team. We have orders to do a thorough inspection of the computer system to insure it hasn't been hacked."

He stepped back and waited for the reaction.

The man's shoulders straightened and he did a double-take. "Is this for real?"

"Do you think for one minute a couple of saps would try to bluff their way into the main hub station with a forged document? Give me a break. What do we look like, the Three Stooges?" Will leaned closer as he spoke making the shaken guard lean the opposite way.

"Yes, sir, I mean no, sir. You are here on official business. I can see that. I was just making sure." After signing the offered clipboard, the guard opened the gate.

"Thanks, buddy." Will said and gave the man a crisp salute. The shaken guard returned it with wide eyes.

"Okay, we're in. Let's get to work. Lily, you and Troy go to Computer Central. Make your way to the fifth floor. You can use your pass keys to gain access to the mainframe. You'll know what to do."

As he turned, Troy asked, "Where will you be?"

He pointed to the massive electric power production plant. "In there. Once you've shut down the grid's command and control units, I'll cause an interruption in the power supply. It will only last a few seconds before rebooting. When that happens, I will have destroyed the power surge protection system. The jolt of electricity released in the rebooting process will fry the satellite uplink. With any luck, it will knock the satellite right out of the sky. Now check your coms. Make sure we time everything to the second."

Troy and Lily checked their communication devices and headed in the direction of the computer center while Will made for the power plant.

***

Not wanting to draw any undue attention to herself, Lily resisted the urge to cling to Troy's arm.

With a steady stride, they passed several technicians and entered the facility. The cool air prickled Lily's skin and she inhaled deeply to calm her racing heart. They approached a desk where several guards stood poised and ready for action.

"We are part of the President's advanced team," Troy said, handing the guard his clipboard.

The man inspected it and handed it back.

"The President should be here within the hour. Do you think you will finish before he arrives?"

"Sir, we know what we're doing. That's why they are paying us the big bucks. Now if you are through delaying us, we'll be on our way."

The bravado worked and the guard ushered Lily and Troy though the security scanner. They immediately headed for the elevator. Once in, Troy pressed the button for the fifth floor. When the doors opened, they found themselves standing in a wide corridor leading in two directions. Lily quickly unrolled the blueprint and pointed. "This way," she said, and took off with Troy close behind.

They joined a group of lab-coated technicians and stayed with them until they reached a door marked Main-Frame.

Two guards stood on either side of the door looking bored.

"I'll take it from here," Lily said.

With a slight twist of her hips, she sashayed toward the guards who eyed her with interest. "You boys sure look like you could use a little female company. Anyone interested in taking a walk?"

The two guards exchanged looks.

"We're on duty and we can't leave our post." The taller one said, his eyes wandering the length of Lily's petite body. "Well, that's too bad. Looks like I'll just have to find someone else to fill my time with. By the way, my daddy's the new commandant of this facility. He's tied up in some boring meeting and said to find a handsome guard to give me the tour."

With a swish of her hair, she pivoted and started to walk away in a girlish fashion. "Hey, wait a minute," the taller guard said. "There's nothing much going on here anyway. I'll show you around."

At his chauvinistic comment, Lily cringed, but held his gaze. "How about we start over there?" she said, pointing to a room down the hall.

Like a sheep to the slaughter, the guard hooked his arm in Lily's and strode off.

The moment they disappeared, Troy stepped around the corner and presented the clipboard to the remaining guard.

He thumbed the signature, it smeared and the color drained from his face. As he reached for his weapon, Troy caught his wrist and shoved it into his chest.

Pop!

His body muffled most of the blast. He coughed, splattering blood all over Troy's uniform. As his knees buckled, Troy grabbed him under the arms and dragged him to the room where Lily waited. She had just rendered her guard unconscious with one swift punch to the throat.

As he entered with the dead guard, he saw Lily dragging her guy across the floor.

She turned, "Troy, you're hurt."

Glancing down, his eyes widened. "That's not my blood. It's his," pointing at the newly formed corpse.

"Well, you certainly can't go walking around with blood on your uniform. We need to get another shirt or something to cover it up."

Footsteps approached. It was a technician wearing a white smock. Troy swung the door open, grabbed him by the throat and yanked him inside. The shocked man's eyes bulged under Troy's powerful grip. He slammed the butt of the guard's gun on his head and he slumped to the floor. Then he grabbed him by the armpits and dragged him over to where the guards lay. He quickly donned the man's lab coat and stood.

"How do I look?" A wide grin tugged at the corners of his lips.

"You look mauvelous," Lily said, patting him on the shoulder. Troy's smile quickly faded as he rechecked the time. "We've got to hurry. Let's go."

They reentered the corridor and made their way to the unguarded door.

Fingers slightly trembling, Lily slid the security pass key through the magnetic sensor. A soft click followed and Troy pushed the door open.

"Okay, let's do this," he whispered.

Stepping inside, they found several technicians huddled around a computer screen. One of them glanced up.

"We're the advanced team—" Troy said.

The technician waved him off. "We know. You're the guys getting paid the big bucks," his fingers formed air quotes. "Just get it over with," he sneered.

Lily felt heat creep up her neck as the others stared at them enviously. She smiled broadly, pulled out a chair, and took a seat at a console. Letting out a nervous chuckle, her fingers flew over the keys. She hacked through one protocol after the other and in a few minutes was staring at the activation codes for all twenty-six grids. "Troy, would you look at this," she pointed.

He leaned in close enough to feel the heat radiating from her body.

One of the computer nerds spoke up. "Hey, someone's hacked into the main frame."

Heads turned in Lily's direction. The man stood and took a step.

Troy straightened and pulled the guard's gun from the small of his back. "Stop! Another step and I'll shoot," he ordered, his two hands gripped the butt of the weapon.

The technician jerked to a halt and backed away. As he did, one of the other technicians dove for the door.

In a smooth move, Troy tracked his movement and squeezed off a round. The bullet struck the man in the chest sending him sprawling. "You were warned."

Lily kept her eyes averted. "Okay, I'm in." She withdrew the list of codes from her pocket and began entering them as quickly as possible.

Still holding the technician at bay, Troy checked his watch. At any time, the President would arrive. It would take him about fifteen minutes to get to the computer center and another seven to get to the fifth floor. "I wish I'd thought to deactivate the elevators." he said through pinched lips.

Lily nodded and licked the sweat from her upper lip. She had changed a dozen codes and still had fourteen to go.

While Troy kept one eye on the computer nerds, Lily's fingers tapped away. Five minutes passed and she still had ten codes yet to be entered.

Troy glanced at the other technicians who eyed them warily. "Hurry," he whispered.

"I'm going as fast as I can." Her tone was laced with tension.

Three minutes . . . two codes. One minute . . . And she entered the last code. Breathing a sigh of relief, her finger hovered over the enter button. Once she hit that button, the codes would change and the border grids would come crashing down. There wouldn't be enough time for the President to correct the damage.

"Do it," Troy said.

She smiled wickedly and hit enter.

***

On the other side of Hub Central, Will had bluffed his way past the security desk and was making his way to the Electrical Room.

His ear piece crackled.

"Okay, we've changed the codes. The borders are safe to cross." Troy said.

It sounded like they were running.

"I'll pass the news to HQ. Now get out of there."

"Roger that," Troy said between gulps of air.

From a pouch in Will's cargo pants, he removed a small plastic tool kit. He lifted a couple of probes and knelt in front of a door marked, "ELECTRICAL, KEEP OUT." He inserted the probes and twisted. A moment later, the door swung open and he slipped inside.

The air conditioner was running full blast making chills run the length of his body. He ignored the temptation to mop his brow and kept working, He found the unit which controlled the flow of electricity coming from the power production plant going to the computer control center. It acted like a giant surge protector. With a pair of rubber handled wire clippers, he cut the end. Sparks flew and the unit flashed, "Warning, power interruption. Manually reboot the system."

Klaxon's began their deafening scream. He knew within a few minutes the place would be swarming with armed guards with a shoot on sight order.

He had to stay focused.

He unbuttoned his shirt revealing a set of abs any man would die for and any woman would love to cling to and stripped several pounds of C-4 which he'd taped to his midsection. With trained hands he placed the explosives near the electrical panel marked main bus.

Then he carefully inserted the probe and set the timer for five minutes. Just long enough for him to get out. The blast would temporally shut down the electrical supply chain momentarily before the redundant breakers would take over. Since he'd rendered the surge protector useless, the surge of electricity coming from the power plant would fry the super computer. The microwave signal coming from the super computer would act like a LASER beam knocking the satellite out of orbit.

He remembered the day he and Lily rammed the Garda truck into the CDC building. He told Lily that he thought he'd found his calling . . . blowing up things. He smiled at the memory.

Sweat beaded on his brow and he swiped them aside. His watch buzzed. He had less than ten seconds to get out. With the clock ticking, he exited the room and raced for the stairway.

Boom!

Then the lights went out.

Chapter Sixty-Five

"Like a chameleon, their only hope was to blend in and their movements go undetected."   **A. Nonymous**

Troy and Lily had to take the stairs since the elevators went into lock down.

The alarms blared at every cross corridor making the fleeing technicians and engineers cover their ears as they ran down the stairs.

Troy and Lily pulled their helmets down and joined the crowd. But they knew it was only a matter of time before someone recognized them.

Suddenly, Troy pulled up short.

A squad of soldiers armed with automatic machine guns formed a barrier between them and the last exit.

"This way," Troy whispered.

He grabbed Lily's arm and tugged her through an unmarked door. As the door closed, the ground beneath their feet shook from the explosion. Thin dust filtered through fissions in the ceiling and lights swayed.

"Oh Troy," Lily buried her face in his chest, shaking.

He laid a trembling hand on her shoulder. He tried to speak but no words came.

The explosion drew the guard's attention away from them long enough for Troy and Lily to rush from the Computer Center.

"Where is Will?" Lily asked, still breathing hard.

"I don't know." Troy's answer did nothing to allay her fear.

The entire facility swarmed with soldiers and teams of first responders.

All at once, the power surge hit the super computer. Computer Central lit up like a Roman candle. A jolt of lightening shot skyward from somewhere deep within the building. Lily and Troy stopped long enough to catch a glimpse of something bright in the upper atmosphere. It was the satellite bursting into a million pieces.

There was no time to celebrate.

Amidst billowing clouds of smoke and debris, Troy and Lily dashed along the sidewalk headed for the main gate.

All at once, Lily skidded to a stop and stared.

The gate was closed and heavily guarded.

"Troy, how are we going to get out of here?"

He glanced around, looking for a secondary escape route.

In the distance, an engine roared to life.

Wheels screeched as a pickup truck smashed into the guard rail. It splintered sending chunks of wood in every direction. Troy and Lily had to duck to keep from being hit. The guards opened fire into the engine block and cab of the vehicle. Mayhem erupted as the guards continued to fire at the vehicle, but its momentum kept it moving until it struck a concrete embankment.

While the guards were distracted, Troy and Lily slipped past them and dashed across the campus. As they approached the perimeter gate, they found several dead guards laying in the street. It was obvious what had happened. Whoever was driving the van had gunned them down.

"This way!" Troy said. Taking Lily by the hand, he led her across the street.

"Stop right there!"

***

President Bleakly stood between them and freedom.

His helicopter had just landed and he stood amidst dust and leaves from the chopper's blades.

Lily slammed into the back of Troy nearly knocking him off his feet. She grabbed him and faced the President.

Another explosion rocked the ground sending smoke, glass and metal skyward.

"You're too late, Mr. President. We've blown your whole operation," Troy said between gulps of air.

"That may be so, but I'm not finished with you," extending his hand, he continued, "now give me the codes."

"Don't do it," Troy spat.

Lily dug in her pocket and produced the list of codes. "It doesn't matter," Lily said. "I've changed the codes before the power surge. The entire super computer has been fried."

Bleakly's face registered shock. "Nicely done. You just admitted to espionage."

"Lily!" Troy shouted.

She remained unmoved. "That's nothing compared to leading a coup."

The President smiled wickedly. "The problem with history is, it depends on who's writing it. And right now, I am in the position of power." He gave a quick nod to his men.

A moment later, they dragged Millie from the helicopter and tossed her on the ground.

"I find all of you guilty of treason and espionage. And now, we are going to execute you."

Lily's eyes rimmed with tears. Not for herself, but for her dad. She longed to tell him she loved him just one more time.

Troy steadied himself. He'd faced death before. He could do it again.

As they lined them up and prepared to fire, the commander of Grid Central came rushing up. "Mr. President, Mr. President! You've got to see this."

He carried an iPad which carried the news of the day. An anchorman was in the middle of describing a large movement of militia coming across the borders and attacking local grid hubs. "Sir, we are being overrun on every front. What should we do?"

Bleakly grabbed a gun from one of his security details hands and pointed it at Lily's head. "Call off the attack or so help me—"

In a flash of teeth and fur, Wag lunged for Bleakly's gun arm and sank his teeth into his flesh. The gun exploded striking the man next to him.

All at once, a pack of wild dogs sprang from behind the helicopter. The small Presidential detail was not prepared for such a vicious attack. Within seconds, they were overwhelmed. Their cries were drowned out by the sound of the rising helicopter.

In the jet wash of the rotating props, Troy grabbed the gun which had fallen from Bleakly's hand. He didn't know what he'd do if the President got his footing and came after him and Lily, but he knew he couldn't stay there. Shooting a sitting President, even if he was illegitimate, wasn't an option, but leaving him to the mercy of a pack of wild dogs wasn't either.

"Call off your dog," Bleakly cried out angrily.

"And what, surrender? Not on your life." Lily fired back.

"Go ahead, Lily, call him off, I've got him covered." Troy stood, poised to anyone who made a move toward them.

She nodded reluctantly. "Wag, that's enough."

He snarled angrily, then released Bleakly's arm. Still growling, he stepped back ready to pounce again if given the word.

"Don't move or he'll pick up where he left off. Now stand up." Troy's commanding tone left no doubt he meant business.

Bleakly pushed himself up on shaky legs. His designer suit had been ripped to shreds as well as his neck, hands and face. He wiped the blood from his eyes and glowered at Troy. "You'll never get away with this. I'm the President of the—"

"Shut up!" Lily spat. "You're nothing but a fraud and a hypocrite. You've done nothing but bring sorrow and pain to me and my country."

Troy touched her arm. "Simmer down, Lily or I might change my mind about not shooting him."

She kicked a loose rock and sent it flying in Bleakly's direction. His hands flew up as the projectile whizzed past his head, missing him by inches.

Wag yipped and the other dogs released the Presidential detail, leaving them torn and bloody. They fumbled to their feet and gathered around their fallen leader.

An instant later, the air screamed with hot lead. The soldiers in charge of protecting Grid Central mounted a counterattack and were charging through the gates.

Troy squeezed off several rounds, striking the closest men.

As bullets ripped the air apart, Lily looked around for cover.

There was none.

***

In the distance, an engine roared and a jeep appeared through the dust and smoke.

It parted the approaching soldiers and skidded to a stop.

"Get in." Will ordered with urgency, his face stained with soot.

Needing no encouragement, Lily, Troy and Wag, dove in. Amidst a hail of bullets, Will hit the gas. The truck fishtailed, sending pebbles and rocks all over the President and his men. The ding of bullets pelting the cab was deafening. Fortunately, none of them penetrated the glass.

In the confusion, Millie dove for cover behind a disabled car.

"Will, where did you come from?" Lily asked over the roar of the engine.

He glanced in the mirror and smiled, "I had the blueprints, and a handgun. After I left you two, I disabled the surge protection system and sabotaged the power plant. That's what's firing off behind us. When the alarm went off, the corridors filled with employees and soldiers. Those who were firing at me dove for cover. Those who weren't, well … let's say, I emptied my magazine and headed into the sewer. It led straight out to a holding pond next to the employee parking lot. I found this jeep, hotwired it and here I am."

Her eyes rounded with wonder. "But what about that pickup truck? Who did that?"

Will swiped his hand over his face. "Oh, that. Well, just before I stole this jeep, I found the keys in a pickup truck in the ignition. I pointed it in the direction of the first check point, tied off the steering wheel and placed a large rock on the gas pedal. The rest is history."

Troy patted him on the shoulder. "Man, you're one cool dude." He offered him a high five. As the three of them clasped hands, Lily glanced around at Wag. "And how did you get off your rope?"

Lifting the ragged end, Troy said, "I guess he snapped it and followed us to the first security check point. When the Marine One landed, he and his buds must have hid and waited for their chance."

With her hand running through his fur, Lily hugged him. "You came through for us again, my friend. Cami will be so proud of you."

"Speaking of Cami, I was going to tell you, when I cranked up the jeep, she was on the radio. She was telling the nation all about President Bleakly."

Troy and Lily gaped at Will. "You mean she's on the air right now?"

"Yep." Will slowed as they entered the outskirts of town where a large group of men holding rifles and shotguns stood guard. The moment they entered, the locals closed the road behind them with cars and trucks. If the International Guard tried to follow them, they'd have a fight on their hands.

Once they reached the other side of town, Will took a rutted dirt road into the country. It led to an abandoned farm house with a rickety old barn. He nosed the jeep through the open door and killed the engine.

"Let's get the barn door closed before anyone sees us," Will said as he jumped out. In an instant, he was joined by Troy and Lily. With their help, he shoved the heavy door closed and covered the truck with a tarp.

Mopping his brow, Will turned and said, "We'll be safe for now. The town's people are on our side. They'll take care of any trouble that might come our way. For now, we rest and let the national militia do their job." Will took a seat on a bale of hay and let out a tired sigh. Troy joined him and extended his hand.

"Will, you're one cool dude." He patted him on the shoulder. "I'd be proud to call you my brother-in-law as well as my brother-in-arms."

Lily's eyes glowed with admiration. "Troy, if that was your way of proposing ... well then ... I accept." She dove into Troy's arms and kissed him passionately.

***

President Bleakly stood helplessly as the jeep, carrying Will, Troy, Lily and a dog, raced away.

"After them," he raged.

But his men were in no condition to chase anyone. The commander of the military force protecting the grid hub called a cease fire. Once the shooting stopped, he approached the President. "Sir, we need to get you to safety. I'm getting reports of a large military force moving in our direction."

Bleakly filled the air with a curse. "Get me on Marine One."

His head of security, though badly injured, lifted his walkie-talkie. After relaying the message, he took a seat on the fender of a bullet ridden car. "They said they'll be here in five minutes. That we need to secure the LZ. He has no intention of setting down in the midst of a war zone."

POTUS let out another curse. "Get me in touch with General Haggerty. Have him—"

"Mr. President, General Haggerty has been arrested. All but one of your advisers and cabinet member have either been taken into custody, are dead or on the run. All except for your secretary, Millie Kendall." Bleakly stared at his head of security. "Take me to Camp David. We'll make our stand there."

As he spoke, Marine One began its descent.

Amidst flying dust and debris, a lone figure stepped from behind a disabled vehicle and approached him. A Colt .45 was pointed directly at the President.

***

"You've got no place to run, Bleakly."

It was Millie. She was flanked by two secret service agents. Their weapons were trained and ready to fire if the President made any sudden moves.

As the blades of Marine One churned, time seemed to have stood still.

"You!" Bleakly spat. "I trusted you."

"No, you used me. You used all of us to do your bidding. Not anymore. You're under arrest." She held up her credentials.

Bleakly froze half way between the helicopter and his would-be-captors.

"Raise your hands and turn around slowly," her voice cut through the pounding thunder of Marine One.

Turning, he lifted his hands. This was not how it was supposed to end. He was supposed to be holding the weapons, commanding his enemies to surrender. Instead, he was faced with humiliation, with defeat, with the fear of being labeled a lunatic, an enemy of the state. Like Hitler during the last hours before Berlin fell, his choices were quickly evaporating. He either allowed himself to be taken alive or . . .

He slid his hand into his shredded coat pocket and withdrew a small device. It controlled the ID chips within a twenty yard perimeter. If he activated it, the people around him, his protective detail, the commandant of Hub Central, et-al, would die. It was a costly exchange, but one he had to make.

"Do you see what I'm holding?"

Her glare never left his eyes. "I know what it is. But the grid is down. That thing is worthless."

"That may be so, but this has a range of twenty yards. If I press the button, all of you will die. Are you willing to take that chance?"

Millie hadn't anticipated this turn of events. She had an ID chip as well as the two men standing next to her. One flick of that button and they'd all be dead. Seconds ticked as she grappled with a life and death decision. She knew she was a good shot, but not that good. She figured she had a fifty-fifty chance at best at hitting his hand before he squeezed the trigger.

"Take the shot," the man on her left whispered.

Pop!

Blood splattered the side of the hovering Marine One. Bleakly's hand flew back as the bullet ripped it from his body. Clutching the bloody stump, he staggered backward. The pilot of Marine One lowered the aircraft and hollered. "Get in!"

Millie held her breath as the wounded man dove for the side of the helicopter. His good hand gripped the rail but slipped. His eyes grew wide as he fell into the pack of wild dogs.

In an instant, they were on him. The smell of blood and the taste of man flesh drove the wild animals into a feeding frenzy.

Before his security men could react, the beasts had torn Bleakly to ribbons. They fired their weapons wildly into the pack, but it was too late. All that remained were a few shreds of bloody clothing and a few bones.

Chapter Sixty-Six

The moment the grid barriers came down, the national militia took to the streets.

They charged across the no man's zones and stormed the local grid authorities. The unsuspecting International Guard was not prepared for the massive attack. Within hours, their defenses collapsed and they were overrun.

When the sun rose the following day, the stars and bars flew over most state capitols and by noon, it flew over the White House.

As soon as it was clear that the partisans had taken over of the command and control centers, President Richardson took to the airwaves with his prerecorded message to the country.

In the White House Press Room, Millie had a large screen television set up. After making a brief statement, she stepped aside. The screen sprang to life and President Richardson's face appeared.

With the help of a few computer gurus, they had uplinked the press conference to every news outlet in the country. The moment the President went on the air, his image appeared on every television screen, every remote billboard, every iPhone, iPad, and every computer across the country.

His message was clear ... 'I'm back!'

"My fellow Americans! For the last eleven months this country has been under the delusion that I caused the bird attacks. You have been deceived! You have been lied to! I am here to tell you, I have the proof that this entire debacle was planned and orchestrated by a shadow government. These masterminds of evil have gone undetected until they were ready to spring their plan perpetuated by their willing accomplices, the media. But make no mistake about it; we have been working relentlessly to take this country back. Today, I stand here to tell you … we have succeeded.

In the coming weeks we will tear down the grid border crossings, and reestablish the state borders as defined by the Constitution of the United States. After a brief election, we will hold a gala ceremony in which we will swear in new governors, Senators and Representatives.

I will draft legislation prohibiting the use of any personal tracking devices. I am also charging the CDC and the new Homeland Security Commandant to open our vast medical community to remove your ID chips at no cost to you.

In addition, the power grid is gone … history. It may mean some inconveniences for a short time, but we will return to localized power plants. With the help of our creative and ingenuous entrepreneurs, we will seek full employment making America great again." He concluded his comments with "And may God bless America … again."

***

Later that day, President Richardson stood before a group of airmen and addressed the men and women of the California Army Air National Guard.

Eleven months earlier, the 177th Fighter Wing comprised of the decorated F-106 pilots, had been replaced with a new breed of pilots from other countries; countries not friendly to American interests. He now reviewed these "Delta Dart pilots," with pride and confidence.

"Ladies and gentlemen, it has been a long time in coming, but I am happy to tell you that we have gained the initiative. The National Guard is in retreat and with your help, we will gain air superiority. I am tasking you with the responsibility of giving air cover to our advancing forces and to cut off the enemies retreat. It is vital that you leave the enemy quarter, with no place to hide, no place to run and no ability to make a counter attack."

A smile tugged at the corners of each of the pilot's lips as they dashed to their fighter jets. Within a few short minutes, they roared off the tarmac hunting for targets of opportunity.

AFTERWORD

R ed, white and blue banners flapped lazily in the wind over the US Capital and surrounding buildings.

From around the world and across the nation, dignitaries stood shoulder to shoulder with common citizens as they gathered on the steps of the White House. Among them, Olivia Emerson and Carnes stood hand in hand. They both had survived the ordeal and were reunited after years of being separated. Their plans were still unfolding.

A small platform had been quickly erected and a bank of microphones stood at the ready for President Richardson to address the nation and the world.

With little fanfare, he emerged from the front door of the people's house and strode to the podium. To his left stood his friend, fellow-patriot, and recently appointed Vice President, Joe Franklin. To his right were five of his most trusted and loyal supporters; Mr. and Mrs. Trace O'Reilly, Mr. and Mrs. Troy Ashcroft and Will, aka Nigel, O'Reilly.

In the weeks since the liberation of America a lot had happened. A government had been formed along with two new homes; Trace and Cami had exchanged their vows in a little chapel located at the center of Point Pleasant Township under the guidance of the Reverend

Horus T. Blankenship with Mr. and Mrs. Lawson and their son, Jed as witnesses. Troy and Lily found marital bliss after a brief ceremony in the little town on the outskirts of St. Louis. With Will and Wag as their best men, and an army of local militia as their attendees, they celebrated and danced most of the night away in the old barn.

Together, they faced a bright future, one that didn't involve Brewer Blackbirds, ID chips, and Grids.

Speaking without notes, President Richardson addressed the nation for only the second time since his arrest.

"My fellow Americans, our nation's history is littered with wars and hard times. The war for our independence, the Civil war which pitted brother against brother, the Great Depression which drove us to our knees, the Great War and its sister World War II which cost us dearly, the Korean War, and the Vietnam conflict once again divided our nation. And we will never forget September 11th and the conflicts in the Middle East fighting radical Islam wherever it reared its ugly head. And now this; the second war for our independence. In it our brave sons and daughters fought side by side with our loyal military to take our country back from those who would corrupt it. Today, we salute you. We owe you a great debt of gratitude for your sacrifice, your blood, sweat and tears, and especially, your prayers. For without them, we would have surely failed.

We stand here on the dawn of a new day of peace and understanding. After feeling the oppressive hand of a government drunk with power, I pledge to you this day, an era of transparency and openness, a respite from our hard labor, a time of refreshing from the Lord when we will beat our swords into plow shears, the lion and the lamb will lie down together and we'll study war no more."

At his last statement, the appreciative crowd rose to their feet in thunderous applause.

***

"Does this mean you won't be staying in Washington, D.C. to finish with the transition?" Trace whispered to Cami.

Keeping her eyes straight ahead, Cami continued to smile and applaud. "Yep, we've got a long awaited honeymoon planned and nothing is going to stand in our way."

"And what about Lily and Troy, what's their plans?"

"I think they have their own plans and I don't think it involves O'Reilly and Ashcroft Detective Agency."

Trace leaned forward, caught his new son-in-law's eyes and winked. "Do you think Will can handle things in our absence?" His question brought a smile to Cami's face.

"Will is on his new career path and I think he'll enjoy it very much. I overheard the President offering him the job of dismantling the Central Grid Unit and refitting it for the production of nuclear energy. He couldn't have picked a better candidate for the job. He also introduced him to his daughter."

"Oh?" Trace could barely control his surprise. "I forgot all about him having a daughter."

Another cheer went up and Trace and Cami joined the applause.

"I did. She's a beauty. She's got the looks of her mother and the brains of her father."

Trace gave Will a thumbs up.

He returned the gesture.

"What's her name?"

Cami couldn't control herself. "You'll never believe it. It is Millie."

"Millie!?" Trace nearly shouted. "You mean to say, Millie is the President's daughter? But I thought her last name was Kendall."

"It is, or at least was. Her husband was killed in Afghanistan. Shortly after the President was elected, he hired her to be his personal secretary."

Grinning broadly, Trace considered Will's good fortune. "Hmm, with any luck, you and I might be invited to a state wedding."

Her elbow gently jabbed his ribs. "Don't get your hopes up. He's got to prove himself."

"Oh, he has, in spades."

As the crowd rose to their feet one last time, Cami threw her arms around Trace's neck and warmed his lips with hers. "You must be so proud."

"Oh, I am, Mrs. O'Reilly. Now let's go celebrate."

The Chase Newton Series
The Order

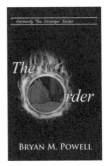

Follow investigative reporter Chase Newton as he goes undercover in search of the truth. What he finds puts him and those he cares for in mortal danger. Fast-paced and high-energy describes this first of three mystery and action thrillers.

The Oath

The President and Vice President have been attacked. The vice President survived, but he is a hunted man. The man who was sworn in is an impostor and Chase must get a DNA sample from him to prove who the real President is.

The Outsider

After a thousand years of peace, the world is suddenly thrown into chaos as Satan is loosed from his prison. These action-packed stories will hold you breathless and capture your imagination until the exciting conclusion.

The Jared Russell Series
Sisters of the Veil

Jared Russell, a former Marine turned architect, must navigate the minefield of hatred and prejudice to find the meaning of love and forgiveness.

ISBN - 978151057994

Power Play - #8 on Amazon Political Fiction

Jared and Fatemah Russell go to Beirut, Lebanon, to establish the Harbor House, a refuge for converted Muslims and find themselves caught in a Middle East conflict of global proportions.

ISBN – 9781511402750

The Final Countdown – #25 on Amazon

The clock is ticking and Jared once again finds himself battling against forces beyond his control. Can he and his friends unravel the mystery in time to stop two radical Muslims from perpetrating a horrible crime against our country? ISBN – 978153297825

Non-Fiction Series
Seeing Jesus: A Three Dimensional Look at Worship

Seeing Jesus is a thought provoking and compelling expose' on what is true worship. ISBN -9781511540582

Show Us the Father

A thirty-day devotional showing how Jesus demonstrated His Father's character and qualities.
ISBN -9781517633905

Faith, Family, and a Lot of Hard Work

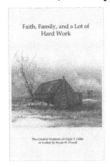

Born the year the Stock-Market crashed, Mr. Gillis grew up in South Georgia with a 3rd grade education. After being challenged to get the best job in the company, he worked hard and got a degree from the University of Georgia and Moody Bible Institute in Finance. By mid-life, he owned 14 companies. ISBN -9781467580182

The Christian Fantasy Series

The Witch and the Wise Men

An ancient medallion is discovered, an evil spirit is awakened, a witch's curse is broken ... and the wise men of Bethlehem are called upon to face the ultimate evil

The Lost Medallion

Beneath the Hill of Endor is a Temple, inside the Temple is a Chamber, inside the Chamber is a door, behind the door ... the abyss. And the key to the door is the witch's medallion.

The Last Magi

Israel has signed the Peace Accord. The Third Temple is under construction. The world holds its breath as the Ark of the Covenant is rediscovered, and then stolen. It is up to the Magi to find it but then what?

Journey to Edenstrae

What if the Tree of Life survived the Flood and is living in a valley guarded by a Dragon and a warring people?

Southern Humor at its best!

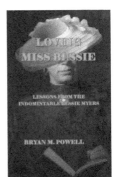

Although Miss Bessie Myers is a figment of my imagination, she is every bit real in the sense that we all have a Miss Bessie in our lives.

Miss Bessie is everyone's crazy aunt, spooky neighbor, beloved grandmother, and dearest friend. She can be brutally honest, painfully funny, sweet as honey and prickly as a pear. She is both the preacher's staunchest supporter and sharpest critic. Of all the words used to describe this godly saint, there is one which stands out above them all … unpredictable

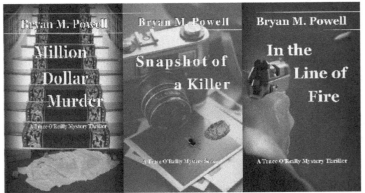

Falsely accused of killing his ex-wife and facing execution, Trace O'Reilly can think of only one thing—what's next?

About the Author

Novelist Bryan M. Powell is a full-time author. Having worked in the ministry for over forty-two years, Bryan is uniquely qualified to write about Christian topics. His novels have been published by Tate Publishing, Lightening Source, Create Space, Kindle Direct Publishing and Vabella Publishing. His novel, The Witch and the Wise Men, held the #23 slot on Amazon's best seller's list and The Lost Medallion hit #22 on Amazon Christian Fantasy.

In addition to his novels, Bryan's short stories and other works appeared in *The North Georgia Writer* (PCWG's publication), *Relief Notes* (A Christian Authors Guild's book, released in 2014), and in the *Georgia Backroads* magazine.

Bryan is a member of the following organizations: American Christian Fiction Writers (ACFW), The Christian Author's Guild (President, 2016), The Paulding County Writers' Guild (PCWG), and the local chapter of ACFW, the New Life Writers Group.

www.facebook.com/authorbryanpowell
www.authorbryanpowell.wordpress.com
authorbryanpowell@gmail.com